THE HUMMING GRIZZLY BEAR CUBS

Amelia Lionheart

Amelia Lionheart
The Humming Grizzly Bear Cubs
978-0-9937493-8-4 softcover
978-0-9937740-2-7 ebook (mobi)
978-0-9937740-1-0 ebook (epub)

The paper used in the publication of this book is from responsible forest
management sources.

Printing
Minuteman Press (Calgary North), Alberta
Information and Sales: info@mmpresscgy.com
Printed & bound in Canada

Other titles in this series:
Peacock Feathers
The Dolphin Heptad
An Elephant Never Forgets
Can Snow Leopards Roar?

Website: http://www.jeacs.com

Dedicated to

my Canadian friends and readers

with a special dedication to all those involved
with the JEACs.

You inspire me and make
our little corner of the world
a better place.

I could not have so much fun with my books
without each and every one of you.

Thank you for EVERYTHING!

FOREWORD
by
Dr. Doug Whiteside

"Those who have packed far up into grizzly country know
that the presence of even one grizzly on the land elevates the mountains,
deepens the canyons, chills the winds, brightens the stars,
darkens the forest, and quickens the pulse of all who enter it."

John Murray, The Great Bear

Grizzly bears (*Ursus arctos horribilis*, which translates to the 'horrible brown bear') are an iconic keystone species in North America. Few species can evoke such a wide range of emotions from wonder and amazement to healthy respect and fear. While this iconic giant is often associated with images of breathtaking and unspoiled wilderness, the sad reality is that human-bear conflicts, and destruction and loss of habitat, are driving populations towards extinction.

Historically, grizzlies ranged from Alaska to Mexico, and as far east as the Mississippi River. Over the past two centuries their population number and range have declined dramatically. In Canada, the remaining population of approximately 20,000 bears is confined to British Columbia, Western Alberta, the Yukon and Northwest Territories. At the southern end of their range which extends into northern Idaho, Montana and Wyoming, grizzlies are in trouble with approximately 1,800 bears left and their habitat reduced to only 2 percent of their historical range.

In her new book *The Humming Grizzly Bear Cubs*, Amelia Lionheart highlights many of the issues facing grizzly bears today. In order to survive, grizzlies need abundant undisturbed wilderness. Males (boars) can have an average home range up to 2,000 square kilometres, while females (sows) can have ranges up to 500 square kilometres. Loss of habitat to commercial property development, expansion of highways through their natural corridors, oil and gas exploration and development, logging, hunting, illegal poaching, and conflicts with humans in their natural space, have had detrimental consequences to their population. Owing to their slow reproductive rate, any decline in their population size has a negative impact on their long-term recovery. And grizzlies are not alone in this plight. Six of the eight bear species found worldwide are listed as threatened or vulnerable by the International Union for Conservation of Nature (IUCN).

Over the years, many orphaned or problem bears (those that have come into conflict with humans) have ended up in zoological institutions as their last hope for survival. The sad reality is that people are the usual cause of the conflicts. At the Calgary Zoo, our male grizzly, *Skoki* (formerly Bear #16), was a young male that became a "problem bear" due to human activity. Skoki spent his summers in the Bow Valley eating to gain enough weight to sustain himself for his long winter hibernation. However, people started to stop and get out of their cars to take pictures of him, causing traffic jams known as "bear jams". While conservation officers and researchers tried adversive techniques to try to keep him afraid of humans, over time he was introduced to discarded human food from the thousands of people stopping to see him. He started to associate people with an easy meal, and became bolder and more aggressive towards people when they invaded his personal space. He was relocated by Parks Canada conservation officers; however, owing to the amazing homing instinct in bears, he came back to his territory within a short period of time. When he poked his head into the bakery at Lake Louise, it was decided that he was too dangerous to remain in the wild, and fortunately the Calgary Zoo had the space to take him. While Skoki has adjusted very well to his life at the zoo over the past eighteen years, and is often seen playing in his pool, what is most unfortunate is that he never had a chance to reproduce and now his genetics have been lost to the wild population. His story serves as a reminder of the devastating consequences that can occur due to the careless actions of people.

We can all do our part to keep bears safe in the wild. Become *Bear Aware*, never feed or approach wild bears, and never leave food or garbage out for them to find. Drive with care through bear habitats such as the National Parks. Finally, support conservation organizations that will help protect their habitats and support research to keep them healthy in the wild.

The creation of the Junior Environmentalists and Conservationists (JEACs) by Amelia Lionheart has served to inspire today's youth to become passionate about the conservation of wildlife and wild spaces. I have had the pleasure to interact with Amelia and the Calgary-based JEACs on several occasions, and have witnessed their amazing work and their contributions to save endangered species. Through Amelia's vision and guidance, they are a beautiful example of the ripple effect of conservation education and how powerful it can be for achieving global change one small wave at a time.

Dr. Doug Whiteside
Senior Staff Veterinarian, Calgary Zoo
Clinical Associate Professor,
University of Calgary Faculty of Veterinary Medicine

ACKNOWLEDGEMENTS

I would like to extend my fervent thanks to everyone who has contributed to the production of this book. While I would love to write a detailed paragraph about each person, I will, however, restrain myself as that would fill another book. ☺

Dr. Doug Whiteside, DVM, DVSc, Dipl. ACZM, Senior Staff Veterinarian at the Calgary Zoo, is also an Adjunct Associate Professor at the University of Calgary and a renowned expert in the protection of wildlife who speaks at numerous conferences. Dr. Whiteside set aside many hours of his limited time, meeting with me and assisting me in understanding the technicalities of tranquillizers; writing the foreword for this book as well as the previous one; reading the manuscript and ensuring that all technical information was accurate; and providing helpful insights and suggestions in order to make the story more plausible. In addition, Dr. Doug has attended two of my book launches – speaking at them and signing books for children. He also attended a JEACs – CAC[1] – No. 3 fundraising event, and gave some of our groups a tour of the medical facilities at the zoo. Thank you, Dr. Doug, for your ongoing support of our cause.

Amaris, Louise, Brinn, Corben, Sorena, and the rest of their families – Sorena's dad, Steven, and brothers Gabriel and Joel, and Corben and Brinn's dad, Pat: Corben and Sorena, as leaders of *JEACs – CAC – No. 3*, you have taken my concept of the structure, goals and activities of the JEACs to a whole new level. Thank you for your **dedication** in helping to make this little corner of the world a better place;
Joanne Bennett, for editorial assistance;
Glenn Boyd, for handling the printing of the books and production of all marketing materials in his consistently exceptional and efficient manner;
Mary Anna and Warren Harbeck, for editorial assistance, excellent suggestions and ongoing encouragement and support;
Sheri Gouglas, for advice in the cover design of these new editions, and for keeping me laughing and on track with matters involving the JEACs;
Michael Hartnett, for know-how, business advice and never-failing support;

---

[1] CAC – Canada Alberta Calgary – #3

Grace and Hubert Howe, for assistance in innumerable ways;

Sarah Lawrence, for her advice, support and commitment in bringing these new editions, and the new book, to publication;

Elaine Phillips, my cheerful editor, who proofread the pre-print manuscript with her inimitable attention to detail. Your enthusiasm is unbelievable;

Robin Phillips, for business advice and ongoing support;

Rani Theeparajah and her husband, **Theeps**, long-standing, special friends are more precious than gold;

Lisa Trotta, for her unfailing and constant encouragement and support in everything I undertake, and for being an ineffably wonderful friend ever since I came to Alberta. Also, her husband, **Remo**, and their children, **Anthony** and **Giuliana**. I cannot imagine what my life in Calgary would be like without them;

A few special Calgarian supporters: **Annamarie Bergen, Janice Buckingham, Marlou Gandia, Anna-Marie Martin, Kelly Swanek** and **Angela Wong** – thank you for all your support and advice in countless ways;

My **amazing readers**, aged six and a half to ninety years old – you are awesome;

And, once more, **my family and friends**, especially all my **Canadian** friends, for their ongoing encouragement and support.

In 2012, 2013 and 2014, I have done, and am booked for, close to 200 book signings – at Indigo, Chapters and Coles book shops, and Monkeyshines Children's Books. Once again I would like to express my appreciation to the owners, managers and staff of all the book shops – thank you for opening your doors to me and to the JEACs groups, and for making the JEACs series such a success.

YOU
CAN MAKE A DIFFERENCE

You are UNIQUE! This means YOU have special gifts to help change the world. Talk to your parents about ways in which you can recycle or conserve at home. Ask the wonderful folk at zoos and conservations close to you how you can get involved in all kinds of fun and educational activities. Get your friends and neighbours involved. Look up websites for zoos and wildlife conservations, and check out what's going on around the world!

THEME SONG

Jun-ior Environ-menta-lists and Con-ser-vation-ists!

When we think about our world, all the animals and birds
Who are losing their homes day by day
If each person does their part, it will cheer up every heart
So let's take a stand and act without delay!

We've decided we will strive to keep birds and beasts alive
And to make CONSER-VA-TION our theme
We will talk to all our friends, try to help them understand
That our world must come awake and not just dream!

All the creatures that we love, from the ele-phant to dove,
Must be cared for and well protected, too
So all humans, young and old, have to speak up and be **bold**
Or we'll end up with an 'only human' zoo!

Where environment's concerned, in our studies we have learned
That composting at home can be a start
And recycling's very good, each and every person should
Be aware of how we all can do our part.

To the JEACs we belong, and we hope it won't be long
Till our peers and our friends all will say
They believe that con-ser-vation and environ-menta-lism
Is the only way to save our world today!

Will you come and join our band? Will you lend a helping hand?
Though it's serious, it can be great fun!
Tell your friends about it all, let them join up, big and small
And our fight against destruction will be won!

Jun-ior Environ-menta-lists and Con-ser-vation-ists!

ABOUT THE JEACs

The JEACs (*Junior Environmentalists and Conservationists*), a group created by *Amelia Lionheart* in the first book of her series, attempts to enlighten children – through the means of adventure stories – about conservation and environmental issues. The author is delighted that the JEACs, once only a figment of her imagination, have become a reality in recent years.

The JEACs firmly believe that some of the key factors in **saving our planet** are:

- Participation
- Awareness
- Co-operation
- Education

****

JEACs MISSION STATEMENT AND GOALS

We are an international group of Junior Environmentalists and Conservationists who long to **save our planet** from destruction. We will work towards this by:

- educating ourselves on the importance and necessity:

  o of protecting *all wildlife* – especially endangered species – and the techniques used by conservation groups all over the world to reach this goal;

  o of preventing our *global environment* from further damage, and finding out how we can participate in this endeavour;

- creating awareness of these issues among our peers and by sharing knowledge with them, encouraging more volunteers to join our group;

- becoming members of zoos, conservations and environmental groups in our region, actively participating in events organized by them and, through donations and fundraising efforts, contributing towards their work.

Table of Contents

1. O Canada!.. 1

2. At the Sanctuary 11

3. Ataneq and Atka... 20

4. Conservation Community 27

5. Settling in at Grizzly Watch............................... 33

6. Beginning the Investigation 54

7. The Humming Grizzly Bear Cubs...................... 60

8. Camouflaged Trails and Clues 70

9. A Fortuitous Rescue 75

10. Discoveries at and around BSC-1 83

11. Following up on Leads... 91

12. Is There a Hidden Entrance to MWCC? 96

13. Another Good Friend 100

14. Cranes, Crooks and Captures 107

15. Possible Assumptions Based on Pooled Information 116

16. Teams at Work 127

17. Divide and Conquer 132

18. So Many Crooks.. 147

19. The Victorious Chase....................................... 159

20. We Saved Our Grizzly Bears!.......................... 165

CHAPTER 1

O Canada!

'Are you comfortably settled, JEACs?' said Janet Larkin, starting the ten passenger van.

'Yes, thanks!' chorused the JEACs. The van left Calgary airport, heading west to Banff, from where they would carry on to Manipau Wildlife Conservation Trust.

'It's marvellous to be together again,' said Anu, who was seated behind Janet. 'It's the seventh of July, and I can't believe we're actually in *Canada*, and on the way to Manipau!'

'We've been so ecstatic that we couldn't concentrate on anything,' said Amy, hugging Anu and Rohan who were seated on either side of her. 'When we heard the announcement that your flight had landed, Mich gave such a shriek that the boy in front of her fell off his chair.'

Michelle, known as Mich to family and friends, chuckled. 'It was hilarious! I had to apologize, and get his grandmother another bottle of water since she dropped hers when I yelled.'

'Gina only gave a small yelp when we landed,' chuckled Nimal. 'But the shrieks she and Mich let out when they met must have been heard all the way to Manipau.'

'You wait . . .' began Gina, but Umedh laughingly interrupted.

'Peace, kiddo. Nimal, put a sock in it – you know they'll get their revenge.'

'It's Nimal who . . .' said Mich.

'Calm down, JEACs,' laughed Janet, as everyone joined in the fun.

'Okay, Aunty Janet. Please tell us how Hunter's doing,' said Rohan.

'He's fine, and has made friends with Sam and Codey, dogs belonging to two staff members who are currently on vacation. Hunter's at our place today, eagerly awaiting your arrival.'

'He *knows* you're coming and kept going to the door, his tail wagging nineteen to the dozen,' added Mich.

'We couldn't bring him since he was scheduled for one last injection this morning,' said Amy. 'Everyone loves him.'

'He's a lovable dog! Are any of you hungry?' asked Janet.

'Nimal's simply STARVING!' yelled Gina and Mich, promptly.

'Cheeky brats,' muttered Nimal sotto voce. 'Aunty Janet, I'm a tad peckish, but will valiantly staunch the hunger pangs until we arrive at a watering place, which I assume will be soon.'

'Poor lad,' said Janet, as the others laughed mockingly. 'Mich, pull out the cookies. Nimal, you'll have a good meal in an hour's time at the Fairmont Banff Springs Hotel.'

'Thank you, Aunty Janet,' said Nimal. 'The way these kids bully me is simply one of the . . .'

'. . . saddest stories of his life,' chanted everyone.

Teasing one another, catching up on news, and admiring the beauty of the Rocky Mountains they were driving through made time fly, and they were soon entering the parking lot of the hotel.

'It looks like a castle,' said Gina.

'It was originally built in the nineteenth century, constructed in the Scottish baronial style, and opened to the public in 1888,' said Amy. 'Over the years it underwent several renovations and is now quite different from the original structure.'

Inside the elegant hotel, seated at a table with a gorgeous view of the Rockies, the group had a delicious brunch at 10:15 a.m.

'What time will we reach Manipau, Aunty?' asked Anu.

'When we leave here we go north-west past Jasper on the Yellowhead Highway; then we take Highway 40 north-west from Hinton and branch off on Manipau Trail. We'll be home around six this evening.'

'That's quite a drive,' said Rohan. 'Would you like us to share the driving, Aunty?'

'Once we're in quieter areas that would be great, thanks – you, Amy and Umedh can take turns.'

'What time does Chris-J arrive, Mum?' asked Mich. 'We call my cousin Chris-J for "junior" to avoid confusion since our dad's name is also Chris,' she explained. 'When Dad's not around, we just say Chris.'

'Chris will get to *Tranquillity* between three and four this afternoon,' said Janet. 'As you know, that is the name of our home.'

'Yes, and it's a lovely name!' said Anu. 'I'm glad Chris-J's joining us. He sounds like a fun chap from what you've said. Will anyone else from Manipau join us?'

'Corazon, for sure,' said Amy. 'She's fanatical over animals, and longing to meet all of you – especially Nimal.'

'What an unusual name,' said Umedh.

'She's a First Nations kid and her name means *heart*,' explained Amy. 'Her father's one of our new rangers, while her mom, Ahnah, assists with fundraising. Her brother, Nanook, is four.'

'You have a cosmopolitan group at Manipau, right?' said Rohan.

'Absolutely – a veritable United Nations,' said Amy. 'Greek, First Nations, Italian, Indian, Jamaican, Spanish, Irish, Chinese, Arabian, African, British, Russian, Korean, South American and American – those are the main ones.'

'That sounds great,' said Nimal. 'Are there lots of kids?'

'Yes, but most of the kids in our age range, other than Corazon, are currently either on vacation or at various summer camps,' said Amy. 'They'll be back by the twenty-third of July, and we'll all work together for the fundraiser on the sixteenth of August.'

'The youngsters were reluctant to leave Manipau,' laughed Janet, 'because you JEACs are famous. We assured them that you were here till the twenty-fourth of August, and they'd have plenty of time with you.'

'So I don't get to sign autographs? No queues of adoring fans?' sighed Nimal dramatically.

'Dumbo!' said Amy, pulling his hair affectionately. 'But I *can* call up my girlfriends who want to meet you: Kioni, Haley, Lianne, Alexa, Mo

Li, Kaitlyn, Queisha, Susan, Cara, Meg, Nancy . . .' She trailed off as Nimal groaned and the others laughed.

'Golly gumboots! Don't you dare, Amy,' protested Nimal, looking horrified.

'Scared?' challenged Amy.

'Petrified! Now, tell us more about Manipau.'

Janet's cell phone rang, and she moved away to answer it.

'I know Manipau's humongous, Amy, and you mentioned that you've added an animal shelter,' said Anu. 'How's that going?'

'Extremely well. People bring animals to us, or tell us about them, and we go on rescue missions. We have over 60 animals.'

'What news of the Conservation Community . . .' began Umedh. He stopped, as Janet returned to the table, looking upset. 'What's happened, Aunty Janet?'

'Hassan, one of our rangers, called to check when we'd be home. We're facing a serious problem at Manipau but I didn't want to spoil your reunion. If you've finished eating, let's go, and I'll update you in the van.'

'Sure, Aunty,' said Anu.

The JEACs bustled around, and within fifteen minutes they were on their way.

'What's up, Mom?' begged Amy.

'We didn't tell you and Mich, hon, since you got home from school just two days ago,' said Janet. 'As everyone knows, we specialize in grizzly bears, which are on the threatened list. There were approximately sixteen in our Centre last year. In the summer we carry out our annual census. Hassan and Shawn, our specialists in grizzlies, spent all May tracking the bears. They found eleven bears, including one mother who should have given birth three weeks ago.'

'But there should have been five more adults, and the men kept searching. Last month, they found the tracks of two male grizzlies, and further on there were blood trails, each trail ending in a big patch of dried blood. The bears were never found, although more rangers joined the search. Then Tulok offered to assist. He's an *incredible* tracker, and within a day he discovered the tracks of the other three grizzlies.'

'Did he find the bears?' asked Rohan.

'No, and we can only assume they were killed,' said Janet sadly. 'However, the main reason Hassan called was to inform me that he, Tulok and Corazon tracked the mother bear with the late pregnancy, and found her hiding in a small cave. There were two tiny cubs clinging to her – two and a half weeks old. She was badly injured, and although she tried to charge the men, she stumbled and fell down.'

'What about the cubs?' asked Anu.

'They followed their mother and climbed on top of her when she fell,' said Janet. 'Once transport arrived the mother was tranquillized, put in the vehicle and taken to the Sanctuary, where Lisa, our vet, is looking after her. The cubs were taken to the animal nursery, and our head zookeeper, Rani, is trying, unsuccessfully, to feed them.'

'Poor little things,' said Nimal.

'They're crying for their mother and won't be comforted. The mother, too, is very anxious, and Lisa says she won't calm down. We're hoping you can help, Nimal.'

'I'll do my best,' said Nimal, whose amazing charisma with animals was renowned.

'Nimal will make them feel better,' agreed Mich.

'Definitely,' added Gina. 'He'll help the mother, too. Remember how he calmed the injured snow leopard when we were in Scotland?'

'Thanks for the vote of confidence, kiddos,' said Nimal. 'But that was in a captive breeding setting – this grizzly is completely wild.'

'True, yaar,' said Umedh, 'but you also worked with wild elephants when we were in Sri Lanka.'

'The elephant situation was also different, since we had Mal-li and other working elephants,' said Nimal.

'We have confidence in you, yaar,' said Rohan, 'and know you won't do anything foolish.'

'You okay, yaar? Don't have a *temperament* or anything?' teased Nimal, who inevitably joked to cover his embarrassment.

'What do you mean by a "temperament", Nimal?' said Mich.

Nimal laughed. 'Blame Anu for that, Mich. When she was little she confused the word "temperature" with "temperament" – so now, when we're kidding we ask if someone has a *temperament*, rather than a temperature.'

The others chuckled, and Rohan said, 'I'm not *non compos* due to a high temperature, yaar, but I'll stop making you blush. Aunty Janet, do you suspect foul play?'

'What else can we think? Several centres in Western Canada have lost grizzlies and the culprits weren't caught – are they now in our Centre?

Anyway, let's forget that for now, JEACs. You've had a long flight, and there's a twelve and a half hour time difference between India and here; I suggest you sleep for a bit.'

'We're not too tired, Aunty,' said Anu, 'but it's a good idea.'

A little later, only Janet and Amy were awake, and the others slept for nearly two hours. The highways were not crowded, and they reached Hinton in good time.

Rohan woke up as they drove into a gas station, and Amy got out to refuel. 'Where are we, Aunty?'

'Hinton. How do you feel?'

'Refreshed, thanks,' said Rohan. 'May I get out for a couple of minutes?'

'Sure, hon,' said Janet. 'Are you cramped?'

'It's not too bad, Aunty; we're all used to long trips, but I wouldn't mind stretching a bit.'

'We'll join you, yaar,' said Umedh, as he and Nimal woke up, and they climbed out of the vehicle.

The others were still drowsy and didn't feel the need to get out of the van. The boys walked around for five minutes, glad to stretch their legs. Amy paid for the gas, and they helped her carry out more bottles of water.

'We'll stop for a drink, some snacks, and a washroom visit, at one of our favourite coffee shops – about an hour away,' said Janet. 'Okay, JEACs?'

'Great!' chorused the JEACs, as the van started off again.

They sang their favourite songs or chatted, and at the coffee shop they took their drinks and snacks outside and sat on some rocks, enjoying the spectacular views.

'I can't believe how warm it is,' said Rohan. 'What are normal temperatures at this time of the year?'

'It's a good summer,' said Amy. 'Today it's 23°C, and in Manipau we have an average temperature ranging from 19 to 22.'

'By the way, we've put you in the GW residence – acronym for *Grizzly Watch* since there are lots of grizzlies in that area. We know your love of independence,' said Janet. 'And, since three of you are sixteen and can drive, we'll leave two Land Rovers at your disposal.'

'Thanks, Aunty Janet,' chorused the Indian contingent.

'Who generally stays at GW?' asked Nimal.

'People experienced at living on conservation centres,' said Amy. 'It's fully equipped for rangers, researchers or visitors, and is the closest bungalow to the north boundary wall.'

They piled back into the van, Amy taking the wheel. 'What a wonderful country this is,' said Anu, taking lots of pictures. 'It must be beautiful in the winter, too.'

'It's a winter wonderland,' agreed Janet. 'The trees sparkle with icicles, and snow abounds. However, from November to April these roads can be treacherous, and are only used by those who live around here or by skiers. During the other six months, there are thousands of campers and holidaymakers. By the way, after the fundraiser we'll take you to Ontario to see the Niagara Falls, a couple of shows at Stratford, Niagara-on-the-Lake and Toronto. Naturally, African Lion Safari is a must, and you'll fly back home from Toronto.'

'That's so exciting, Aunty,' said Anu. 'I can't imagine the reality of the Falls – such an awe-inspiring body of water!'

'It sounds wonderful,' said Gina.

'Aunty Janet, how's the new venture with the Conservation Community progressing?' said Umedh. 'Please tell us more about it.'

'Actually, you'll get a clearer picture of the situation from Remo, who's the manager of the construction company and in charge of this project. He's invited you to lunch and a special information session at noon tomorrow,' said Janet. 'Can you wait till then?'

'No problemo, Aunty,' said Umedh, as he took over the wheel from Amy.

They reminisced about their fun winter adventure with the snow leopards at the Kinnaird Wildlife Conservation Centre in Scotland six months earlier. Rohan drove next and then Janet took the wheel once more.

'We're nearly home,' sang Mich. 'Manipau begins where you see that heavy green forest.'

'And we'll enter the main gates in fifteen minutes,' said Janet. 'Are you kids exhausted?'

'Not at all, Aunty,' said Rohan. 'And it's only 4:10.'

'We made excellent time on the highways,' said Janet. 'Amy, call Dad and tell him we'll be home soon.'

'Hi, Dad,' said Amy, a few minutes later, and passed on the message. She listened intently, laughed at something he said, and then hung up. 'Dad says hello to everyone, asked if the Indian JEACs were asleep, and also said that Chris-J arrived with a pal – someone named Ricky. Who's he, Mom?'

'I don't know the parents, but Ricky met Chris recently, and they hit it off. Chris's mother called last night and asked if Ricky could join Chris. Apparently, the kid had problems at school, and she felt that Chris and you kids could be good role models – especially the boys.'

'What sort of trouble, Aunty?' asked Rohan.

'I'm afraid that's confidential, son,' said Janet. 'Perhaps one of the boys will tell you – Ricky needs support and encouragement.'

'Sure, Aunty – we'll keep an eye on him,' said Umedh.

'I'll be a model of saintliness,' said Nimal. 'Once he meets me, all his troubles will vanish into thin air.'

'Huh! A likely story,' said Anu, punching him in the arm. 'If anything, he'll become worse. I remember the mischief you and Eadan got into while we were touring Scotland and England, and . . .' She trailed off, laughing, as Nimal gave her a humongous hug, and covered her mouth with his hand.

'Now, Aunty,' he pleaded, 'if you're going to remember all the sins I committed when I was a kid, I'll have to hug you to bits!'

'Kid! It was a mere six months ago, my boy,' chuckled Amy.

'Peace, ladies,' begged Nimal. 'You kids are always joking around. It's time you grew up, and – right, I'll stop, Anu,' he said hurriedly, as Anu threatened to smack him. 'But one last word – don't worry about Ricky, Aunty Janet. We'll help him in any way we can.'

'I know you will, Nimal,' said Janet, as they reached the entrance to Manipau and waited for the gates to open. 'I have complete faith in all of you.'

The drive through Manipau was lovely, and the JEACs fell silent, drinking in the beauty of their surroundings. They loved reserves and conservation centres, and the intriguing glimpses of birds and animals, moving hastily into the forest, made them impatient to spend time tracking these North American animals in their native habitat – especially the grizzly bears.

'Uncle Chris! Hunter!' shouted Gina, waving madly as they entered a huge clearing and stopped in front of a house where a tall, broad-shouldered, blond-haired man was waiting to greet them. Dancing around him was the Patels' beloved dog, Hunter – a jet-black Alsatian.

'And how are you, Gina?' said Chris, gathering Gina into a big hug. Hunter leapt on everyone, prancing around ecstatically.

The JEACs greeted Chris affectionately. They hugged and kissed Hunter, whom they adored. Hunter was thrilled to be with his family again, and after barking madly, he raced off to gather flowers for Anu and Gina – it was one of his special tricks.

'I see Mich is still over the moon,' said Chris, as his daughter jumped up at him, too, shouting with joy. 'Who'd believe that when you kids aren't around, Mich is a shy, quiet little thing? Welcome, JEACs! It's wonderful to finally have you in our home. Rohan and Umedh, you've both outstripped me, and Nimal, you're my height – what *have* you been doing – on the rack at school, again?'

'No, sir!' said Nimal, saluting smartly. 'We've just been – er – *growing in an upwardly mobile direction!*'

'I see you haven't really grown up, though, cheeky one,' smiled Chris, cuffing him affectionately.

'It's great to see you, Uncle Chris,' said Anu, who had an extra soft spot for Chris Larkin. He was a gentle man, with a great sense of humour. Despite his crazy schedule, he emailed her weekly, encouraging her with her writing – he was writing the foreword for her third book. 'Thanks so much for your emails and advice.'

'You're welcome, honey,' said Chris. 'We'll have some long chats about your books when I return from Ontario – unfortunately, I leave tomorrow morning.' Chris was a renowned speaker at international conferences on wildlife and conservation issues in Canada and North America.

'What news from Uncle Jack, sir?' said Rohan, as they unloaded the van.

Jack Larkin, Chris's brother, lived in Australia, but was in demand worldwide as a consultant on the setting up and management, as well as day-to-day running, of conservation centres. He was a favourite with the JEACs, and they looked forward to seeing him again.

'He's coming back with me for three weeks,' said Chris, and covered his ears as the JEACs yelled with joy. 'This is Kafil, our computer expert,' he continued as a tall Kenyan joined them.

'Good to meet you,' said Kafil, shaking hands with everyone and assisting with the luggage. 'Hunter's a wonderful chap – and we're good friends.' He patted the dog, who gave him a friendly lick. 'Chris, Lisa called just now.'

'Right,' said Chris. 'How tired are you, kids? Lisa and Rani are eager to see you, especially Nimal.'

'We're fine, thanks, Uncle Chris,' said Nimal. 'How can we help?'

'Let's get to the Sanctuary. The mother grizzly's in bad shape; we're trying to help her, but she needs to calm down first,' said Chris.

'Don't worry about the luggage,' said Kafil. 'I'll look after it.'

'Where are Chris-J and Ricky, hon?' asked Janet.

'At the Sanctuary,' said Chris. 'Here come Hassan and Tulok with the Land Rovers. Hunter, I'm afraid you'll have to stay here a little longer – sorry, boy.'

'Stay, Hunter,' said Nimal, hugging Hunter and patting him. 'We'll be back soon.'

Hunter barked, sat down, and waved one paw. He was a smart dog and knew they would return soon.

The JEACs and Chris piled into the waiting vehicles. Introductions were made as they all set off; the men were very pleased to meet the JEACs.

'My daughter, Corazon, is eager to meet you – she's at the Sanctuary,' said Tulok, who had Nimal, Rohan and Chris as three of his passengers. 'That poor mother bear's severely injured, has lost pints of blood, and is mourning the loss of her cubs. But she needs to calm down before we can attend to her.'

'Do you know how she was injured?' asked Rohan.

'No,' sighed Chris. 'But Tulok and Hassan will give you the low down and tell you about the five missing bears. I suspect poaching. Frankly, JEACs, I'm hoping you can resolve the problem – we're up to our eyes in work and are extremely short-staffed.'

'We'll do our best, Uncle Chris,' promised Rohan.

CHAPTER 2

At the Sanctuary

Tulok stopped outside a building with high walls. Chris led everyone into the Sanctuary, which was huge; large and small enclosures held several species of wildlife.

'Injured animals are kept here with minimum human contact until they can be released back into the reserve,' said Hassan as they walked towards the medical facilities. 'This building is a mini veterinary hospital, with accommodation for staff.'

'And here's Lisa – a highly qualified zoo veterinarian' said Chris, as a young woman came hurrying to meet them. 'Lisa, these are the JEACs, and *this* is Nimal.'

'I'm looking forward to getting to know all of you, but Nimal, we need you urgently,' said Lisa, smiling at everyone as she took Nimal's arm and led him down a narrow passage, the others following. 'Corazon, Chris-J and Ricky are watching Hurit – Corazon named the bear, and it means beautiful. Hurit's struggling to crawl from place to place, searching for her cubs. It's heartbreaking.'

They entered an area where three teenagers, looking anxiously into the enclosure, turned as the others came up. The groups nodded at each other, but didn't say anything – everyone was focused on Hurit whose fur was matted with blood. The bear made popping sounds as she sucked in air, clicked her teeth and moved her cheeks, while stumbling around the enclosure; she fell down near the mesh.

'She's scared. Move away from the enclosure, folks, and let Nimal approach,' said Chris. 'Tulok, turn on the fan behind Nimal so that his scent wafts strongly towards Hurit.'

Nimal, his gaze focused entirely on the bear, moved smoothly and fearlessly towards the enclosure. He placed the palm of his hand against the heavy mesh, speaking in a low, caressing voice.

Hurit continued making popping sounds for a few minutes, and then began listening to Nimal. Her keen sense of smell discovered his scent – she seemed to like it. Who was this creature? She stopped clicking her teeth and lay still for a few moments, licking the wounds on her chest. As Nimal continued speaking to her, she began to vocalize with tongue clicks and grunts – she was calming down. She pulled herself close to the mesh and listened to Nimal. Lisa shot a tranquillizer dart into her rump, and the bear fell asleep to the soothing tones of Nimal's voice.

Despite having seen Nimal 'charm' innumerable animals, the JEACs never ceased to be amazed at his gift; those who had never seen him in action were astounded and gazed at him, awestruck.

'Let's get her into the treatment room quickly so I can work on her,' said Lisa.

Hurit was rolled onto a sled attached to a motorized ATV, and wheeled into a lab.

Nimal stayed with Lisa, Chris, Tulok and Hassan, in order to lend a hand, while the young folk introduced themselves.

'That was *awesome*,' said Chris-J. He hugged his cousins, Amy and Mich, and shook hands with Rohan, Anu, Umedh and Gina. 'My cousins told me about Nimal, but to actually see a completely wild animal react to anyone like that – it's incredible.'

'It's amazing,' said Corazon. 'I want to see him with the cubs, too. Aunty Rani's waiting for him at the animal nursery.'

'Yeah,' said Ricky, bemusedly. 'It was *totally* – er – . . .' He broke off, clearly at a loss for words.

'Are the three of you going to join us at GW?' asked Amy.

'That's if you don't mind a loony bin!' chuckled Anu. 'With seven crazy JEACs, the three of you, plus Hunter and whatever other animals attach themselves to Nimal, it's likely to be slightly insane.'

'Sounds like fun – I'm in!' said Chris-J.

'And I,' said Corazon.

'Me, too!' said Ricky.

'Goodo,' said Amy.

'What do you mean by *JEACs*?' asked Ricky.

'We'll tell you about it tomorrow at GW,' said Umedh, hearing voices in the passage.

Nimal and the adults put the still dozing grizzly back in the enclosure, close to the mesh, and Nimal knelt outside, waiting for her to wake up.

Five minutes later Nimal said softly, 'The reversal agent's working – her eyelids flickered.' He began to speak to Hurit as she opened her eyes, and she listened to him calmly, before falling asleep again.

'Let's leave her alone,' said Lisa. As everyone left the area, Lisa gave Nimal a hug. 'Thank you. That was awesome. I wish I could see you with the cubs; but I need to stay here.'

'Will she be okay?' said Nimal anxiously.

'We don't know, son,' said Chris. 'Grizzlies can make amazing recoveries, although this one's in bad shape; she'll miss her cubs which might send her into depression.'

'I see,' said Nimal, looking upset. Chris patted his shoulder.

'I'll keep you posted on her situation,' said Lisa. 'If she survives the next two days . . .' She trailed off, said goodbye, and returned to the room from where she could monitor Hurit's enclosure.

'We have to find out who did this and *stop* them,' said Nimal fiercely.

'You will – I have confidence in you JEACs,' said Chris. 'Let's take you to see the babies. They've got to feed, or we'll lose them.'

'Sure,' said Nimal, squaring his shoulders.

As the group left the Sanctuary, Chris-J, Corazon and Ricky shook hands with Nimal, speechlessly, mounted their ATVs, and led the way to the animal nursery.

'You must be the JEACs,' said a motherly lady who had a little dog in her arms. 'I'm Rani, and this is my dog, Lulu; it's lovely to meet you. The cubs are distraught – they're refusing the milk and scream with fear if any of us try to hold them. Which one of you is Nimal?'

'I am – Mrs. – er?' said Nimal stepping forward.

'Call me Rani,' she smiled, as the JEACs quickly made friends with Lulu. 'Let's go to the kitchen.'

In the kitchen, huddled fearfully in a corner of the cage, were two tiny cubs weighing around four kilograms each.

'Poor little mites,' whispered Anu.

'Hello, kiddies,' said Nimal softly, sitting on the floor beside the open door of the cage, and reaching out his hands slowly towards the scared creatures. 'Come and have some milk. You're hungry, tired and haven't eaten in a while.'

He spoke soothingly, not making any quick movements which might frighten them, and they listened. The cubs sniffed at Nimal's hands, crept slowly towards him, and two minutes later they were in his arms, cuddling up to him.

Rani handed Nimal bottles of milk, and he gently inserted the nipples into the tiny mouths, holding a cub in each arm. The onlookers watched in amazement as the cubs drank their milk. Then, satiated and comforted, they fell asleep in Nimal's lap. He placed them gently in the cage, covering them with a furry blanket, and closed the door.

A deep sigh of delight went around the room. 'What shall we do with them, Uncle Chris?' said Nimal. 'They'll need to be fed again.'

'We'll take them with us, son,' said Chris, lifting the cage carefully. 'Will you be mama grizzly for tonight?'

'No problemo,' grinned Nimal. 'I could look after them at GW, too, as long as required.'

'That's perfect,' said Chris gratefully, leading the way to the Land Rovers.

'That was wonderful, Nimal,' said Rani, coming out to the vehicles with them. 'Thank you. I look forward to seeing you with the other animals and hope you'll visit us soon.'

'Absolutely,' said Nimal.

'Nimal, when will the cubs feel safe with us?' asked Mich.

'We'll try tonight, kiddo,' said Nimal. 'You and Gina can be mama grizzlies, too.'

Waving goodbye to Rani and giving Lulu a final pat, everyone climbed into the Land Rovers and followed the three ATVs to Tranquillity. Tulok and Hassan bid them goodnight, saying they would see them the next day.

'Boys' rooms first,' said Janet, as she and Hunter met them at the door, Hunter welcoming his family back joyfully. Her husband quickly updated her on the grizzly situation.

Rohan and Umedh, standing near Chris-J, Corazon and Ricky, noticed that the trio were extremely quiet, throwing Nimal sidelong glances as if in awe of him.'

Rohan winked at Umedh, and said, sotto voce, 'I must say, yaar – the boy's weird! See his head – swelling by the second.'

'Time to sit on him – grab his arms, and I'll get his legs,' grinned Umedh.

Seconds later, there was a scramble, as the three older boys fell on the sleeping bags in a tangle of arms and legs, Gina and Mich shrieking with laughter and egging them on. Chris-J and Ricky were enjoying the fun, when Nimal and Umedh pulled their legs from under them and they fell on top of the group. The boys had a rough and tumble – Hunter joining them – which everyone thoroughly enjoyed.

'Men!' said Amy, winking at Anu and Corazon. '*We'd* never dream of behaving in such an – er, Anu?'

'Unrefined and uncouth manner,' said Anu promptly.

'Are you calling us *uncouth*, Anu?' said Nimal, rolling out of the tangle and rising too swiftly for Anu's comfort. 'Where do you pick up such *abysmal* language? Not at all PC. Apologize immediately, or I'll tickle you till . . .' He advanced on her menacingly.

'I 'pologize! I 'pologize!' shrieked Anu, dramatically going down on her knees in front of Nimal. 'Please, Uncle, I *will* be good,' she pleaded.

By then everyone was laughing uproariously, and the tension around Nimal's gift had dissipated.

'Little wretch!' said Nimal affectionately, pulling her to her feet and giving her a rib-cracking hug.

'Ouch! Kindly remember that you're a humongous heffalump, and I'm not,' gasped Anu, pulling his hair.

'You two take the cake – in fact, you take the entire bakery,' chuckled Amy. 'Chris-J, you know how dignified, calm and, er . . . *sophisticated*, I usually am? But with these two around . . .'

Chris-J interrupted, 'You're *what*? If my memory serves me correctly, it was *you* who got Mich and me into trouble during Easter break, with a banshee-like shriek when a call from Rohan came through. You charged for the phone, leaving a disaster zone in your wake, and *we* got blamed for three broken mugs and coffee all over the table.'

'Oh, I forgot that,' grinned Amy, slipping her arm through Rohan's.

'Time for dinner, everyone,' smiled Janet. 'I'm sure . . .'

'. . . Nimal's simply STARVING!' yelled Gina and Mich, and Mich led the way to the dining room.

They served themselves and sat around the dining table.

'Chris-J, Corazon and Ricky,' said Rohan gravely, 'you've only had a glimpse of Nimal's character so far – and it *might* have given you the impression that he's something special – he is!' The other JEACs, excluding Umedh, stared. This was quite unlike Rohan.

'Hey, yaar . . .' began Nimal, but Rohan raised a hand, and he trailed off.

'When you hear about the insane tricks . . .' he paused at the shout of laughter, 'he has played – and will play – you'll be grateful for the fact that you only have to put up with him for a few weeks. And, if your name's Mohan, you'll soon wish you'd *never* met him.'

'Was it a new trick? Oh, do tell us,' begged Mich.

'What mischief did you get up to this time, kiddo?' added Amy.

'Moi? Je ne comprends pas,' said Nimal. 'I'm a saint these days – serious, studious, stupendously kind – see the halo around my head?'

'Oui, mon ami,' said Amy, 'but it's slipped and become a noose around your neck. For those who haven't heard of him before, Mohan's a guy who attends the same boarding school as Nimal, Rohan and Umedh – he's arrogant and a pest! Anu's the storyteller in our group – you're on, hon.'

'Right,' said Anu. 'Their school planned a compulsory educational trip to a wildlife centre north of Delhi. It was just before school broke up, so Gina and I heard the tale on the flight here. Forty boys and five masters camped in the jungle; they'd been warned that their tents should always be zipped up, and no food left outside since animals would be attracted to it. The largest animals were cheetahs at that centre, and they generally stayed away from humans. But Mohan was paranoid and insisted in setting up his tent right in the *centre* of the group, so that he would be well protected. The campsite had fifteen to twenty clearings, each of which held six tents. Mohan's tent mate, Prasad, a good pal of Nimal's – the two of them are known as "I Squared" which stands for *incorrigible imps* – wasn't a "Mohan fan". I^2 knew the masters had deliberately separated them in the hopes of having relatively peaceful nights.

'The first three nights Mohan screeched at every shadow – be it boys, branches of trees, a rustling in the shrubbery, a mongoose running past, a hopping bunny, or an early bird looking for the worm. He insisted on Prasad accompanying him everywhere. Prasad, the other chaps and the masters were getting pretty cheesed off with Mohan. "I wish we could give him something to *really* screech about", grumbled Prasad to Nimal over lunch the next day. "I have a plan, yaar", said our boy.'

Ricky raised his hand and asked, 'What does "yaar" mean?'

'It's an informal Hindi word, used mainly by males in India, and it means mate or buddy,' explained Umedh, 'and you don't have to raise your hand, *yaar*.'

'Thanks,' grinned Ricky. 'Sorry, Anu, please continue.'

'No problemo. One of the rangers had a large cat which, naturally, adopted Nimal; Ranil, Nimal's tent mate, a quiet chap who loved wildlife and enjoyed watching Nimal with animals, had no objection to the extra room-mate.' The Indian JEACs began to chuckle, as Anu continued the tale. 'The next night at 9:15, when the camp was in total silence, I^2 carried out their plan.

'Mohan was in his sleeping bag when a loud rustle was heard in the shrubbery. "What's that?" squeaked Mohan, sitting up quickly. "Nothing, man, go to sleep." Mohan lay down. A few seconds later, a low growl was heard, and Mohan jerked upright, trembling in fright. "I *know* there's something out there, Prasad. The rangers told us that cheetahs growl. *Do something* – don't just lie there laughing! Call a ranger, call the masters, call the cops", he moaned. The growl came again as well as the rustling, and Prasad, hiding a grin, said, "Okay, give me your torch, and I'll check".

'He unzipped the tent and disappeared. Mohan zipped it up quickly and sat in the middle, shaking with fear. Suddenly a bright light shone onto the tent, and the shadow of a huge figure, with a catlike head, was projected onto the side of the tent. Menacing growls ensued, and then the figure flung itself at the tent. Mohan hollered for help, screeching wildly, and all the boys and masters raced over, along with two rangers with tranquillizer guns. They unzipped the tent and pulled Mohan out – still screaming blue murder. Then, two prefects, trying to keep straight faces, pushed something into the middle of the ring of people – I^2 and a cat!'

Everyone roared with laughter.

'Needless to say, Nimal and Prasad were punished – they each had to write out two thousand lines saying "I will not play incorrigible tricks",' concluded Anu. 'Mohan was furious that the punishment was not more severe, but everyone was tired of him, and told him not to be so pusillanimous – a word Mohan had to look up in the dictionary later on. When more than twenty-five boys assisted I^2 with their lines, the masters turned a blind eye on the varying handwriting, and chuckled over the trick.'

'Oh, Nimal,' said Janet, wiping her eyes, 'will you *ever* grow up?'

'Doing my best, ma'am,' grinned Nimal, 'but Prasad and I figured it was our *duty* to help Mohan become an eager conservationist – and less fainthearted.'

Chris-J choked over his food and had to be slapped on the back by Umedh, who said mockingly, 'Sure, yaar, and naturally it had nothing to do with the fact that the two of you can't resist playing abominable tricks on the chap.'

'But . . .' began Nimal.

'Or the fact that Mohan's *never* going to appreciate your stated altruism,' said Anu. 'Sorry, kiddos,' she said, turning to Gina and Mich. 'Altruism means "selfless concern for the wellbeing of others", which is certainly not I Squared's primary intention where Mohan is concerned.'

'Do tell us about other tricks you've played,' begged Ricky.

'It'll take years to tell you about *all* Nimal's pranks,' said Amy, 'but we'll tell you more when the APs aren't around.'

'APs?' asked Corazon.

'Aged Parents,' chanted Mich and Gina.

'Oh!' said Corazon, and she, Chris-J and Ricky looked at Janet and Chris to see how they took this.

'Well, this AP and Kafil are going to stagger off to bed,' laughed Chris, rising from the table. 'We leave at 4:30 and Kafil's dropping me at the airport. It's good to have all of you at Manipau – and please save our grizzlies.'

'We will! Good night, Uncle Chris and Kafil,' chorused the youngsters, 'and thanks for having us.'

'Aunty Janet, how can we help?' said Anu, as they cleared up.

'As Chris said, by solving the problem with our grizzlies,' said Janet, loading the dishwasher. 'Look after yourselves and each other at GW.'

'Will do,' said everyone.

'Do you want Hunter's new pals, Sam and Codey, at GW?'

'Absolutely! Three dogs and ten of us will be a blast!' said Nimal. 'When do we meet the boys?'

'They're at my place and someone will bring them to GW,' said Corazon.

'What's our programme for tomorrow?' said Rohan.'

'In the morning – breakfast at six, feed the grizzly babes, see how Hurit's doing at the Sanctuary, and a visit to the animal nursery. Lunch meeting with Remo to learn about the Conservation Community, then back here to organize everything and set off for GW,' said Janet. 'How does that sound?'

'Wonderful!' said Amy, and the others nodded.

Everyone went to the boys' room to feed the cubs. 'Good, they're waking up,' said Nimal.

Nimal made Mich and Gina sit on a sleeping bag, with a bottle each, and gently took the cubs out of their cage. Speaking soothingly, he gave them to Mich and Gina, keeping a hand on each of the cubs. The babes, cuddled by the girls, drank their milk greedily, knowing they were safe since Nimal was with them. They showed no fear of the girls and as soon as the bottles were empty, cuddled deeper into the girls' arms, and fell asleep again. Nimal put them back in their cage.

'They're adorable,' sighed Gina.

'I could cuddle them forever,' added Mich.

'Nimal, what caused Hurit's injury?' asked Rohan.

'She was shot,' said Nimal grimly. 'Lisa removed seven bullets from her chest – they didn't hit a vital organ but Hurit's in bad shape.'

'Horrid, horrid people,' choked Mich. 'How dare they hurt our animals. Rohan, we *must* catch the crooks quickly.'

'Definitely, kiddo,' said Rohan, hugging her and his little sister. 'We'll discuss the situation and make plans tomorrow evening, okay?'

'Okay, Rohan,' said Mich and Gina.

The girls said goodnight to the boys, and went to their room. It had been a long, exhausting day, and by 10 p.m. everybody was fast asleep.

CHAPTER 3

Ataneq and Atka

'Rise and shine, boys,' said Rohan, leaping out of his sleeping bag at 5 a.m. A chorus of groans answered him, but the boys were ready in half an hour.

'Who wants to feed the cubs?' asked Nimal, giving Hunter a hug as the dog licked him. 'I fed them around 2:30 a.m., but they'll be hungry again.'

'Do you and Ricky want to take first dibs, Chris? I heard that Uncle Chris left for Ontario over an hour ago, so I guess we don't have to call you Chris-J any more,' said Umedh.

'Yes, please,' said Chris eagerly.

'Are you sure it'll be . . .' said Ricky hesitantly.

'Definitely, yaar,' said Nimal. 'Hold them firmly, so they feel secure. I'll introduce Hunter to them first, so that they aren't frightened. Rohan, I need you, too.'

The girls joined them as Nimal opened the cage. The cubs, very lively this morning, scrambled out and climbed all over him. Nimal spoke to them gently, passed one cub to Rohan, and then called Hunter to sit beside him.

The big dog obeyed. 'Hunter, these are friends,' said Nimal. 'They're babies and need to be treated gently, okay?'

Hunter stared at the cub, wondering if it was a puppy – he had a lot of experience with baby animals. He lay down, resting his nose on Nimal's knee. Nimal, holding the cub securely, brought it close to Hunter, speaking softly, and patting both Hunter and the cub. The cub and Hunter looked at each other curiously and sniffed, rubbing noses. Hunter whined softly, and the cub tumbled out of Nimal's arms with a little grunt, and snuggled beside Hunter, putting out a paw to pat the dog. The other cub also climbed out of Rohan's lap and joined its sibling. In a few minutes, the three creatures had become friends.

'Ooh! Look at Hunter licking them,' smiled Gina. 'The cubs aren't scared of him.'

'Maybe they think he's their mother – they're looking for milk,' chuckled Mich.

'Time to feed them,' grinned Nimal, and passed the cubs to Chris and Ricky, who each had a bottle of milk. The cubs drank the milk eagerly, keeping an eye on Hunter and Nimal.

'This is cool,' said Chris, cuddling the cub he was feeding.

'It's so tiny,' said Ricky. 'I find it hard to believe that these little creatures become huge bears. I've never bottle-fed an animal before.'

After the cubs had drained the bottles, Chris and Ricky reluctantly put them down on the sleeping bags. The cubs immediately scampered over to Nimal and Hunter. After a few minutes Nimal beckoned the others, and everyone had a chance to cuddle and pet the cubs.

'They're adorable,' said Corazon, hugging the cub she was holding. 'And friendly, too. I'd never have believed they would become comfortable with us so quickly – I guess it's because you're here, Nimal.'

'They'll soon go to anyone,' said Nimal.

'Are they female or male?' asked Chris.

'One of each,' said Nimal. 'Corazon, give us some nice names for them.'

'Hmmm. What about Ataneq, for the male, which means *king* – and for the female, Atka, which means *guardian spirit*?'

'Those are super names, Corazon,' said Amy. 'Nimal, Lisa called and asked if you could come by this morning.'

'Sure, what time?'

'After breakfast,' said Amy. 'We have time for the animal nursery before lunch at CC.'

'What's CC?' said Ricky.

'Sorry, Ricky – Conservation Community,' chuckled Anu. 'We use tons of acronyms. For example, GW is the acronym for *Grizzly Watch.*'

'Gotcha,' grinned Ricky.

'Sorry, mate, I should've warned you,' said Chris. 'I've adjusted to my cousins talking in acronyms, but it's confusing at first. I was stumped when Mich asked me how my MB was going – she had to explain that she meant mountain biking.'

The others laughed, and after Nimal had put the cubs back into their cage, snuggled around a couple of Mich's teddy bears, they went to the dining room.

'Good morning, Aunty Janet,' said Nimal, hugging her exuberantly. 'My nose tells me that there are heavenly concoctions in the vicinity.'

'Now, young man,' said Janet, trying, unsuccessfully, to push him away, 'I nearly cracked a rib when you hugged me at the airport, and I have too much work on my hands without additional injuries.'

'Nobody loves me,' sighed Nimal, giving her a gentle hug and releasing her. 'It's . . .'

'. . . one of the saddest stories of your life,' chanted Mich and Gina.

'I give up,' said Nimal sadly, going over to the buffet table, and handing out plates. 'Kids these days! Do have some manners, Mich, Gina – and here's a huge dish of it. No, these are sausages. Aha – allow me to serve you half a sausage each, everyone – which,' he muttered sotto voce, 'leaves the rest for me.'

'Back of the queue, yaar,' said Rohan. 'Ladies first.'

'Sure, as long as it's also *first into the lion's den*,' said Nimal, going to the back of the queue.

Amidst much laughing and teasing, the group settled down to eat quickly.

'Gosh, it's 7 a.m.,' said Rohan, as his watch beeped. 'How do we get to the Sanctuary and animal nursery, Aunty – walk?'

'Take two Land Rovers. Rohan and Umedh, you can drive, with Amy and Chris beside you. Get back by 11:30, and we'll send you to the CC meeting. Nimal, do you think the cubs will take milk from us when you're not here?'

'I think so, Aunty. They were very friendly, and we'll leave Hunter to help.'

'Thanks,' said Janet.

Piling into the vehicles, they drove off and were soon at the Sanctuary, being greeted by Lisa, Hassan and Tulok. Two of Lisa's best assistants, Anthony and Giuliana, who also helped at the animal nursery, were pleased to meet the JEACs.

'How's Hurit, Lisa?' asked Nimal, following her to the enclosure.

'If you can calm her down and persuade her to drink some of the medicated water, she'll sleep for a couple of hours,' said Lisa.

'Okay,' said Nimal.

'Nimal, go ahead and we'll observe from here,' said Tulok.

Nimal sat on the floor opposite the food and water which had been placed for the grizzly, and spoke to the bear. 'How are you, Hurit? We named your cubs for you – Atka and Ataneq. They're good kids, drinking lots of milk and getting plenty of sleep. You need to eat and drink too, so that you heal quickly.'

Hurit listened intently. She recognized the comforting voice and scent of the human. She moved painfully towards Nimal, came up to the mesh and sniffed at his hand which he had once more placed against the mesh. She made a soft sound, lay down contentedly, and listened to the boy. After a few minutes she drank half the water in the large bowl, put her head down, and five minutes later she was asleep.

Lisa and the others did a silent jig of joy. Nimal kept talking to Hurit a little longer; when the bear didn't wake up, he joined the others.

'Excellent,' said Lisa softly. 'Thanks, Nimal. I'm thrilled you're here. I have to go and deal with some of the other animals, but I'll see you around 10 a.m. after you've visited the animal nursery.'

'Okay, Lisa, unless you'd like some help here,' offered Nimal.

'No, thanks. Giuliana and Anthony are available to assist this week,' and Lisa hurried off.

Tulok and Hassan joined the youngsters at the animal nursery, where Rani and Lulu greeted them. 'How's Hurit?' asked Rani.

'Sleeping peacefully, thanks to Nimal's charisma,' said Hassan.

'That's wonderful, and hopefully she'll continue improving,' said Rani. 'Shall we go and see the babies?'

'Yes, please,' they chorused, after saying hello to Lulu.

'Swift foxes first, and I'll tell you the story of how we acquired the first pair,' said Rani, leading the way to an enclosure from which a great deal of excited barking was heard.

'Are there swift fox babies, I mean, *kits* – did I get the name right?' asked Gina.

'Yes, Gina,' said Rani. 'The babies are known as kits, cubs or pups. And we have lots of them.' She stopped in front of a large enclosure, and fifteen kits raced up to the barrier, yipping joyfully when they smelled the meat and berries.

'They're adorable,' cooed Gina. 'Can we feed them, Rani?'

'Sure, hon. We'll lure them through the creep into the smaller enclosure on the side, and you can play with them.'

Once the kits were in the sectioned-off enclosure, Rani let the group inside, having given them each a large bowl of food.

'They're so friendly and cute,' said Anu, as a kit sat in her lap and ate hungrily, pausing to give her a quick lick now and then.

'And they adore Nimal,' laughed Hassan, who, along with Tulok, was watching from outside. Five cubs sat either in Nimal's lap, stood on his legs, or pressed themselves close to the boy as they gobbled up their food.

'How did you get the first swift foxes, Rani? I understand they were once an endangered species,' said Anu. 'I assume this lot will be used for captive breeding purposes.'

'That's right, Anu, and we have eight centres waiting for them. You've heard of Clio Smeeton who did an incredible job of breeding swift foxes in captivity and then releasing them back into the wild, right?' They nodded. 'We got our first four pairs from *The Cochrane Ecological Institute*, started by Clio's parents.

'The CEI, located just west of Calgary, has been breeding swift foxes for many years. We were eager to participate, and some of their staff taught us everything. It's been a successful project.'

'Tell us about them, please,' said Chris.

'Their Latin name is *Vulpes velox*, and technically speaking, a group is called a "skulk",' said Rani. 'Foxes make short, yipping barks, high-pitched wails, and also chuckle and churr; they live in dens, have a keen sense of smell and hearing, and, in general, mate for life. They're community oriented, and a cub, if the parents aren't around, will be looked after by other adults. They are omnivores, and eat mammals and insects, as well as fruit and grasses. Tulok, do you want to continue?'

'Sure. Their name originates from their speed – they've been known to achieve speeds of nearly 60 kilometres per hour. They're very small animals, weighing an average of 2.5 kilograms; kits weigh very little at birth, but they soon look like adults – this lot were born in May. The females produce three to five kits at a time, but on occasion there can be eight in a litter. In the wild, if they're lucky, they may survive for eight to ten years, but in captivity they live for thirteen to fifteen years.'

'Wow! They're incredible animals, given they're so small,' said Ricky.

'They are, and if you want to know more details, you should visit the CEI sometime, Ricky,' said Amy. 'It's close to where you and Chris live.'

'I will,' said Ricky.

'These kits have had a great time,' said Rani, 'but we must feed the other babies.'

They left the enclosure, and had fun feeding the many species of baby animals and watching their antics with Nimal.

'Time to get back to the Sanctuary, folks – it's 9:45,' said Rohan, as his watch beeped.

Reluctantly they left the animal nursery, after thanking Rani, who promised to bring Lulu over to spend a day at GW, and drove back to the Sanctuary.

'How's Hurit?' asked Nimal as they joined Lisa.

'Incredibly well! Look,' said Lisa, pointing to the screen in front of her.

They gathered around the monitor. Hurit was eating; then she drank more water, lay down and went to sleep again. The group sighed with relief.

'She woke up five minutes ago and drank a little water before eating,' said Lisa. 'I'm going to be optimistic and say she'll be fine. Would you agree, Tulok and Hassan?'

'Absolutely – she looks so much better,' said Hassan, observing the grizzly closely.

'Her breathing's less tortured,' added Tulok.

'Brilliant!' said Nimal. 'Is there anything else you'd like us to do?'

'No thanks, Nimal,' said Lisa, gratefully. 'It's been great to have your assistance with Hurit. Perhaps, one of these days, all of us can have a fun evening together.'

'We'd love that, Lisa,' said Anu, 'and we're looking forward to hearing your stories.'

They left the Sanctuary and returned to Tranquillity to park their vehicles; they would drive to the CC with Tulok and Hassan.

'Once we're at GW, will you and Tulok have time to tell us what happened yesterday when you were tracking the bears and found Hurit?' asked Rohan.

'It would also be helpful to have details of what you found when tracking the missing bears,' added Nimal.

'Sure,' said Tulok. 'We'll come to GW around 5:30 p.m. today. We'll get Shawn, too, and I'll bring Sam and Codey when I come. Does that work for you, Hassan?'

'Sure. My family are in Vancouver and leave for Dubai today; I'll be speaking with them at 4:30, before their flight takes off.'

'Will we meet them before our holiday's over?' asked Gina.

'Absolutely! They wouldn't miss the fundraiser for anything,' chuckled Hassan. 'Fadi's longing to meet you. He's fourteen this year and, together with his best friend, Marco, started a JEACs group in their school. They're both keen fundraisers, and want to become conservationists.

'Marco's father, Omar, a highly qualified surgeon, went to Dubai six months ago and was appointed as the doctor for one of the sheikhs. He wanted his family to come to Dubai for their vacation. My wife and Marco's mother are best friends, and were going to be in Dubai at the same time. However, neither boy wanted to go until we told them they should recruit kids and get them to start a JEACs group in Dubai.'

'Good for them,' chuckled Rohan. 'Do you have other children, Hassan?'

'Twin daughters, Farah and Falak, who are six – they're determined to save the world. My youngest son, Nabil, at three and a half, has learned the words: JEACs, funraining, save our plant and consation. He's convinced that *recooting* is an animal which looks like a racoon.'

The others chuckled, and Anu said, 'I can't wait to meet them, Hassan – and your son, too, Tulok.'

'Time to leave for CC, folks – Remo's a busy man,' said Hassan.

They piled into vehicles and set off.

CHAPTER 4

Conservation Community

'Where are we on the map, Rohan?' asked Chris, looking over Rohan's shoulder.

'Right here, yaar,' said Rohan, pointing. 'We're going south at the moment. Hassan, do we cross a bridge?'

'Once we're through the gates, the first bridge over the Akie River is fairly close. It was completed last week and leads right into the CC.'

'Are they already building houses in the CC?' asked Anu.

'The show home was completed at the same time as the bridge. Other than that, we have several large, temporary buildings – accommodation for the workers,' said Hassan as they approached the gates.

The gatekeeper recognized the vehicles and opened the gates, waving to the youngsters as they passed.

'I can't believe how quickly the bridge was completed,' said Amy, as they approached the bridge.

'Remo sent out an appeal to construction companies in Alberta, British Columbia and Saskatchewan asking for construction workers,' said Hassan. 'You'll hear details at the meeting. And here we are.'

He parked and took them into a large building. A number of construction workers in the dining room waved to the youngsters.

'Too bad we're not joining them,' said Nimal, following Tulok through a door into a smaller room where a meal was being laid out in buffet style on a side table. 'Some of them look fun, and barely older than us.'

'Hello, Xing and Solon,' said Tulok, greeting the men who were placing dishes of food on the table. 'Kids, these two are highly qualified chefs.'

'And I'm Remo Mancini,' said a big man, entering the room right behind the children. Everyone introduced themselves.

'Amy and Mich, it's great to see you,' said Remo, hugging the girls and shaking hands with the others. He looked like a very fit soccer player. His brown eyes studied the group, thinking that they looked a fine lot of youngsters. 'Let's serve ourselves and get to know each other. We'll talk about the CC over dessert.' He began handing out plates.

'So you're the famous JEACs,' said Remo, as everyone sat down, Xing and Solon joining them. 'I've known the Larkins for years. When my kids heard about the JEACs, two years ago, they were determined to start a group in their school and with their cousins.'

'They formed the first group in Kamloops, right, Remo?' said Amy.

'Yes. JEACs – CBCK – #23. Sergio, Pietro and even Carmela, who's only six, have all recruited members. I was told last night, before I left to come here, that I should inform Amy, Mich and all the other Indian JEACs that JEACs #23 have raised over $3,000 in eight months, and will donate the money to Manipau – their unanimous choice for this year.'

'That's wonderful! It's so exciting to hear how well the groups in Canada are doing,' said Anu.

'How old are you, Gina?' asked Solon.

'Ten; Mich and I are twins,' said Gina.

'I see that!' twinkled Remo. 'It's tough telling you apart.'

The girls grinned at him, and the others laughed. It was a jolly meal.

'Has everyone had enough?' asked Xing.

'Yes, thanks! It was superfantabulous – absolutely delish,' sang out the youngsters.

'Excellent! We'll clear up and bring in dessert,' said Solon.

'We'll help,' said everyone.

Plates and dishes were loaded onto trolleys, which were wheeled into the large kitchen, and a tray of desserts was brought in.

Once everyone was served, Remo began the meeting. 'Jump in with questions as we go along,' he told them. 'How much do you know about the concept behind the CC?'

'Not much. Amy told us about it a year ago, when the concept was initially formed,' said Rohan.

'We also know that you got government approval for the project incredibly fast, and that there's tremendous support from the community and businesses,' said Anu.

'Ricky and I don't know anything about it,' added Chris.

'Okay, these are the facts. Last summer we had a big fundraiser with a fantastic turnout from the community. Yes, Umedh?'

'When you say *community*, what's the extent of the region you're referring to? Are we talking about Alberta only, or British Columbia, too?'

'Good question,' said Remo. 'We're referring to both provinces – Manipau is close to BC, and is one of the largest centres in this region. A highlight of the fundraiser was a general discussion about educating the public on the importance of conservation, learning about endangered species and why it was critical to protect their habitat. Something which caused Chris to bring up this topic, sooner rather than later, was an increasing demand for housing communities for our ageing population in both provinces, and the government's looking for suitable venues. Canada has land in plenty, but what's suitable and most attractive to retirees and their offspring?'

'What did you do?' said Anu.

'Chris, Janet, Bella – my wife – and I discussed the matter at length and called a meeting of an eclectic group of people. The group included conservationists, environmentalists, politicians, managers of construction companies, philanthropists, educationalists, et cetera. It was a mind-boggling meeting! We were all on the same wavelength – a rare occurrence – and reached a unanimous conclusion.' He paused and looked around the eager young faces.

'And the decision?' said Nimal.

'It was threefold. *First*: we would petition the governments of Alberta and BC to allocate a large strip of land north and east of the Akie River for a Conservation Community for retirees. *Second*: we would contact all interested parties, to begin with, and obtain donations towards the building of this project – these donations would be either in kind, or monetary. *Third*: the purpose of the CC would be to fulfil several needs: housing for retirees, community, education on saving our planet, and protection of the habitat for the many species of animals living in Manipau, especially the grizzlies. Naturally, Manipau would take the lead in the education on environmental and conservation issues, and enhance their education programmes.'

'Awesome!' exclaimed Amy. 'When you put it like that, Remo, I can't imagine why nobody thought of it before.'

'There's a time and place for everything, hon,' said Remo.

'True,' said Rohan. 'It's amazing how such a humongous project moved so rapidly in a year.'

'What will the CC look like?' asked Chris.

'Here's a drawing,' said Remo, turning on a projector and using a pointer as he spoke. 'The area's outlined in blue. We'll have varying types of accommodation and everything that a retiree city would require, like shopping malls, hospitals, et cetera. We're in the process of building three bridges across the Akie, and we've completed the first one, which you probably came over today.'

'That's right,' said Gina and Mich.

'Hassan mentioned that you sent out a request for construction workers. The response must have been stupendous,' said Umedh.

'It was – 849 volunteers offered their services, and this was before I told them that each of them must sign their name on the walls of the bridge once it was completed. It was going to be part of the educational aspect that a community must pull together and help one another. The beauty of the bridge was not the goal.'

'Ingenious. How did you handle the multitude?' asked Rohan.

'Split them into batches so that each person only gave up a couple of vacation days. They were a hard-working, joyful group, with many experienced hands, and the job was completed in record time.'

'Why were so many people interested in volunteering for this project?' asked Corazon.

'Everyone either had family, or knew of people who would benefit from this project, and they wanted to contribute. They also wanted their children and community to learn about conservation, the environment, and community efforts.'

'Did they volunteer for the other bridges, too?' asked Mich.

'Yes, and we thanked them for their generosity,' said Remo. 'However, as part of our ongoing education, we asked them to share their experience with colleagues and friends, and said we would choose from the new offers first. Since we would need ongoing assistance with the building of the rest of the community, we assured them we would be grateful for any further support they could offer. We'll recognize all volunteer work.'

'What a marvellous concept! People are incredibly generous,' said Anu.

'They are,' smiled Remo. 'Now, although I hate to bring a negative note into this room, we're very upset about the missing grizzly bears. You know what's happening, right?' The youngsters nodded. 'You JEACs have resolved similar issues at four other conservation centres and I hope you'll be able to do the same here.'

'Absolutely, Remo,' said Rohan, 'and we'd like to hear your ideas.'

'My first thought is poachers, looking for big money. Secondly, the crooks *must* be people who live around the area.'

'Would any of your construction team have information?' asked Rohan. 'Perhaps something they noticed while building the bridge?'

'I don't know, Rohan,' said Remo. 'I've told the teams to keep their eyes and ears open, and they've assured me they'll do so. Feel free to talk to them – they know about you, and that you have my support.'

'Sure – thanks, Remo,' said Umedh. 'Which bridge will be built next?'

'We're working on the one in the north-east.'

'That's the one just north-east of GW,' said Hassan, pointing it out on the drawing. 'I wish we could assist you in catching the crooks, but we're extremely short-staffed.'

'No worries, Hassan,' said Rohan. 'There are ten of us, and we're used to getting around.'

'So I've heard,' laughed Tulok. 'I see Corazon's all set to help catch the crooks.' He winked at his daughter affectionately and she smiled.

'Also, JEACs, Corazon's an excellent tracker,' added Hassan. 'She found the first tracks of the pregnant mother.'

'I'm so glad we found Hurit and her babies,' said Corazon, and quickly updated Remo about Hurit's condition.

'It's nearly 1:15 p.m.,' said Rohan, looking at his watch, 'and I know you're extremely busy. Before we leave, Remo, may I ask a few more questions?'

'Go ahead.'

'How many construction workers are there?' said Rohan. 'Does everyone live on site? Do they work in specific teams, and if so, how many teams are there? How many supervisors do you have?'

'Good questions. Briefly: we have 174 workers. Six supervisors and 76 workers live on site; the others travel from nearby communities. There are eleven teams, each led by two supervisors – a total of 22 supervisors. Occasionally a few teams work together, depending on the project.'

'Super, thanks,' said Rohan.

'You're welcome,' said Remo. 'Here's my business card – call me any time.'

'We should take off, now, folks,' said Tulok.

'Thanks for spending time with us, Remo. We'll do our best to protect the grizzlies,' said Amy, giving him a hug.

'Yes, thanks a ton, Uncle Remo,' chorused the others.

The youngsters said goodbye to the men, thanked Xing and Solon for the delicious meal, and drove back to the Sanctuary.

CHAPTER 5

Settling in at Grizzly Watch

'It's just past 1:30,' said Rohan, as they entered the Sanctuary. 'I hope Hurit's continuing to improve.'

Lisa assured them that Hurit was on the way to a speedy recovery; the grizzly had eaten more food and was sleeping peacefully.

'We're off to GW shortly, Lisa,' said Nimal, as they said goodbye, 'but call if necessary; we'll come over ASAP.' Lisa thanked them warmly.

A few minutes later they jumped out of the vehicles at Tranquillity, and thanked Hassan and Tulok.

'You're welcome, JEACs. We'll see you at 5:30 p.m.,' said Hassan.

'And try not to play with the adult grizzlies, Nimal,' grinned Tulok.

'I doubt he'll listen,' said a cheeky voice from the doorway.

The men drove off and the youngsters turned to the house.

'Sheri!' exclaimed the Canadian crowd. 'What *have* you done to your hair?'

'Oh? Is there something weird about it?' laughed the woman in the doorway.

'It's pink and green,' shrieked Mich, 'and it's a Mohawk! Look at those spikes!'

'Right, I forgot,' said Sheri. 'Won't you introduce me to these famous JEACs?'

'Er . . . sure,' said Amy, staring at the woman bemusedly. 'JEACs, this is Sheri, our office manager and also chair of our fundraising committee and . . . hang on a sec. I've seen that hairstyle before!' She advanced towards a grinning Sheri and lunged at her head, grabbing the hair and . . .

'It's a wig!' yelled the others, and roared with laughter as it came off in Amy's hand. Sheri's brown curls danced around her head as she shook with mirth.

'Gotcha!' laughed Sheri, pulling Amy into a hug. 'So you recognized it from last year's fundraiser, did you, hon? I couldn't resist.'

Amidst much laughter, teasing and explaining, the JEACs were introduced to Sheri, and she and Nimal got along like a house on fire.

'Quick drink before we get going, folks,' said Janet, who, along with Kafil, had been observing the fun.

'The Land Rovers are loaded, and the cubs are in their cage, ready to go with you, Nimal,' said Kafil. 'Hunter helped us feed them and they're fast asleep now.'

'How did Hunter help?' asked Ricky.

'The cubs were upset when they didn't find Nimal or any of you others,' said Kafil, 'but Hunter whined softly, and they recognized him at once, clamoured to get out of their cage, and cuddled up to him. They drank their milk without protest, letting us hold the bottles for them. That's one amazing dog! He just sat there, a feeding cub on either side, and once they'd finished he licked them gently, and stayed still until they fell asleep again.'

'Where's Hunter now?' asked Gina.

'Keeping an eye on them,' said Janet. 'Come and see.'

They followed Janet into the boys' room. Hunter's tail wagged frantically and he loped over to lick everyone. He didn't bark or make a noise.

'He knows they're sleeping,' said Nimal, hugging the intelligent dog, 'and doesn't want to wake them with a shock.'

The others fussed over Hunter, too, and he followed them to the dining room.

'You're one smart cookie, aren't you, Hunter,' said Sheri, giving him a hug. 'If you kids don't want him at GW, you can leave him with me.'

'Er . . . thanks, Sheri,' began Anu, 'but we can't really do without him. He's part of . . .' she trailed off and grinned at the woman who was watching quizzically while Anu strove to answer politely. 'Okay – I completely understand what Amy meant when she described you as "a little wretch".'

'Pax!' laughed Sheri. 'I'll be good now. Shall we move, folks? Janet and I have a meeting tonight, and need to get rid of you – I mean, naturally, we'd like to *settle you into* GW comfortably before we return.'

'You're *never* good, Sheri,' said Chris cheekily. 'We're always on pins, wondering what trouble you'll get us into next.'

'Washrooms and then into the vehicles, folks,' said Kafil, as Sheri pretended to throttle Chris. 'No murders allowed, Sheri.'

A few minutes later, a merry group of people climbed into three Land Rovers, along with the cubs and Hunter. They crossed the lake in motor boats, then took the Land Rovers waiting for them on the other side, and reached GW at 3:20 p.m. The baggage was unloaded and the group trooped into the house.

'The boys can sleep in the basement, while the girls have a dormitory on the second floor. On the ground floor there's a large eat-in kitchen and a comfy living room,' said Sheri.

'And there's enough room in the basement for the cubs,' said Janet. 'We'll have to assign these two for captive breeding at Manipau – they'll be far too tame to be released back into the wild.'

Hunter barked and ran into the lounge, sniffing at the cubs and licking them. The cubs were awake and eager to get out of their cage, and when Rohan opened the cage, they tumbled out, grunting happily at being able to get close to Hunter. Hunter lay down and they fell on top of him, patting him excitedly.

'Perhaps Hunter will play nursemaid,' grinned Nimal. 'Come on, Hunter, round up your kids.'

Hunter jumped up and went to Nimal. To everyone's delight, the cubs scampered behind him, but the minute they scented Nimal, they clutched at his legs, clamouring to be held, and he sat on the ground so they could climb into his lap.

'Hard to believe he's *that* irresistible,' sighed Rohan.

'They're adorable,' crooned Gina, stroking the cubs gently. 'May I hold one, Nimal?'

'And I'd like the other, please,' begged Mich.

'Sure,' said Nimal, passing over the cubs. 'Sheri, are there any toys the cubs can play with?'

'In the cupboard,' said Sheri, and fetched two teddy bears. 'Will these suffice?'

'They're perfect! Gina and Mich, see if the cubs will play with these.'

The cubs gazed at the teddy bears, and approached them cautiously. Ataneq, the male, grunted and then pounced on one of the teddies, trying to wrestle it. When the teddy didn't fight back, he gave it a good smack, sending it skittering along the floor to Gina, who promptly returned it. This became a great game for Ataneq, and he got cross with Atka, who intercepted the teddy bear and hugged it tightly. Happily Mich distracted Ataneq by pushing the second teddy bear across to him.

'I could watch them for hours,' said Janet, 'but we have to get going, so listen up. There's a fully equipped lab and medical cabinet, the fridges and freezers are loaded, and there are several meeting rooms.'

'Amy and Corazon know where everything is,' added Kafil, 'There are computers and telephone extensions in most rooms, along with phone lists. Cell phone reception is impossible, except occasionally near the boundary walls. In the cabinet next to the bookshelf there are walkie-talkies, in sets of six. There are three sets, and they're very powerful. Take them with you whenever you leave GW.'

'You're quite isolated at GW,' said Sheri. 'Since we're currently short-staffed at Manipau Wildlife Conservation Trust, please take extra precautions.'

'We don't know what the situation is with respect to the grizzlies being hunted, so familiarize yourselves with MWCC,' said Kafil. 'The gatekeepers, Min-jae and Su-bin, as well as the construction workers over the wall, are the closest adults to GW. If necessary, try to reach them and they'll get messages to us.'

Kafil's watch beeped. 'We need to leave. There are smaller maps of Manipau, and each of you should keep a copy handy at all times.'

'We will, sir,' said Rohan, reading the concern in Kafil's face.

'They're a responsible lot, Kafil,' said Janet. 'Most of them are experienced in handling both tranquilliser equipment and rifles, and are used to looking after themselves and one another.'

'You're right, Janet,' said Kafil, smiling at the group. 'Sorry, folks. I know you'll be careful.'

'No problemo, Kafil,' said Umedh.

'JEACs, we're all on a tight schedule with lots to do, in addition to being short-staffed, so you won't be able to reach us easily,' said Janet. 'Try to leave us an occasional message so we know you're okay.'

'We will, Aunty Janet,' said Rohan.

'Time to run,' said Sheri, opening the door.

The youngsters saw the adults to their vehicles, and waved goodbye.

'It's a few minutes past four,' said Rohan, closing the door and returning to the lounge.

'Shall we prepare some food so that we can eat as we chat with the rangers? They'll be here soon,' said Amy.

'Sounds good to me,' said Nimal and Chris promptly.

'Yes – we know, you're simply *starving*,' chuckled Anu. 'Any suggestions – oh, look at Ataneq! What a comedian.'

They laughed at the cub's antics; he was trying to climb onto the sofa, and kept slipping off with little grunts of surprise.

'Here, Ataneq, I'll help you,' said Gina, and lifted the cub onto the sofa. 'Golly! Don't do that, you'll . . .'

Ataneq had peered over the edge and tumbled off. He looked most astonished, but in a minute he was attempting to climb up once more.

'He's hilarious,' laughed Mich. 'And now Atka wants to do the same.'

'How about making pizza?' suggested Amy. 'I saw all the ingredients and Chris makes the most delish pizzas – game, Chris?'

'Sure, cuz,' said Chris, who enjoyed cooking.

'Chris, yaar, old chap, machang, amigo mio,' said Nimal, slapping him on the back, '*I'll* be your chief assistant.'

'No you won't, my lad,' said Umedh. 'There won't be any ingredients *left* to make the pizza. Chris, how much help do you need?'

'It depends; Amy, with thirteen of us, will ten large pizzas be enough?'

'Eight will do the trick. We'll make a salad to go with it and put out nachos with guacamole.'

'Great idea,' said Anu. 'Nimal, you prepare the formula for the cubs, and the rest of us will manage the food.'

'Okay, Aunty,' said Nimal bowing extravagantly, 'your wish is my command.'

'If only,' retorted Anu. 'Ricky, Mich and Gina, will you keep an eye on the babies for a bit?' They nodded eagerly. 'Corazon, what would you like to do?'

'I'll join you,' laughed Corazon, leading the way to the kitchen.

The pizza was nearly ready when excited barking ensued.

'That's Hunter,' said Rohan, 'and I guess Sam and Codey have joined him. Come on.'

They ran out of the kitchen to welcome Hassan, Shawn and Tulok, who had arrived at the same time. The barking was deafening.

'Whoa! Settle down, boys,' said Nimal, who was on his back, the dogs on top of him, while the cubs were on the sofa with Mich and Gina, making little chuffing noises and whimpering. 'Hunter, show your manners!'

Hunter promptly sat up, barked once and waved a paw in the air. Sam, a beautiful cream, light brown and black Border Collie/Sheltie cross, rolled over and played dead, all four paws in the air. Codey, a little black Shih Tzu, went straight to the sofa to investigate the creatures he did not know.

He tried to jump up on the seat, but Nimal grabbed him quickly – even a gentle smack from a cub would have hurt the little dog. 'Codey, let me introduce you to the cubs,' said Nimal, sitting on the floor near the sofa, and holding Codey in one arm. The dog licked him but kept looking at the cubs.

'Mich, Gina, hold the cubs and sit beside me. Chris, hold Sam for now.' Nimal took Ataneq and calmed him down. 'Hunter, here, boy. Show Codey and Ataneq how to be friends.'

The intelligent dog obeyed at once. He sat in front of Nimal and licked Ataneq, who grunted in delight, climbed out of Nimal's lap and cuddled up to Hunter, feeling quite safe between his paws, while Codey watched. 'Codey, these are Hunter's friends; they're babies and need looking after. Come and make friends.' As he spoke, Nimal stroked all three creatures. Codey whined softly as Nimal held him close to Hunter and Ataneq, licking first Hunter and then the cub.

'Oooh, look, Ataneq wants to hug him,' said Gina, as the cub reached out his paws to the dog.

'And they're friends,' sighed Corazon.

'Codey's a nursemaid of sorts,' laughed Tulok, as they watched Atka make friends with Codey quickly. 'Whenever he hears a baby crying, he gets very anxious and always runs to find an adult.'

'And I guess Atka believes that any friend of her brother's is a friend of hers,' chuckled Nimal. 'Chris, bring Sam over.'

Sam joined the other four animals and made friends with the cubs, who were, by now, so secure that they sniffed at him and then wandered off to make friends with Shawn. But that did not please Sam.

'He's trying to herd them back together with the other two dogs,' laughed Shawn, as Sam nudged the cubs gently. 'He grew up with a sheepdog and used to help herd cattle and sheep.'

'And the cubs don't mind at all,' said Mich, as the five creatures settled down in a cosy huddle.

'Finally the human zoo can introduce themselves,' said Shawn, shaking hands. 'Obviously, you're Nimal. I heard about Hurit and that's an incredible gift you have, my boy – see you use it well.'

'I'll do my best, sir,' said Nimal, rising to shake hands.

'And I'm sure you'll all work hard to stop our grizzlies from being killed.'

'Absolutely, sir,' said Rohan.

'There's the timer for the last two pizzas,' said Amy, running out of the room, Chris and Anu on her heels.

'We thought you may not have had time to eat before coming to meet us,' said Rohan.

'We didn't – thanks,' said Shawn.

'Let's eat in a meeting room where there's a projector,' suggested Tulok, 'so that we can refer to a map of Manipau.'

'Excellent,' said Shawn. 'We'll use the room right off the kitchen.'

Ten minutes later everyone was served and the meeting began, with a large map of the Centre projected on an overhead screen. Rohan took notes.

'In the north and east, Manipau's boundaries are created by the Akie River, which flows from the low mountain ranges in the north-west, across the northern boundary, and curves south along our eastern boundary,' said Shawn. 'It flows past our Centre and branches off eastwards. There are many tributaries of the Akie, several of which flow through Manipau. The new CC is on the east side of the Akie, and will stretch from the north to the south, along the river.

'The lake practically divides the Centre, the northern section of Manipau being much denser and larger than the southern area. The Muskok, a large tributary of the Akie in the east, flows into Manipau in the north-east, runs through the Centre, joins the lake, and exits through the south boundary of Manipau – it runs parallel to the Akie which is *outside* Manipau, and joins it further south-east.'

'Since poaching's on the rise, worldwide, Manipau decided to put up a solid wall around the entire conservation, as a deterrent to poachers. Our walls are 6.10 metres high and 0.76 metres deep,' said Tulok.

'There's a 1,000-metre gap between the boundary wall and the Akie in the north, where the second bridge is being built,' he continued. 'We'll construct a narrow road so that folks from the CC can cross the bridge and go west to the north entrance.'

'The main area inhabited by grizzlies is north of the lake,' continued Hassan, 'which is excellent territory for them. GBH stands for *Grizzly Bear Haven*, and there's enough room for all our bears. Here's GW, far up in the north-east section.'

'Does this map give you a good picture of the Centre?' asked Shawn.

'Absolutely,' said the youngsters in unison.

Hassan continued. 'When Shawn and I began our annual census of the grizzlies, we searched the entire northern section of Manipau. It was easy enough to track the bears, since they mark their territory clearly. When we discovered that five bears were missing, we commenced an extensive search.

'We discovered two sets of tracks for male bears, beginning in the mountain range. They went south for a few klicks, east over the Nakina, another tributary of the Akie, passed the trail to the gates, and then turned north again. We could tell they were speeding for short distances – you know they can run at nearly 60 kilometres per hour over short distances, right?'

The youngsters nodded, intent on the tale.

'The tracks were close for a short distance, and then separated, continuing north towards the boundary wall, approximately fifteen metres apart at the widest distance. I followed one set of tracks while Shawn followed the other. About 450 metres south of the boundary wall, I discovered blood in the paw prints, and it was apparent the bear was limping. I was nearing the boundary wall – about 300 metres away – when I began to see copious amounts of dried blood, but it was another ten metres before I found two huge patches of blood in a small clearing, and no more tracks. A few minutes later Shawn joined me, following the tracks of the second male to the other patch of blood.'

'That's horrible!' wept Gina, and Anu put an arm around her as she brushed away her own tears.

'I know, hon,' whispered Amy, handing out tissues to Mich and Corazon.

The boys were furious, and Rohan muttered, 'We'll catch the crooks! How far west from GW, measuring along the boundary wall, were these blood patches?'

'About a kilometre west, would you figure?' said Shawn, looking at Hassan and Tulok.

'That's right,' said Tulok.

'What happened next?' asked Anu.

'Shawn and I searched, unsuccessfully, for the bodies in case the bears had fought each other,' said Hassan. 'Then Shawn discovered a couple of bullet holes in a large tree which was behind the patches of blood. Shawn?'

'We called in the police and asked for Chief Inspector Geraldine Montgomery – she's a brilliant officer and crazy about animals. They dug out the bullets, examined them and said they were from a heavy-duty rifle which could kill large animals.

'We also checked with our gatekeepers, but they hadn't heard a thing. They would have reported gunshots or other unusual activities.'

'A silencer on the rifles, obviously,' commented Rohan.

'Yes. Geraldine's team searched the area for human blood, and found a few drops near another tree, where there must have been a scuffle of some sort,' said Hassan.

'Accompanied by the police we searched diligently for several days, but couldn't find anything else. We didn't have sufficient staff to continue the search on a daily basis, and we were still looking for three more bears,' said Hassan.

'Then Tulok joined our search – he's brilliant at tracking. Within a day he found tracks of the other three bears,' said Shawn. 'You take over, Tulok.'

'I began my search from the last known den of the grizzlies,' said Tulok. 'From earlier records, we knew that these three were siblings – a rare case of a mother having three male cubs. They were orphaned early, around the age of two, a couple of years ago. For some reason they stayed together and, my colleagues inform me, hibernated together, too. I was able to track them and found old tracks in April which ranged north to the boundary wall, went around GW, across the Muskok, and then back west.

'So I crossed the Muskok and found relatively fresh tracks – going east towards the boundary wall. I followed the tracks, and discovered blood in them and bullets in trees. Finally, in a small clearing 350 metres east of the Muskok and a few metres away from the eastern wall, I found large patches of dried blood.'

'Was the clearing near the northern wall?' asked Umedh.

'A couple of hundred metres south of it,' said Tulok. 'Although the police came again, and Shawn, Hassan and I spent half a day searching the area, we found nothing more. It was frustrating, but our consolation was that you JEACs were arriving soon, and we hoped we could leave it with you. Anything more, Hassan, Shawn?'

'One point,' said Shawn. 'I've been turning this over in my mind, and one thing stands out – the bears were being *driven to the boundary walls* – eastwards; and my question is, why?'

'Good point. Thanks for sharing this information with us,' said Rohan. 'May we contact you later with any questions, once we've assimilated this info?'

'Certainly,' said Hassan. 'We *must* stop whoever's doing this.'

'Absolutely!'

The youngsters thanked the men and said goodbye, before clearing the meeting room and kitchen.

'It's 7:50,' said Rohan, 'and I need to assimilate everything we've heard, prior to making plans. What about the rest of you?'

'Agreed,' said the others.

'Let's get to know each other this evening,' said Anu, 'and we can tell Ricky about the JEACs.'

'Good idea,' said Nimal, picking up the sleeping cubs. 'I'll put the babes to bed and join you. Come on, Codey – you can tuck them in and kiss them goodnight.' The little dog followed him to the basement, jumped into his basket beside the cage and curled up – he was not going to leave the cubs alone.

Nimal joined the others in the lounge, saying, 'We have a babysitter for Ataneq and Atka – Codey didn't want to come with me.'

'Let's do a round of introductions, but first we'll tell you about the JEACs, when we began the group, and what our goals are,' suggested Anu, when everyone was settled comfortably.

Taking it in turns, the JEACs explained how their group began, spoke about their mission statement and mandate, and said how many JEACs groups had formed around the world.

'I knew a little bit,' said Corazon, 'and I've looked at your website. I'd like to join, please.'

'Excellent,' said Amy. 'You can join our Manipau group. All the kids who live here are members and they start groups in their various schools as well.'

'I'm in, too,' said Chris. 'How do we get badges like yours?'

'I've got spares,' said Amy. 'What about you, Ricky?'

'It sounds really cool,' said Ricky. 'I don't know much about wildlife, but would like to learn, and definitely want to protect them. I'd like to join, too.'

'Excellent,' said Amy. 'Now, introduce yourselves, JEACs.'

'Sure, and let's begin, for a change, with the old man,' mocked Nimal. 'Age, height, hobbies, ambition, a major fault, and how many JEACs you recruited, Grandpa; and try not to fall asleep in the middle of your tale.'

'You, I'll deal with later,' growled Rohan. 'I'm sixteen, six foot half an inch tall, and have a third level black belt in karate. I want to be a detective, and enjoy studying. I'm getting better at controlling my temper, but occasionally it gets me into trouble. In the past six months I recruited eleven JEACs – chaps I met at a fitness camp.'

'And he's an academic who's won several medals, and came first *in the country* in the major exams he took in December,' added Amy.

'Wow! That's some achievement,' said Ricky. 'Doesn't India have over a billion people?'

'That's right,' said Umedh. 'This major achievement also gives Rohan a scholarship to do his graduate and postgraduate degrees anywhere in the world.'

'Now, Umedh, it's . . .' began Rohan, and stopped as Gina interrupted him.

'He's also very good at sports.' She was very proud of her brother.

'But more than that, he's a decent chap,' said Anu. 'Naturally, when his head starts swelling, as it's likely to do any second, we sit on him to deflate it.'

The group burst out laughing, and Rohan, slightly red under his tan, turned quickly to Umedh and said, 'Your turn, yaar.'

'I'm four days younger than Rohan,' said Umedh. 'I'm striving to catch up with him in height, but he keeps ahead easily, so I'm only 5 foot 11.5 inches tall. I also have a third level black belt in karate, and want to be a computer engineer. I'm very impatient, and am striving to change. At a computer camp I recruited fifteen people to the JEACs.'

'He did excellently at his exams, too,' added Anu, 'and came second in their class, also winning scholarships.'

'Another academic,' sighed Nimal. 'What I have to live up to – but I don't!' The others chuckled.

'Umedh,' said Ricky tentatively, 'if you don't mind my asking, how did you lose your eye?'

'I don't mind, yaar; I was born this way.'

'We have a guy in our class who also has only one eye,' said Chris, 'but he feels awkward and some of the kids make fun of him.'

'They don't any more,' said Amy. 'Chris had a few, shall we say, "words with his fists" with them, and they quickly learned not to be mean.'

'Do people laugh at you, Umedh?' asked Chris. Umedh nodded. 'How do you deal with it?'

'Rohan's been my buddy from the first time we met at boarding school and was always jolly big for his age. A few "words" like yours, Chris, and very few kids in our age group made comments in our hearing.' Chris nodded. 'When we were nine, Rohan, Nimal, who was only eight, and I were rescued from being pounded into mincemeat by a group of thirteen-year-olds; we had a combination of five black eyes and three bloody noses among us. A wise master sat the three of us down and told us that it was up to us to educate and teach others to accept me as I was, but that I first needed to be comfortable with myself. He said each of us was unique.' He looked at Rohan and winked.

'He told us that *we* were in charge of how we felt, and nobody could impose feelings on us,' continued Rohan. 'If *we* felt that Umedh's disability made him inadequate and less than a whole being, then others would sense it. Then he asked what we were going to do about it.'

'We talked it over with Umedh's parents and his Aunty Jay – naturally the school had contacted them,' said Nimal. 'We decided that Umedh should focus on all his talents and we'd try our best to ignore nasty comments. Most of the time we succeeded, but sometimes – well, that's history. By the time I was ten, we'd begun to appreciate the fact that Umedh was a genius. We call him "Q" or "U" at school, and not one person ever laughed when they saw his inventions.'

'Queue?' asked Corazon, looking puzzled. 'Do you mean the British word for "line-up"?'

'Sorry, Corazon,' grinned Nimal. 'Not a line-up, just the capital letter Q – referring to the inventor in James Bond movies.'

'Got it!' laughed Corazon, Chris and Ricky.

'Umedh's a genius at inventing all kinds of things,' said Amy. 'If you . . .'

'Whoa, Amy, spare my blushes,' laughed Umedh. Amy smiled and took pity on him. 'To cut a long story short,' said Umedh, 'when I realized that I could do a few things nobody else could, I forgot to be self-conscious about having only one eye.'

'We were proud of our friend, and he gained confidence in himself,' said Rohan. 'As our master had said, it's our choice if we allow others to make us feel inadequate.'

'That makes sense,' said Chris. 'When I met you yesterday, I didn't think twice about you having only one eye, though it struck me when I first saw a picture of you.'

'What did you say, Chris?' asked Ricky.

'I didn't have a chance to say anything other than, "What happened to his other eye?" before Mich and Amy told me about your inventions, and by then I'd forgotten you had only one eye. I say, do you mind my sharing your story with my pal at school, Umedh? It might help him.'

'Feel free,' said Umedh. 'Now, Amy – your turn.'

'I'm also sixteen, and two days younger than Umedh, five foot five inches tall, and I am *not* an academic. However, since I want to become a psychologist and work with animals at conservation centres, with dolphins in particular, I'm studying hard. I love sports, especially skiing both on water and snow, and have a brown belt in karate. My biggest fault is a combination of a quick temper and impatience – and I have absolutely *zero* tolerance for discrimination. I believe everyone has good and bad in them, so why focus on the bad. I recruited twenty-five people at a conservation camp I went to during the spring break. They loved the concept and eighteen have already started their own groups.'

'She did very well at her exams, too,' said Rohan, 'and despite her modesty about academic achievement, she got top marks in psychology and conservation studies, both at school and also at the conservation camp.'

'That's because I love it,' muttered Amy, blushing slightly.

'And though she says she's very impatient and has a quick temper, she's tolerant, caring, and compassionate of human nature. She's counselled many youngsters in her school. She also won the prize for cake baking, during term time,' said Anu. 'I saw a picture of the cake she made and Mich told me it was *the* most delicious cake she'd ever eaten.'

'Thanks, hon,' laughed Amy. 'Whose turn is it next? Ricky, when's your birthday?'

'February sixth,' said Ricky.

'Chris is the thirtieth of January, and Nimal's on the twenty-fourth of January,' said Amy. 'It's your turn, Nimal.'

'I'm fifteen, five foot eleven inches tall. I'm going to be a conservationist, am no academic, and studies are a painful task. I recruited eighteen people last term – mainly new chaps who had joined the school. I love all nature and animals, have my second level black belt in karate, and generally win any karate fight with Rohan. And you lot can stop laughing like drains – you didn't see our last fight where I came out top.'

'Very true, folks,' chuckled Umedh. 'Nimal was right on top *of the pile of six other boys*, in the mock karate fight they had challenged Rohan to. I helped pick up the pieces.'

'As for faults,' said Nimal, grimacing at Umedh, 'who said we had to name them?'

'*You* did,' yelled the group.

'Oh! Right – I don't have *any* faults . . . okay, put a sock in it, JEACs. My biggest fault is being such a saintly . . . man, you kids are boisterous! Don't let a chap get a word in edgewise. Hunter, you think I'm the cat's whiskers, don't you?'

'Woof!' said Hunter, licking him lavishly.

'Hunter's prejudiced,' said Anu. 'Cut slack, Nimal, and confess – unless you'd like one of us to elucidate.'

'I confess,' protested Nimal hurriedly. 'I'm a klutz, I play outrageous tricks, I don't always use my brain to its capacity, and my masters say I'm impossible, incorrigible, mischievous and, in fact, as un-saintly as it gets. There – am I now off the hook?'

'More or less,' said Gina cheekily. 'But the way animals trust and love him is . . .' She had to stop as Nimal placed a hand over her mouth.

'Yes, we're very proud to have brothers like him, Rohan and Umedh,' added Mich, and Gina nodded.

'We're confusing young Ricky,' grinned Nimal, seeing Ricky's puzzled look. 'Factually, Rohan, Anu and Gina are my cousins – our fathers are brothers. But we've lived together all my life, and we're one family. Umedh is not related to us at all, thank goodness.'

'But the three of them are as good as *our* brothers, too,' said Mich, smiling shyly. 'Friends are the family we choose for ourselves. Amy and I have *chosen* to be part of their family, and they're part of ours.'

'Thanks, hon,' said Anu, giving her a hug. 'I love having three sisters.' Mich, the youngest of the group and usually the quietest, was thrilled.

'Now you, Chris,' said Nimal. 'Tell us how brilliant you are!'

Chris grinned, and said, 'Not brill at all, and definitely not an academic. I'm five foot nine inches tall, am six days younger than Nimal, and love welding, mountain biking and cooking. I want to work in construction when I'm done school, and do my biking for as long as possible. My worst fault is being more interested in biking than in my books – and I struggle academically.'

'Chris – how can you be so modest when you're *constantly* showing off?' teased Amy. Chris threw a cushion at her. 'He holds number one position in the Alberta under seventeen expert category for downhill mountain bike racing, which he won last year, and is sure to win this year, too. These hols he'll be away for numerous races, but return here for the fundraiser; his final race is in September. And, since most of you don't know him, I'll be honest and admit that Chris *never* shows off.'

'You must be jolly good, yaar,' said Rohan, admiringly. 'I understand mountain biking's strenuous and the competition is tough. Are there any extra mountain bikes at Manipau? I would love to try it out if you don't mind teaching me.'

'Us too,' chimed in Umedh, Nimal, Mich and Gina.

'There aren't any extra bikes,' said Chris, 'but you're welcome to try mine. One day before you leave, we'll go to Kicking Horse which has some good mountain bike trails, and we'll rent bikes and gear.'

'Deal!' said Nimal. 'By the way, those pizzas were absolutely horrible. I tried another couple of slices when we were putting things away, and I doubt I'll acquire a taste for your cooking until I've eaten at least two dozen more slices!'

'Thanks for the compliments, yaar,' chuckled Chris, punching him lightly. 'Ricky, you're next.'

'I'm fifteen, too, seven days younger than Chris, and I'm five foot seven inches tall. I'm not an academic, but until last year I used to get okay grades. I'd like to be an electronic engineer, but . . .' He trailed off. 'I love mountain biking, but I'm not as good as Chris. I don't really have any talents.' He paused, shot a quick glance at Chris, and continued hesitantly, 'I got into trouble a couple of years ago – got mixed up with a group who did drugs.' He looked at the others, expecting a shocked reaction.

'That must have been rough,' said Rohan, sympathetically. 'What happened?'

'One day my dad caught me when I tried it at home. My parents were very upset and immediately took me out of school and enrolled me in a rehabilitation programme.'

'Did it help?' asked Anu gently.

'Yes – I got off drugs and haven't touched them since. But when I got back to school, none of the other kids would speak to me, let alone look at me. The kids I'd done drugs with had been expelled since they wouldn't go for counselling, and word had spread that I'd been involved. Then I met Chris last summer while mountain biking. Another guy from my school happened to be there, too, and told Chris about me and advised him to avoid me. Chris listened and then asked me if I had taken drugs after my rehab. I told him I hadn't touched them. Chris turned to the other guy, said that I'd learned a lesson the hard way, and that he'd be my friend. Thanks to my parents, Chris and I now go to the same school.'

'Good for you, Chris, and I agree with you,' said Umedh.

'Thanks for trusting us, Ricky,' said Amy. 'We're behind you, too.'

'Ricky's started a group at school to educate youngsters about the drug problems in our schools,' said Chris. 'It's a huge help to lots of kids, and is very successful.'

'Excellent!' said Rohan. 'As for talents, Ricky, everyone has one, as well as a particular strength, and I know what yours is, yaar.' Ricky looked surprised. 'You have courage, strength, determination and caring – anyone would love those qualities.'

'Me?' squeaked Ricky.

'Yes, *you*,' said Nimal serious for once. 'It took great courage to admit what you've been through. As for your strength and determination in attending the rehab programme, and now helping others through your personal experience – that's *huge*, yaar! I hope if I make a serious mistake, I'll have even half your courage.'

'I concur,' said Rohan. 'It takes a lot of moral fibre to face our weaknesses and overcome them. Hat's off to you, Ricky.'

'Anu next,' said Umedh tactfully, seeing that Ricky was overwhelmed.

'I'm also fifteen – hurray, we finally have four fifteen-year-olds and only three old sixteens! Okay, bro, I'll put a sock in it,' said Anu hurriedly, as Rohan pretended to glare at her. 'I'm a bookaholic, I enjoy studying, writing is my favourite pastime, and I hope to be a writer one day. I'm five foot four inches tall. Last term I recruited six girls. One of my worst faults is untidiness. When I'm in the midst of writing, within seconds my entire work space looks like a tornado's been through it – I start off neatly, but it never lasts.' She sighed sadly, shaking her head.

'And, let me elucidate why she only recruited six girls,' said Amy. 'She was editing her first book – she's not *hoping* to be an author some day, she already *is* one. *Peacock Feathers*, her first book, was scheduled to come out in December this year. When the publishers heard about the other books, they wanted her to start doing book signings in December with the first book and tried to pressurize her to finish the other books quickly, too. But Anu and her parents decided that for the next few years, she would work on finalizing all her books and completing her education before engaging in full-time writing and book signings.' Amy was proud of her friend. 'It was a wise decision.'

'That's awesome, Anu,' said Corazon, while Ricky and Chris nodded. 'What's the first book about?'

'It's a children's book – about an adventure we Patels had on our Centre in India, two years ago,' said Anu shyly.

'It's brill,' said Gina. 'It was fun to read a story with all of us in it; it also explains how we got Hunter, and how we founded the JEACs.'

'She has three more books in the offing,' said Rohan. 'Mich, I know you want to talk about the second book, right?'

'Yes, please,' said Mich excitedly. '*The Dolphin Heptad* is also a story about our adventures as JEACs, and the first time the Patels, Amy and I met in Australia, at Uncle Jack's Conservation. The seven of us – which includes Hunter, naturally – are in it, along with a heptad of dolphins – a heptad means a group of seven.'

'The third book includes Hunter, Umedh, and Mahesika, a Sri Lankan friend, and is based in Sri Lanka, where we had an adventure with elephants,' said Nimal. 'It's titled *An Elephant Never Forgets*, and so far she's done the outline.'

'The fourth book's about our adventure in Scotland, six months ago, with three Scottish boys, and it's called *Can Snow Leopards Roar?*' added Umedh.

'So far Anu's jotted down rough notes for it,' said Amy.

'Please write a book about solving the problem with our grizzlies, Anu,' said Chris.

'It would be awesome if the three of us could be in it, too,' breathed Ricky, while Corazon clapped her hands in delight.

'Sure, and of course you'll be in it – you're part of our group, aren't you?' smiled Anu.

'I want all your books, autographed, please,' said Corazon, and the boys nodded.

'As you can tell, JEACs, we're proud to be in Anu's books. And the minute *her* head begins to swell, we'll sit on her, hard!' said Rohan, taking pity on Anu and making the others laugh. 'Autographs later, JEACs, and since I'm her oldest brother, I'm in charge of whom she gives them out to – I *am* open to bribery.'

'Appalling!' said Nimal. 'Our police force should be above corruption.'

'Corazon, it's your turn,' said Anu.

'I'm fourteen, will be fifteen in October, and am five foot one inch tall. I love reading and singing, but most of all I adore animals and want to be a conservationist. When I was eleven years old, my dad took me to the North West Territories where we have family. Dad taught me to drive a team of huskies – it was awesome. I want to start a conservation centre in the north, and protect polar bears, seals, penguins, sea lions and other wildlife. My worst fault is neglecting my studies because I love being in the forest. So I'm trying to change since I must do well to get into university.'

'You were the first to find Hurit's tracks,' said Nimal. 'You must be brill at tracking.'

'I was lucky,' said Corazon.

'Not really,' said Amy. 'We've heard that you're an awesome tracker and have a natural talent in the forest. My mom also told me that you're an amazing organizer and she's hoping to involve you in our events.'

'And we'll encourage each other in our studies and thereby realize our dreams,' grinned Nimal.

'Thanks, *yaar*,' smiled Corazon. 'If I had *your* charisma with animals . . .' She smiled round the group. 'I'm so glad that I've met you all, and I will definitely be recruiting lots of JEACs next term. It's wonderful.'

'Gina, hon, you're next,' said Amy.

'I'm the proud owner of a brill family,' began Gina. 'I'm ten years old, four foot nine and a half inches tall and not at all academic. I love sports, music and composing songs, and when I grow up I want to be a musician. One of my faults is that I disappear into a dreamworld, especially when thinking of my music – it really bugs my teachers at times. I recruited eight girls last term, and we did a fundraising and awareness campaign, and raised a hundred thousand rupees to donate to our Conservation Centre. Most of the money came from large companies that the girls' parents worked at. And that's it for me.'

'You forgot to mention, hon, that you wrote the words and music for our theme song,' said Amy. 'She's an accomplished musician, plays seven instruments, and composes lots of songs, both words and tune, quite often on the spot.'

'She's also a fine gymnast and athlete,' added Nimal. 'Won the Best Sports Girl award in the lower school two years in a row.'

'Oh – right. Thanks, Amy and Nimal,' said Gina, who often forgot her talents. 'Now it's your turn, Mich.'

'I'm the same age as Gina,' said Mich, 'and I'm four foot, ten and a half inches tall. I'm not good at studies, either, and love all sports. I can be very shy and then I don't speak out when I should, but I'm trying to overcome this problem by recruiting JEACs. I got six girls to join us this year, and hope to get six more in the winter term. I like reading, music, and love singing Gina's songs. But my favourite hobby is drawing cartoons, and when I grow up I want to work with Disney.'

'Did you know that Mich draws all the cartoons for Gina's songs?' added Rohan. 'She and Gina make a wonderful team, and complement each other beautifully.'

'But we don't pay a lot of compliments, Rohan,' said Mich, as she and Gina looked slightly confused.

'Sorry, kiddo,' apologized Rohan, 'but c-o-m-p-l-*e*-m-e-n-t, rather than c-o-m-p-l-*i*-m-e-n-t, means that as a team you enhance each other's skills. That is, you each have skills which work well together. Does that make sense?'

The girls nodded.

'So when do we see the cartoons and hear the theme song?' asked Corazon.

'Soon, but not tonight,' said Nimal, glancing at his watch. 'Do you realize it's almost 9 o'clock?'

'Thanks for sharing, JEACs!' said Amy. 'Rohan, what's our programme for tomorrow? Sorry, Corazon, Chris and Ricky – we JEACs usually turn to Rohan for leadership in our detective work, since he's Mr. Sherlock Holmes II. Is that okay with you?'

'Absolutely!' chorused the three.

'We're completely inexperienced in adventures like this,' added Chris, 'and we're happy to have Rohan as head of the force.'

'I'm only *one* head,' laughed Rohan. 'As the old JEACs know, we work in partnership, each using our various talents to complement each other – team work is our strength.'

'Hear, hear!' said Umedh. 'And what are we going to tackle tomorrow?'

'Brekker at 5:45 – don't groan, Nimal,' said Rohan. 'I'm going to sit up a bit and think things out and we'll have a plan of action for you in the morning.' He looked at Umedh and raised his eyebrows inquiringly.

'Sure, yaar,' said Umedh obligingly.

Chris, Corazon and Ricky looked puzzled, and Amy explained. 'They're going to brainstorm for a while. Anyone for hot chocolate?'

A loud chorus of 'yes' answered her, and after Nimal had taken mugs of hot chocolate to Rohan and Umedh, who were deep in conversation, the others went to bed.

By 10 p.m. everyone was sound asleep.

CHAPTER 6

Beginning the Investigation

Rohan and Umedh were dressed and in the kitchen by 5 a.m. the next morning, accompanied by dogs and cubs. The animals were fed, pots of coffee and tea were brewing, and the boys were frying eggs and sausages by the time Amy and Anu joined them twenty minutes later.

'Did you sleep well?' asked Amy.

'Like logs,' smiled Rohan. 'Amy and Anu, would you babysit the cubs for part of this morning?'

'Sure,' nodded the girls, setting the table and starting on the toast.

'Thanks, ladies – we were 99.9 percent sure you'd agree,' said Umedh. 'We'll have to split up in groups, frequently, and ensure there's protection where required, whether it be for the kiddies, or Ricky and Chris – the boys, compared to the rest of us, aren't experienced in wandering through forests and dealing with wildlife.'

'Agreed,' said Anu. 'Here come the others.'

'Good morning, JEACs!' said Rohan. 'Breakfast's ready, so have a seat and we'll serve.'

'Thanks, Amy and Anu,' said Ricky. 'You must have been up early.'

'Actually, the chefs for the meal are Rohan and Umedh. We only arrived a few minutes ago,' said Anu.

'Gee, thanks, guys,' said the others.

'And how are you, my four-footed buddies,' said Nimal, as the cubs scampered over to greet him. 'Have they been fed?'

'Yes, and so have the dogs,' said Anu. 'Our senior JEACs have done a good job – come to think of it, we should start a group of *YEACs.*'

'I'm stumped! What does *that* acronym stand for?' laughed Corazon.

'*Young* EACs, kiddo – get with the lingo,' chuckled Anu. 'I first thought of SEACs, that is, Senior EACs, but figured that would have other connotations, especially with the CC close by.'

The others laughed.

'Help! Lingo?' protested Ricky. 'I need a dictionary when you guys talk.'

'It means *language*,' chorused Gina and Mich, hugging Hunter, Sam, Codey and the cubs, before sitting down at the table.

'I doubt it has that precise meaning in the dicky,' said Amy. 'It's our own special brand of chit-chat.'

'I'm sure you understand what *dicky* means,' chuckled Nimal, and Ricky and Corazon nodded. 'Is it really safe to eat . . . ouch!' he yelped as Rohan punched him on the arm before serving him with two eggs and four sausages. 'Yummy – it looks delish. Muchas gracias, amigo mio. I'm thrilled that Amy's training you well.'

'Where exactly would you like the toast, kiddo?' threatened Amy. 'On your plate or down your shirt?'

'I'll be good, Aunty, I promise. The plate, please. Thank you, merci, grazie . . .'

'Put a sock in it, yaar,' laughed Umedh, pouring out juice.

'What's our programme for the day, yaar?' asked Nimal, changing the subject.

'Amy and Anu have agreed to look after the cubs this morning,' said Rohan, 'and the rest of us will go to the BCS – sorry, bridge construction site. We'll take both vehicles and WTs – yes, Ricky? No need to put up your hand, yaar.'

'What are WTs?'

'Walkie-talkies. Nimal said the cubs could be left with Codey as babysitter for a few hours at a time from tomorrow,' continued Rohan. 'So today, we'll do shifts at GW – fair play as always – and work out the programme as we go along.'

'Good idea,' said everyone.

'We checked with Remo last night and he informed the supervisor that we'd be along,' said Umedh. 'There's a break at 7:30. We'll meet everyone and get their views on the situation.'

'What time do you want to leave?' said Amy.

'By 6:45; Rohan will take Mich, Gina, Ricky and Sam,' said Umedh, 'and I'll take the others. We each need a pocket map of Manipau.'

'What's the plan at the site, yaar?' said Nimal.

'We'll assess the situ and I'll take the lead if everyone's comfortable with that,' said Rohan.

'Aye, aye, sir,' agreed the others.

A short while later the eight JEACs were on their way.

'We'll take the main trail, Umedh,' directed Corazon.

'Right,' said Umedh. 'There seem to be numerous trails branching out from this one.'

'The area's pretty dense and you can't see much through the shrubbery. Corazon, are there trails for the vehicles from GW to the blood spots?' said Nimal, who had his binoculars out.

'No – the forest's too dense and the trails are narrow.'

'We figured we'd try to check the two blood patches in this section, and search the entire area,' said Umedh.

'Are we also going to check the patches of blood that my dad found when he followed the other three bears?' asked Corazon.

'Definitely,' said Umedh. 'Is it possible to make our way east from the first patches to the second lot, Corazon?'

'Sure, but it's *very* dense; we'll have to meander, finding trails where possible.'

'Good point,' said Umedh, slowing down as they approached the gates.

The gatekeepers, Min-jae and Su-bin, a lovely Korean couple, opened the gates, waving to the JEACs as they drove through. Turning east, the vehicles drove along with the Manipau boundary wall on their right and the river on their left, until a wire fence with a gate in it prevented them from advancing further. They parked outside the gate where a sturdy young man came up to Rohan's vehicle.

'You must be the JEACs,' he said.

'That's right,' smiled Rohan, getting out of the Land Rover to shake hands. Umedh, Nimal and Chris joined him. 'Are we allowed in?'

'Sure thing, buddy. We're expecting you this morning. My name's Jason.'

'Good to meet you, Jason. I'm Rohan, and these three are Umedh, Chris and Nimal. Do we park here?' said Rohan.

'No, come inside,' said Jason, opening the gates. 'Then follow me to the cabin. I have helmets for everyone. It's a good thing you came a bit early.'

'What about the dogs?' asked Nimal.

'As long as they're obedient, they can come with us,' said Jason. 'And they don't need leashes or helmets,' he added with a grin.

'Thanks, yaar,' grinned Nimal, who had taken to the young man immediately.

'What's . . .' began Jason, when Chris, climbing back into the vehicle with Umedh said with a chuckle, 'Yaar means buddy or mate. We're all learning a whole new lingo with these *foreigners*.'

'Hey, yaar, that's not at all PC,' said Nimal, promptly.

'See what I mean,' winked Chris, poking his head out of the window and continuing, 'PC means *politically correct*. These kids are crazy. If they say *pavements*, they mean sidewalks; the *boot* of a car is the trunk and the *bonnet* is the hood, and . . . the list of strange words goes on and on. They also talk in acronyms – so BCS means *bridge construction site*,' he concluded with a chuckle.

'We're not *completely* crazy, yaar, seriously,' said Nimal.

Once parked, everyone joined Nimal and Jason in the cabin beside the gates. Further introductions were made, and both dogs immediately took to Jason as he knelt on the floor and hugged them – it was obvious that he loved animals. The JEACs really liked him.

'Where do you live, Jason?' asked Umedh.

'With the gatekeepers, Min-jae and Su-bin – they're my uncle and aunt, and have an extra room for me,' said Jason. 'I eat meals with my co-workers when I'm working, and with the family when I'm off.'

'So you're Korean, too,' said Nimal. 'Have you been in Canada long?'

'Since I was two; but I've visited family in Korea and also speak the lingo.'

'You must come to GW and have a meal with us,' said Gina. 'Anu and Amy will want to meet you.'

'And Amy's a super cook,' added Mich. 'Do you have a friend you'd like to bring?'

'Thanks, ladies, I'd like that,' grinned Jason, 'and I don't have a girlfriend. I'm a bachelor boy, and that's the way I'll sta-a-a-ay . . .' He hummed the tune of the one time hit song by Cliff Richard, and then stopped. 'But you probably don't know that song.'

'We do – all of us,' said Chris. 'Our parents were Elvis and Cliff fans and we know all their songs – we didn't have a choice since they're still played at home!'

Jason laughed heartily. 'That's hilarious – my parents are fans too! Let go and prepare for the break; our day supervisors are Tina and Carl. Helmets on, folks. Come on, Hunter and Sam – follow me.'

Jason led them to a small covered booth, obviously used for food and drinks, and began preparing coffee and tea, assisted by the JEACs. The bridge construction was progressing, and there were twenty to twenty-five people on site.

At 7:30 the break began. The workers lined up in front of the booth, eager for a drink and snack, greeting the JEACs and dogs in a friendly manner. They helped themselves to food and drink, and stood around in small groups or sat on grassy patches.

'JEACs, meet Tina and Carl,' said Jason, as the supervisors arrived, pulling off heavy gloves.

A round of introductions was made, and as she shook hands with them, Tina said, 'We've heard about you and would be happy to help in any way. It's terrible that the grizzlies are being killed. I love animals, and my oldest son's a zookeeper at the Greater Vancouver Zoo.'

'Hi, JEACs,' said Carl, shaking hands and giving Rohan his business card. 'Grizzlies are my favourites. I hope you can resolve this situation.'

'Thanks, Tina and Carl,' said Rohan. 'Do you have a few minutes for us to ask you some questions while you drink your coffee?'

'Sure,' said Tina, 'and feel free to chat with the others.' She raised her voice and addressed the workers, saying, 'Folks, these are the JEACs whom Remo spoke about yesterday – feel free to pass on any useful information to them.'

The JEACs thanked Tina and split up according to Rohan's directions, while Rohan and Jason continued speaking with the supervisors.

The workers were eager and willing to assist, and gave them lots of information. They promised to look out for anything unusual that might occur and pass it on via Jason. After the break the JEACs thanked everyone, said goodbye, and returned to the gate with Jason.

'Thanks very much, Jason,' said Umedh.

'My pleasure,' replied Jason. 'Carl's tale about how Kylie became a night supervisor was interesting, wasn't it, Rohan?'

'Very.'

'Gina, Mich and I heard something weird, as well,' said Corazon. 'What about the rest of you?'

Umedh, Nimal, Chris and Ricky nodded. Everyone looked thoughtful.

'Let's discuss it at GW with Amy and Anu, since Jason has to get back to work,' said Rohan. 'Jason, do you have a phone we can reach you at – if you don't mind us bugging you further?'

'I'd like to catch the crooks,' said Jason, fishing out a pen and paper. 'Here's my cell number, and I have the GW number. One quick point, folks – Kylie and I don't hit it off. We both speak Korean, something I discovered the day we met. She was at the tail end of a phone call and I overheard her saying goodbye and agreeing to meet the person soon, so I greeted her in Korean – she didn't seem to like that.'

'Hmmm, point taken, thanks, Jason,' said Rohan, shaking hands with him.

The others said goodbye, too. The dogs gave Jason one last lick, and the JEACs climbed into the Land Rovers, waving as they drove off. They stopped to meet the gatekeepers and reached GW just after 8:30, where Codey greeted everyone as if they'd been gone for months, and led them to the kitchen.

'Something smells wonderful,' said Ricky, sniffing hard.

'Samosas – and I'm . . .' began Nimal.

'Absolutely STARVING!' yelled Mich and Gina.

'We figured you'd be hungry,' smiled Amy. 'How did it go?'

'Very well,' said Umedh, going over to help the girls.

'I see the cubs are sound asleep,' said Nimal, who had peeped into their cage.

'We fed them half an hour ago, and noticed something really funny,' said Anu. 'Let's eat and we'll exchange news.'

CHAPTER 7

The Humming Grizzly Bear Cubs

The snacks were delicious and for a few minutes nothing was said other than comments like, 'Please may I have more chutney?' or 'I need water – anyone else?' But once the first pangs of hunger were assuaged, the group looked at Amy and Anu.

'What was funny about the cubs?' asked Rohan.

'They hummed as they drank their milk.'

'Come again?' said Ricky.

'It was adorable,' said Amy. 'Anu and I each had a cub and Codey trotted between us, supervising. The cubs were content, and Anu and I hummed and rocked as they drank their milk. Suddenly, Atka began to make a rhythmic noise which sounded like humming – it was quite loud. Anu stopped humming immediately, but Atka carried on, and then Ataneq began.'

'It was hilarious,' grinned Anu. 'Amy and I kept very quiet and the cubs continued to hum. Then Codey seemed to feel that they were happy, because he stopped his supervision and settled down between Amy and me.'

'Did it really sound like humming?' asked Gina, intrigued.

'I can't think of another way to describe it, hon,' said Amy. 'I know that cubs make various noises to communicate contentment when feeding.'

'That's adorable,' said Corazon. 'I wish I'd heard it.'

'Perhaps *your* humming started it off,' said Nimal. 'We'll try it out later. Anu, your book about this adventure must indicate that.'

'Perhaps a title like *The Humming Grizzly Bear Cubs*?' laughed Anu.

'Exactimo!' chuckled Rohan, and the others agreed vociferously, while the three dogs joined in with excited barks.

'Grizzlies are awesome,' said Ricky. 'I don't know much about them, but would love to learn.'

'And so you shall, my boy,' said Nimal, paternally. 'I'm glad that youngsters like you are on a quest for knowledge. A favourite saying of one of my masters at school is, "It is fundamental to your growth and well-being that you absorb knowledge like a sponge while you are still in your youth, young man"; and he keeps throwing information at us as if we were dartboards. Also like a dartboard, it's a hit-and-miss since I'm jolly good at ducking!'

The others chuckled and Chris said, 'I want to know more about grizzlies, too, but what about sharing what we learned at the construction site?'

'We will, Chris,' said Rohan. 'However, a good starting point would be to share info about the grizzlies, their behaviour, habitat, et cetera, and bring to the forefront ideas as to *why* people might want to kill them. It may also shed light on anything we hear and see, and point us in the direction of the crooks.'

'Good plan, yaar,' said Umedh. 'Let's start with the youngest – Mich, tell us a little bit about grizzlies.'

'Okay. The grizzly bear's a huge, powerful animal, and when erect, stands six or seven feet tall. A male can weigh from 158 to about 363 kilos, while a female's about a quarter percent less heavy, but this weight is dependent on the time of year, where they live and what food they have access to. I heard of a humongous grizzly in Alaska which was nearly 10 foot tall and weighed about 544.31 kilos – it was the largest grizzly ever seen. Grizzlies are usually found in Canada, the United States and Mexico. They have bad eyesight, but an amazingly keen sense of smell. Gina.'

'A distinct feature is the muscular hump on its back, above the shoulders. The head's huge, it has long claws, and the fur can be black, brown or a muddy-blond with the tips of the fur usually looking quite grizzled – that's where it gets its name from. They eat a variety of food, depending on where they live since they are omnivorous. Salmon and other fish are their favourite food if they live near lakes or streams, but if available, they'll eat large mammals such as deer, moose, elk and bighorn sheep, as well as rodents, bugs, plants, berries, grasses, flowers and wild vegetables. Also, if there's a shortage of their usual food, they sometimes attack other animals and steal their food. Corazon?'

'Grizzlies live in varying types of territories such as dense forests, mountains, valleys, near rivers and coastal areas. They love safe dens and will return to them, and will use caves, hollows in trees or the ground, under fallen timber, et cetera. They're not *true* hibernators but sleep lightly during winter, and wake up quickly if disturbed. Their tracks are similar to those of other bears, but the base of their paw is more stretched out and oval in shape, while there are also partial or full nail prints which can measure up to 10.16 centimetres long. You have to *really* study grizzly tracks to ensure that you're not following a black bear instead. Anu.'

'While the status keeps changing, grizzlies are currently on the "vulnerable and threatened" list. Poaching, persecution and elimination of their natural habitat are three major causes of their decimation. Manipau specializes in protecting grizzlies, and didn't want the surrounding habitat to be taken over by the general populace who wouldn't care about conservation. Loss of habitat also means loss of food, which in turn means that grizzlies will look for food which brings them in close contact with humans who don't understand them and taunt, kill or protest against them. Ricky?'

'I don't know much, but I've heard that in Canada many groups are doing their best to create awareness; in Calgary, for example, the zoo holds fundraising events and educates the community about the importance of protecting wild spaces. When necessary, captive breeding is encouraged in order to preserve genetics. Chris?'

'I've learned a lot over the past few days – I can't imagine how people can be so cruel to animals. I was speaking with Lisa, before you folks arrived, and she told me about the way they communicate.

'They're very vocal and use a variety of whines, growls, roars, woofs, grunts and groans. If they face you head on, with flattened ears and their bodies low on the ground, this means they're dangerous; but if they turn their heads sideways, they're submissive. Occasionally, a female without a cub may adopt an orphan cub, even to the extent of nursing it. They fight among themselves, but also have playful sparring matches – especially the young bears. They normally spar with partners of the same size. They appear to enjoy sliding down snowbanks, and have been known to go back to the top and slide down again, for no apparent reason other than for the fun of it. Nimal?'

'The Latin name is *Ursus arctos horribilis*. I understand that centuries ago it was assumed that grizzlies, along with most other animals, had very little intelligence. It's now confirmed that this is incorrect. Grizzlies are extremely intelligent, learn from experience, and solve and deal with problems. For example, they find secure hiding spots where they can see but can't be seen. That's cognitive thinking – which simply means they are conscious thinkers. It's also common knowledge that if you teach a grizzly something once, it will remember it always.

'Grizzlies breed every three or four years. After mating, embryos will float in the female's body for months, enabling the female to obtain all the nourishment she needs prior to hibernation in her den. Once the embryos implant, the gestation period is around 235 days, and cubs are generally born in late January or early February. The number of cubs at birth could be from one to four, but two is the average. Grizzlies are extremely protective of their offspring and raise them for four to five years until they achieve sexual maturity.

'Cubs weigh about 0.4 kg at birth, and are around 23 cm long. They're poorly developed, toothless and blind at birth; their eyes open after about three weeks, and they'll nurse for at least six months. The mother's milk is richer than cow's milk and the cubs grow fast. They nurse every two or three hours, and make gurgling, chuckling sounds when they're nursing – or, as Amy and Anu discovered, they hum.

'Man, I could go on for hours – they're fascinating creatures, and Amy recommended some wonderful books with tons of amazing facts. Newborn cubs are quite helpless, and a mother grizzly will give her life to protect them – remember Hurit's behaviour. She'll send her cubs up into a tree and stand at the base of it, fighting off all dangers. Amy?'

'The books were super, Nimal. I'm thrilled that over the past few years, Manipau's been doing more research on the grizzlies. We ensure that when we want to examine them, we use tranquillizing drugs that won't harm them. All necessary tests and examinations are made and recorded, and we sometimes attach a radio collar so we can track the bear. This type of research enables us to discover more about the nature and habits of the bears and, thereby, find ways and means of ensuring its survival in a world which is suffering increasingly because of human greed.

'Research and education are crucial, and lessen the threats not only to grizzlies, but to all other animals. I'm so glad we're involved in conservation outreach. Manipau invites specialists from all over the world to share knowledge and we've already had several grizzly experts here. Once the CC's set up, we hope to educate more of the general populace, too. I'm currently working on an educational article that will go up on our JEACs website. Umedh?'

'Increasing human population results in the necessity to use more land for housing, roads, and shopping centres, and the use of wood from the forests for building purposes is inevitable. Instead of being proactive, governments and countries let themselves be forced into a reactive mode, and use band-aid solutions. But since most educational institutions are now introducing the importance of environmental factors and the need for conservation into their curriculum, people are becoming increasingly aware of these crucial issues.

'However, the greed of criminals for fast money causes havoc in the cycle of life. Poaching is a vice that conservationists have battled for centuries. Then there are people who think they're doing a kind deed by feeding animals who wander into their cities and towns. This deadens some of the natural fear animals have. Results – people lose caution, animals become threatened and attack – the animals are killed. Another factor is when people choose to ignore or disobey rules set by parks and conservation centres, which could result in someone being killed by an animal, and the family suing the organization. Even if the organization wins the case, this creates negative publicity. Yet another danger to animals, when they lose their habitat, is that they wander onto the roads and highways, and are often killed by trucks and other vehicles. Rohan?'

'Thanks for sharing your knowledge, JEACs. Clearly we know a fair amount about the grizzly bear and the problems facing it. In conclusion, let me tell you what Umedh and I discovered last night when we searched books and the internet to try to figure out reasons why anyone would kill grizzlies. It's not a nice topic, but we must try to understand why they're being poached in order to see if it connects with what's happening here at Manipau.

'There's a growing international trade in bear parts, both for the black bear and the grizzly; the parts are mainly used in traditional Asian medicine, and also as food in certain countries. Cubs are sold for large amounts of money, and when they become adults they're killed and their gall bladders, paws, claws and teeth are used. Their heads and hides are also in demand. I'm not going to say more, since it's sickening, but we also read that poachers can sell gall bladders for thousands of dollars.

'I'm sorry, folks,' added Rohan, as everyone around the table looked ill. 'Let's not discuss details of how the bear parts are used, but focus on how we can prevent this happening. Agreed?'

'Yes,' muttered the group.

'Which Asian countries are most heavily involved?' asked Nimal.

'China and Korea were the two main countries mentioned in the research,' said Umedh.

'Does that mean the crooks will be from those countries and we search for Korean and Chinese crooks?' asked Ricky.

'Not at all,' said Rohan. 'We check anyone, no matter what their nationality, who looks or behaves suspiciously. Crooks who poach animals for international trade have contacts in the country from which the animals are being poached, as well as in the countries where they sell them. And take Jason, for example. He's from Korea and has Korean contacts. Can you even imagine him being a crook?'

'No way! I get you, Rohan,' said Ricky. 'Jason's a good guy, and you're saying that we shouldn't make a blanket judgement of nationalities – I agree.'

'Precisely, Ricky,' said Anu. '*Every* country has its good people and its crooks. However, the world is shrinking rapidly: people travel and migrate all over the world, and advancing technology makes worldwide communication that much easier. While this results in hundreds of good things, it also enables crooks to operate internationally more easily.'

'Good point, Anu,' said Amy. 'Returning to our situation here, what did you hear at the site? Did you split up and speak to different people?'

'We did,' said Nimal. 'Just one more point, though. Your mum mentioned a huge reserve named *Kanasu*, in BC, which lost more than 40 grizzlies to poachers over two years, and the crooks weren't discovered.

The poaching stopped as more stringent measures were taken to protect the reserve. It's possible that those crooks have moved here.'

'We'll keep that in mind,' said Rohan. 'Corazon, Gina and Mich, let's start with you – what did you learn at the site?'

'We spoke to a group of five,' began Corazon. 'Some of them work on night shifts, and they were concerned that their previous supervisor, Keith, couldn't return to work for a few months. He was badly injured just over four weeks ago. Mich?'

'One of the women said he was an excellent driver and she couldn't understand how he got into that accident. Apparently his car went off the road and smashed into a tree at a speed of over 80 klicks when he tried to avoid being hit by a truck – there shouldn't have been any trucks on the road at 5 a.m. since the only vehicles delivering goods to the sites come around 7 a.m. Gina?'

'A man made a weird comment,' said Gina. 'He said the accident was deliberate, and clearly someone wanted to harm Keith. Otherwise why would they have been lurking on a side road? The police haven't found the truck.'

'Who discovered the accident?' asked Amy.

'Two other night-shift workers – they left fifteen minutes after Keith, taking the same road. They saw the car with its lights still on, called the police and ambulance, and then tried to help Keith, who was unconscious,' said Corazon. 'He had to be cut out of the car. They weren't sure he'd survive, but he has a strong constitution, and is now recovering.'

'Poor chap,' said Anu. 'How did they know he was trying to avoid a truck?'

'They didn't tell us,' said Gina, 'and then they had to go back to work.'

'Ricky and Chris?' asked Rohan.

'Keith's wife is friends with one of the women in our group,' said Chris. 'She said that about a week after his injury, Keith told his wife that he saw a truck swing out from a side road on his right, and he swerved to avoid it hitting him – he had no choice.'

'And the rest was the same as what the girls heard,' added Ricky.

'I heard a shorter version of the same tale,' said Nimal, 'from a woman named Dinah. She also said it was *interesting* that Keith, who was crazy about animals, should be replaced by Kylie who doesn't seem to care one way or the other about the safety of animals. Apparently Kylie's not popular with the group we met this morning.

'Several other women and men agreed with Dinah, and I was going to ask why she used the word "interesting" when a chap named Andy said, "*Interesting* is the very word, Dinah, and my question is why does Kylie only want to work the *night shifts* and *no* weekends? All our other supervisors rotate shifts and weekends. Kylie claims to be a dedicated daughter who has to go home each night to her home in a small town north of MWCC called Powela, to look after her parents during the day and weekends – but from what we've heard, it's not true". Before I could question Andy, the break was over.'

'I can fill in a bit more, Nimal,' said Umedh. 'One of the women in my group, Ellen, really dislikes Kylie and says she's a liar. Two weeks ago, Ellen had a Saturday off; she met Angela, her friend who works in a jewellery store in the shopping mall in Powela, and they had lunch in a restaurant opposite the store. Ellen said she was venting about Kylie, when through the window she suddenly saw Kylie, with a couple of pals, entering the jewellery store. She pointed her out to Angela, who recognized Kylie and said that she purchases a lot of jewellery and always pays in cash. Angela mentioned that Kylie lives at a local address.'

'I guess Ellen told her story to some of the others, Andy being one of them,' said Amy.

'Sounds like it,' said Umedh. 'Angela told Ellen that Kylie mentioned she'd only been in Powela for about six weeks. Rohan?'

'Jason and I spoke with Carl and Tina. Carl said the police haven't found the truck that caused Keith's accident. I asked how Kylie became supervisor and Carl said that when Keith was chosen, there were two other women who applied for the position, and one of them was Kylie. The other woman got a job shortly afterwards, but Kylie was still available. Since they badly needed someone with experience, they met all her demands to work only on the night shifts and not on weekends.

'What interested me was that *they* didn't contact Kylie when Keith was injured – *she* called them up the very next morning.'

'But how did she know that the position was vacant?' asked Ricky.

'Good question,' said Rohan. 'Kylie told Remo that she'd heard that morning about the vacancy. Since news tends to spread quickly in small towns, Remo and Tina, who spoke to Kylie over the phone, accepted it at face value, and called her in for a second interview. Tina says that if they'd had a choice they wouldn't have hired Kylie – but she had experience and good references, and they needed a replacement fast. She started work that night.'

'Good references? From whom?' asked Anu.

'Point, sis,' said Rohan. 'I asked, and it was from a manager in a construction company in BC – she worked there last year.'

'Hmm. Now that is interesting,' said Anu. The others looked at her questioningly. 'Remember, Kanasu Reserve where they lost lots of grizzlies in the last two years?'

'Right on!' exclaimed Amy. 'And good references can be forged.' The others agreed, and Amy continued. 'We must find out about Kanasu – I'll call Maddison, one of our JEACs, this evening.'

'Excellent. One last point,' said Nimal, 'Jason and Kylie don't hit it off. His negative reaction is instinctive, but it sounds like she doesn't like the fact that he understands Korean.'

'Yeah, I'd like to meet Kylie,' said Rohan. 'We need to go to the site when she's on a shift.'

'Agreed,' said Umedh. 'Now, if we're going out to check the blood spots and do some tracking, we should get moving. What about the cubs?'

'Mich and I'll stay with them,' offered Gina.

'And Codey and Sam can help us,' added Mich.

'Actually, although I'd love to come, I'd better stay, too,' said Ricky. 'I have holiday homework to complete, but I don't want to miss this adventure, so I'd rather finish the homework now.'

'I haven't finished mine either, so I'll also stay and finish it,' groaned Chris.

'Good thinking, chaps – we need everyone after today. The six of us, and Hunter, will do some tracking,' said Rohan. 'Let's get the tranquillizer equipment and sufficient darts, take cameras, binocs and maps in your knapsacks. What about more WTs, Umedh?'

'We'll each carry one – we have three sets of WTs, each with six units. Those of you staying here should also keep a WT handy in case we need to get in touch with each other,' said Umedh.

'Point, yaar. Chris and Ricky, we'll show you how to use them,' said Rohan. 'Corazon, do you know the way from here?'

'Sure, and I know some trails that will get us there quickly.'

'Super,' said Nimal. 'Amy and I'll get the darts and equipment, while you folks get the other things, and some snacks and drinks.' He grinned as the JEACs chuckled, 'I know *you* folks will be stuffing your faces here, and *we* may not get back for several hours.'

CHAPTER 8

Camouflaged Trails and Clues

By 10 a.m. they were ready to leave, agreeing that they would only check the first blood spot site that morning, and everyone would go to the other site, time permitting, in the afternoon.

'Mich and Gina,' said Nimal, 'when the cubs wake up, play with them for a bit, then leave them in the playpen on their own for half an hour. Even if they cry, try not to go to them. The next time, leave them for an hour before you return. That way they'll learn that you *are* coming back, sooner or later, and they won't become upset when we all leave for a few hours. Leave Codey in the room with them when you leave – he'll keep an eye on them.'

'Contact us on the WTs if anything crops up,' said Umedh.

'Will do,' agreed the others.

'Corazon, take the lead with Nimal and Hunter,' said Rohan. 'Do you want a TG?'

'Tranquillizer gun? No, thanks, Rohan,' said Corazon.

'I'll take the blow dart,' said Amy, 'and Nimal, Rohan and Umedh can each carry TGs and guns.'

They set off, Corazon leading the way while Rohan and Umedh brought up the rear. It was a beautiful day, and the flowering shrubs exuded a warm scent as the JEACs brushed against them. They headed deeper into the forest going west and then north. Various small animals, and a herd of deer, avoided the group.

'We're nearly there,' said Corazon, a little later. 'We need to go extra cautiously now, since there may be grizzlies around. Dad and I saw some last week.'

'East or west of us?' said Nimal.

'West – there are numerous hollows and holes.'

A few minutes later they entered a small clearing and Corazon showed them the blood spots.

'Hunter, on guard, boy,' said Nimal. The dog began prowling around the clearing, alert for animals or humans.

'They're pretty close together, and both under huge trees on the edge of the clearing,' said Rohan, as the group started examining the area.

'Look, you can still see the tracks with blood in them,' said Corazon, pointing. 'It must have been fairly damp the day they were running, because the prints are deep.'

'And I guess it hasn't rained since then,' said Anu, rapidly taking as many pictures as she could. 'Did the police or trackers find any *human* prints?'

'I don't know,' said Amy. 'Corazon?' The girl shook her head.

'Let's examine the area, find the bullet holes and check everywhere for signs of human beings. I know the police must have looked thoroughly, but you never know.'

They found the bullet holes easily enough, and took more pictures. It was a disappointing search, and they sat on some fallen logs to have a drink.

'How would they take full-grown grizzlies out of the Centre?' mused Rohan. 'Anu, what do you imagine crooks would do if they couldn't drive out of here with the dead bears?'

Anu thought for a moment and said, 'They'd have several options. Bundle up the parts they wanted, bury the rest and get a chopper to pick them up and lift them over the wall. Or, since a chopper would draw attention, the crooks could move the animals on a small sled, and somehow get it *under* the wall, with a vehicle on the other side to pick them up. If they wanted the entire body, they'd have to choose the latter option.'

'A tunnel makes sense,' said Umedh. 'It wouldn't take long to dig a decent-sized tunnel through which a sled could be pushed,' said Umedh, 'and I'm positive this was all pre-planned.'

'Brill, folks,' said Rohan. 'Let's go and examine the wall, see if there are any signs of people, blood, et cetera, and look for a tunnel. Corazon, lead the way. Nimal and Hunter go with her, since Hunter can warn us of danger.'

'It's very dense going north,' said Corazon, examining the area. 'Wait! This looks like a new trail – we'll take it.'

The JEACs followed her.

'One sec, folks,' said Nimal, kneeling on the ground and pointing. 'See these marks – they could be sled tracks.'

'Question – would any of *our* rangers use a sled to get to the wall?' said Rohan, examining the marks and then the trail. 'Answer – no. Look! These branches have been cut – this isn't a new trail; it's at least a couple of weeks old – the branches are quite dry.'

'You're right, yaar – a handsaw's been used,' said Umedh. He went ahead on the trail with Hunter and Nimal, examining more branches and the ground. 'A path's been cut through this area with a handsaw and there are more sled tracks ahead.' The others followed them.

'Look at this,' said Anu, pointing at a broken branch. 'A piece of cloth in black and gold print 7.62 centimetres in diameter.'

'It's probably from a shirt,' said Amy thoughtfully, examining the branch and measuring herself against it. 'Someone who's my height – could have lost a piece from the back of a shirt if it wasn't tucked into jeans. I know it's stereotypical, but going by the print, I'm positive it's a woman's shirt.'

'But wouldn't they have felt it rip and stopped to make sure?' said Corazon.

'Not if they were in a hurry and if it was dark,' said Rohan. 'They were obviously up to no good.'

'They created a trail,' said Nimal, 'didn't care about destroying the shrubbery, and were pulling a sled – sounds pretty suspicious to me!'

Rohan took the piece of cloth carefully off the branch, and put it in his knapsack. 'Let's move, JEACs – go carefully, keep your ears open and eyes peeled. Corazon, how much further is it to the wall – and does the treeline go right up to it?'

'We're twenty metres away, Rohan, and the trees stop about fifteen metres before the wall. There's a clearing in front of the wall.'

'Let's get closer to the treeline and then Hunter and Nimal can scout ahead.'

'Okay,' said Corazon, and the group proceeded cautiously.

A little later Corazon stopped; Nimal and Hunter moved ahead. A few whispered commands from Nimal, and Hunter knew exactly what to do. At the edge of the forest the dog stopped – he sniffed the air and whined softly.

'Okay, boy,' whispered Nimal. There was a fair-sized clearing in front of the wall. Ten metres west, deer and rabbits were drinking at a small waterhole which was half in the forest and half in the clearing.

'Clever Hunter,' said Nimal softly, and the dog gave him a quick lick. 'I know they'll run away the minute we go out, boy, but we need to check the area. Come on.'

The boy and dog moved into the clearing, and the animals immediately disappeared into the forest. There were no other creatures around; Nimal gave the 'all clear' over the WTs, and the others joined them quickly.

'There's more rock than sand here, and the tracks have disappeared,' said Rohan. 'Spread out, JEACs, and look for clues.'

But no more tracks were discovered.

'Come over here,' called Rohan. He and Corazon were checking branches and rocks piled up against the wall, towards the eastern side of the clearing.

'We wondered if there was a tunnel under these branches and rocks,' said Corazon, pulling away branches.

'I doubt it,' said Umedh, examining the rocks. 'They're too big to move manually and look quite solid.'

They got to work, and as they moved the last branch, they gasped in surprise.

'A hidden firepit – interesting,' said Rohan. 'It looks like people have camped and cooked meals here. Is that a common occurrence, Amy?'

'Absolutely not – there's always a risk of forest fires, and we discourage people from building campfires anywhere they please. We have designated areas, and you've seen the barbeque set-ups we have in the camping grounds.'

'This was possibly used for nefarious purposes,' said Anu. 'Let's cover it and search for cans of food which might be buried in the soil – it's very rocky here, so look around the edges of the forest.'

'How do you come up with these ideas?' asked Corazon in amazement, as they quickly replaced the branches.

'We've had a bit of experience looking for clues during some of our adventures,' smiled Amy. 'Look for soil which looks as if it's been dug up recently.'

They split up again, and within a few minutes, Nimal and Hunter found a large hole in the ground where empty food cans and beer bottles were buried.

'They've either eaten many meals here, or there were lots of people – I'm sure there are at least two dozen cans, and a dozen or more beer bottles,' said Anu.

'We've got the pictures as evidence. Now, if they wanted to kill grizzlies, they'd go deeper into the forest – around BSC-1, for instance. What do you others think?'

'Agreed – and they'd probably climb trees for safety,' said Nimal.

'Let's return to BSC-1,' said Rohan.

'BSC-1? Blood Spot Clearing number one?' grinned Corazon.

'Absolutely, kiddo,' smiled Rohan, as they made their way back to the clearing. 'This is the first one and BSC-2 is where your dad found the other blood spots.'

'It's possible,' said Umedh, 'that the crooks split up: one group chasing the grizzlies to BSC-1 and killing them there. Then they loaded them on sleds and brought them along the trail to the firepit clearing. The second group may have been there, preparing a meal, and assisting the first group to take the bears away, but we don't know where they went.'

'All excellent points,' said Rohan. 'Let's split up and check the trees, then head back to GW to discuss everything. Hold all reports on search results for that meeting. It's nearly noon; if we search for an hour, we should be back by 1:30 p.m. Stay alert, watch out for grizzlies, and if necessary use the WTs to contact each other. Agreed?'

'Sure . . .' began Anu, and stopped abruptly as shots rang out. The JEACs froze.

CHAPTER 9

A Fortuitous Rescue

'That was north-east of us – come on,' said Rohan, as he and Nimal sprinted back along the trail leading to the wall, TGs in hand, the others at their heels.

'I'll check on GW,' said Umedh, pulling out his WT as they ran. 'GW, come in, *urgent*. Over.'

'Hi, Umedh,' said Gina. 'What's up? Over.'

'We heard shots; did you hear anything? Are you all okay? Where are the boys? Over.'

'We're fine, but didn't hear any shots – Mich and I are in the garden with the cubs and dogs, and here come Chris and Ricky – we're all tuned in now. Do you want us to do anything? Over.'

'Get inside, ASAP. Lock all doors and windows, draw the curtains, and stay together. Stay alert, and don't open the door to anyone unless you know them. We're trying to locate the shots. Have to run – keep your WTs handy and headsets on. Over and out.'

'I hear running, east of us, but it's not a bear,' whispered Nimal, stopping suddenly. 'We need to go further east.'

'Follow me,' said Corazon, plunging off the hacked trail and pushing through heavy shrubbery. 'There should be a proper trail just about – good, here it is.'

'Excellent, Corazon,' said Rohan softly. 'Make a big racket, JEACs. Shout as if we've spotted someone and are chasing them. Nimal, you have a loaded tranquillizer; enough to put down a grizzly?' Nimal nodded. 'Good. Go ahead with Hunter and see if you can find signs of any animal that was shot – we're right behind you.'

Rohan yelled loudly, and banged a stick against a tree, as if he were running through the forest and breaking branches. 'There, further east, I saw something. Run – we've got to catch them.'

'I'm with you,' roared Umedh. 'Did someone call the police?'

'Yes, and they're on the way,' shouted Amy.

'Hurry up – don't lose them,' cried Anu.

They made a big commotion, and Corazon hollered, 'They're getting away, but the police should be here soon.'

The group stopped for a few minutes, and in the silence, they heard two sets of footsteps running fast – eastwards.

'There's an animal north-east of us – and it's moving slowly,' said Nimal. 'Could be injured. Hunter and I can find it.'

'I'll go with Hunter and Nimal,' said Rohan. 'The rest of you continue along the trail. Don't shout any more, but make some noise and listen for sounds that people are still running away from us. Someone contact GW, give our location and ask for a couple of rangers to join us ASAP; say we need transport and medical equipment for animals.'

The group split up.

'Here's a trail going north,' said Nimal softly. 'Hunter, smell out the animal. Rohan, we're upwind, so we'll be okay.'

Hunter went along the trail until he reached a small clearing ten metres ahead. Then he froze, growling softly.

'Good, boy,' said Nimal, as he and Rohan joined Hunter. In the clearing, seated on the ground leaning against a tree and panting hard, was an enormous grizzly bear. It licked its chest, pausing every now and then to listen and sniff the air. It was obviously very weak.

'It has two chest wounds,' said Rohan softly.

'I hate to shoot, even to tranquillize it,' said Nimal, 'but it'll die unless the bleeding's staunched. Take Hunter and move towards the right while I get closer on the left side. When I signal, send Hunter out so that the bear sees him and turns, and I'll put a dart in its rump; we'll keep our distance until the sedation works.'

'Okay, yaar,' said Rohan. 'Come on, Hunter.'

Ten minutes later, the injured bear was sedated and collapsed on the ground. Putting Hunter on guard, Nimal and Rohan promptly removed their shirts and tore them up, making pads to staunch the flow of blood.

'I wonder if anyone's on the way,' muttered Nimal anxiously, holding down a pad firmly, while Rohan staunched the other wound. 'This chap's lost a ton of blood and will need a reversal agent soon.'

Just then their WTs beeped and Rohan answered. A few minutes later Shawn and Tulok arrived and took over. The boys watched as the men worked quickly and efficiently on the bear, and nobody said a word until they were ready to move the grizzly.

'Heave-ho! Good work, lads,' said Shawn, when the grizzly was safely in the mobile medical unit.

'He'll be okay fairly soon, we hope,' said Tulok, shaking hands with the boys. 'You saved his life with your quick thinking. We need to get him to the Sanctuary and under Lisa's care ASAP, but we'll call you later on to tell you how he is and find out what happened.'

'We informed Janet and Kafil that there was a problem, but that we didn't know what it was,' said Shawn, leaning out of the window. 'All Mich said was that we were needed urgently for a possibly injured animal. Fortunately, we were only a few minutes away from GW. Chat soon.'

As the men drove off, the others raced up.

'We're okay, honestly – it's just grizzly blood,' said Rohan, as Amy turned white, grasped his arm and looked at both boys in horror. 'Hunter's got some on him, too.'

'Thank goodness,' said Anu, faintly. 'Is the bear . . .' She stopped.

'It'll be fine – Shawn and Tulok have taken it to the Sanctuary,' said Nimal. 'Let's get back – we need a bath. We used our shirts for padding to staunch the bleeding; there were two shots in the chest and it was bleeding profusely.'

'Poor thing,' said Umedh. 'I hope it'll be okay. I'll go ahead and let you in through the basement door, and you can go straight to the showers. I assume you'd prefer Gina and Mich not to see you in this state.'

'Absolutely, thanks, yaar,' said Rohan gratefully.

'We'll give them details when we've cleaned up,' said Nimal.

'Corazon, come with me – you can distract the girls while I go down to the basement,' said Umedh, and the two of them ran ahead.

'We'll prepare a meal,' said Anu, as she and Amy raced away, too.

The boys made their way, through bushes, to the basement door. Half an hour later, the JEACs assembled in the kitchen, along with a freshly bathed Hunter. It was nearly 1:30 p.m. and lunch was almost ready.

'Mom called,' said Amy, placing a telephone in the middle of the table. 'I said we'd call her and conference-in Shawn, Tulok and Hassan.'

'Okay,' said Rohan. 'But since they have so much on their plates, and are short-staffed, let's not bother them with any plans we might make – we'll just update them as to what happened, and say we're looking further into it. Agreed?'

'Absolutely,' chorused the others, and a few minutes later they were updating the adults. The JEACs who had not been involved listened eagerly, too.

'Thank you so much, JEACs,' said Janet. 'The guys told me that if not for your quick thinking, we'd have lost another grizzly.'

'How is he?' asked Nimal.

'Very weak, but he'll be okay in about ten days,' said Shawn.

'I wish we could come and help you find the crooks,' said Tulok angrily.

'No worries, Tulok,' said Rohan. 'We've got ten able JEACs, and three dogs – we'll be fine! Do you need us to help with anything?'

'No thanks, JEACs – just catch the crooks,' said Shawn.

'I trust all of you, so I won't tell you to be careful,' said Janet. 'Keep us posted as often as you can, okay?'

'Will do, Aunty Janet,' said Rohan reassuringly.

'There are a couple of air guns in the cupboard downstairs,' said Hassan. 'Take them with you – at least you can make a loud noise.'

'Sound idea,' said Umedh.

'We have a meeting and must run,' said Hassan. 'Let us know if you need assistance again – the three of us wander all around northern Manipau and could reach you in less than half an hour at any time.'

'Thanks, goodbye and good luck with your work,' said the JEACs, and rang off.

'Fifteen minutes before we can eat,' said Anu, changing the subject. 'What about the cubs – they must be hungry. Anything fun happen while we were away?'

Hunter barked softly as Codey raced into the room and ran off again, Hunter and Sam following him.

'I guess the cubs are awake,' said Gina. She and Mich followed the dogs, and returned with the cubs, the dogs prancing around excitedly.

'And have you been good, infants?' crooned Nimal, sitting on the floor. The cubs climbed into his lap, making funny humming noises as they tried to hug him. 'Yes, I love you, too – but I won't scare everyone away by joining in your song. What did you do today?'

'They slept till eleven and then woke up. Gina and I gave them a red ball to play with, and the cubs and the dogs . . .' Mich broke off, giggling.'

'. . . were hilarious,' continued Gina. 'When I first rolled the ball to the cubs they were scared and climbed into our laps hurriedly. Codey nosed the ball in front of Mich who had Atka in her lap.'

'Atka became curious; she crawled over to it on her tummy and glared at it, but it didn't move,' said Mich. 'She wriggled her behind – you know the way dogs do when they're approaching something cautiously – then pounced on it and tried to take it by surprise. It rolled away and Atka reversed rapidly into a surprised Sam, who was lying between us. Sam leapt up in a hurry, licked her gently and tried to *herd* her towards me – it was simply hilarious because Atka whined piteously, which upset Codey, who immediately went over and licked her, too.'

'Then,' continued Gina, stifling her giggles, 'Ataneq became brave. He approached the ball and somehow managed to kick it towards Atka who, taken by surprise, got it on the nose. She fell on her back, the ball landing on her tummy. Mich and I nearly died laughing, and Chris and Ricky came running to see what all the shrieking was about. You guys had better tell them the rest,' she said as she and Mich collapsed on the floor shrieking with laughter, while the dogs danced around, wondering what was going on.

'We thought they were being murdered,' grinned Chris, 'so we raced in to find Atka trying to bite the ball, Ataneq pawing at her with a puzzled look on his face, while Codey ran around them, whining anxiously, and Sam tried to herd everyone into a tight circle.'

'After that, Ataneq and Atka lost their fear and chased the ball all over the room until everyone was exhausted,' chuckled Ricky.

'We fed the cubs, and they hummed as they drank milk,' said Gina.

'And Gina made up a song about them,' said Mich excitedly. 'Sing it, Gina!'

'Okay, but join in.' And the girls began to sing.

Grizzly cubs are cutie pies
When drinking milk they close their eyes.
Tell me, little cuddly bear,
What's that funny sound I hear?

Chorus:
Slurp, gloop, gurgle and yum, this is great, it fills my tum.
I love milk, it soothes me so, hum, hum, hum-hum, hum, hum!

You like to hum? You're such a pet.
Could someone, please, a picture get?
I hope you will remember me
When you become a huge grizzly.

Repeat chorus:

Let's play with this nice red ball,
Compared to us it's rather tall.
Hit it with your head, my dear,
It won't bite you, do not fear.

Repeat chorus:

Ataneq and Atka, too,
We have fun with both of you.
And we'll do our very best
To protect you, and the rest.
Slurp, gloop, gurgle and yum, this is great, it fills our tums.
We love milk it soothes us so, We love you, too, hum-hum, hum, hum, hum!

'That's hilarious, girls!' said Anu, when everyone had stopped laughing over the song. 'Perhaps we could sing it at the fundraiser.'

'Good idea,' said Nimal. 'What happened after that?'

'We heard Umedh on the WT, came inside, and locked ourselves in,' said Mich.

Gina took out two bottles of milk from the refrigerator and said, 'Who wants to feed them?'

'Me,' said Ricky and Corazon simultaneously.

'Did you discover anything before you heard the shots?' asked Chris.

'We did, but were unable to complete our searches,' said Rohan. 'If everyone's game, let's eat fast, get back to BSC-1 and continue our search. We'll brief you on a few things so that you know what we're looking for, and then we can update each other on all our findings over dinner.'

'Good idea, Rohan,' said Amy. 'I doubt we'll have time to check BSC-2, near the north-east wall, today.'

'True; perhaps we could do that early tomorrow morning,' said Anu.

'Lunch is ready,' announced Amy, 'so brief everyone while we eat.'

Once they were served and had begun their meal, Rohan said, 'When we get to BSC-1 we'll split into two groups – A and B. Search for trees that people could climb easily and sit in, and from where they could shoot a grizzly.'

'Also look for signs that people have cut through the forest and created trails, which they've tried to camouflage,' said Umedh.

'Each group needs at least two TGs – and an air gun,' said Rohan. 'Here's a suggestion: Amy, Umedh, Nimal, Corazon and Gina will be Group A and the rest of us will be Group B. We'll take Hunter and he'll stay with whichever group is searching around BSC-1. Nimal, can we leave the cubs with Codey and Sam as babysitters for a few hours this afternoon so that all of us can go out?'

'No problemo,' said Nimal. 'Gina and Mich say they didn't whimper when left alone.'

'Excellent,' said Anu. 'Question, Manipau JEACs. Who has keys for the various houses, sheds, et cetera, and are they easily accessible?'

'Our staff have access to everything,' said Amy. 'Good point, hon. From now on we lock everything before we leave.'

'Why? It's quite safe here, isn't it?' asked Ricky, looking puzzled.

'With crooks wandering around, we can't take risks,' said Rohan. 'Five of you – do a quick round and check *every* door and window, on all floors, thanks. Take the dogs with you. The rest of us will clear the kitchen.'

'Will do,' chorused everyone.

'Everything's locked and secure,' reported Gina, when the group reassembled.

'Umedh, can you rig up something to connect to our WTs?' said Nimal. 'Then, if the dogs bark and sound angry and upset, we'll hear them and can return quickly.'

'I have an idea,' said Umedh thoughtfully. 'Want to help me, Ricky?'

'Sure, yaar,' said Ricky, and the boys left the kitchen. The others were organized when Umedh and Ricky returned with two units.

'The home crowd are wired, folks,' said Umedh.

'Those look like iPods,' said Chris.

'They function like speakers for microphones,' said Umedh, showing them the units. 'The earpieces will capture sounds in the living room, near the front door, in the kitchen and in the basement – Ricky has planted receiving units in each section.'

'He's brill!' said Ricky admiringly. 'He just looked at the equipment available, and the next minute he was putting it together!'

'That's our Mr. Q,' said Nimal. 'Pure genius!'

'Dry up, man,' said Umedh. 'Ricky helped me. I suggest Gina and Mich be responsible for these.'

'Excellent, yaar,' said Rohan.

The girls were thrilled to be in charge of the speaker units, and quickly plugged in the earpieces.

'Let's go, JEACs,' said Amy.

They left GW, locking the front door carefully behind them. It was nearly 3 p.m.

CHAPTER 10

Discoveries at and around BSC-1

Four hours later, an exhausted but excited group of JEACs and dog returned to GW, where they were greeted boisterously by dogs and cubs.

'I feel sticky and grungy,' said Anu, as they removed their shoes and knapsacks in the hallway.

'Me too – I need a shower,' said Amy.

'Us, too,' chorused the others.

'Right, quick march, JEACs,' said Anu. 'It's a good thing we have three washrooms. Amy, any suggestions for a quick dinner?'

'Chilli?' said Amy. 'There's a big pot in the freezer and all we need to make is a salad and garlic bread.'

'Yes!' yelled the rest.

By 7:20 p.m. everyone was seated around the dining table in the kitchen, eating hungrily. The animals were content and lay in a corner of the room.

'We'll first update you on what we found *before* the incident with the bear, and then share our current news,' said Rohan. 'Corazon, you start – we'll take it in turns.'

They quickly updated the others on what they had found, and laid the piece of cloth on the table. Then Group A gave their report.

'We returned to the firepit clearing, and divided the area in three,' began Amy. 'Nimal checked the eastern side; Umedh and Gina the western end near the waterhole. Corazon and I searched the middle section and began our search around the hacked-out trail from BSC-1 to the clearing, and checked every tree, since we figured crooks may have climbed them. We found one leafy tree which was easy to climb, but was too fragile for a grizzly, and Corazon shinned up, like a squirrel, to the first fork. Carry on, hon.'

'It was large enough to hold at least three medium-sized people and was quite safe. I found no traces of a hammock, but I did find *this* stuck to a branch,' and Corazon held up a piece of fabric.

'It's identical to the piece we found earlier,' said Anu, placing it next to the first clue.

'Wow,' gasped Ricky. 'Anything else?'

'Not a thing,' said Amy. 'Nor did we find any other suitable trees, though we searched diligently. Umedh and Gina?'

'Gina and I first searched all around the waterhole. We were hoping to find footprints – and we did!' said Umedh. The others gasped. 'At the far western end of the waterhole, we found a trail of footprints – which looked like a male size eight or nine, with a distinct pattern. I made a quick drawing of them. Gina?'

'We followed the tracks into a thick bush,' said Gina. 'Clearly, someone had crouched there for a few hours since there were cigarette butts strewn around – they're in the envelope on the side table. From the bush we tracked the prints towards the firepit, but they faded and disappeared because the ground was very stony. Nimal?'

'The bushes were dense on the east side of the clearing and went right up to the wall, so I began with the trees and found nothing,' said Nimal. 'I decided to check the bushes, and as I examined them, I noticed that several branches growing five metres away from the wall were quite dead. Just then I saw *this* piece of cloth.' Nimal held it up for everyone to see, and placed it on the table beside the other two pieces of cloth – it matched.

'Seems like the person who wore that shirt was all over the place,' said Rohan thoughtfully. 'Where did you find it, yaar?'

'Clinging to a twig in the midst of the dead branches – and I wouldn't have seen it if not for a slight breeze which made it flutter. I tried to push through the branches to reach it, and discovered that the branches had only been stuck into the soil. So I called the others to come and help.

'We pulled out all the dead branches which were arranged two metres into the shrubbery, and then found the beginnings of another hacked-out trail, and the sled marks! Amy?'

'There wasn't time to check it out, so we replaced the branches, and hurried to join the others. We also checked along the wall for a tunnel – nothing doing.'

'It's beginning to come together,' said Rohan, who was making rapid notes. 'Let's give you our report, and then we'll discuss things. Okay?'

Everyone nodded eagerly, and Rohan looked over at Anu, who began Group B's report.

'When we got to BSC-1, we split up, too. Ricky and I searched the trees close to the blood spots and soon found a tree I could climb in a jiffy. I did so, and signalled Rohan, who was opposite me, examining the trees with the bullet holes. Rohan's a better shot than I am, and had the air gun, so we exchanged places: Rohan in the tree, Ricky and I near the tree with the bullet holes. Chris and Mich pretended to be a bear running towards the blood spots. Ricky?'

'As we figured from our experiment, if someone was seated exactly where Rohan was, they could have fired at, and missed a bear which was running across the clearing, and if the gun was loaded rapidly, fired again, and the bear was hit, it would have collapsed exactly where one of the blood spots is. Chris and Mich?'

'We began our search around the tree to see if we could find any spent cartridges – we found three!' said Chris. 'They're also in an envelope on the table. They'd been pushed into the earth, and Mich found them because she was crawling around on hands and knees. Carry on, Mich.'

'We also found several cigarette butts at the foot of another tree,' said Mich, 'which I climbed in less than a minute. It was to the left of the blood spots. Rohan?'

'Then Hunter, yes, you're brilliant, boy,' said Rohan, pausing to pat the intelligent dog who jumped up and licked him, 'found our last clue. We let him sniff the piece of cloth we'd discovered earlier and said "find". He sniffed all around the clearing and stopped at a heavy bush, opposite the blood spots. He checked it thoroughly, and then sat down, looked at us and barked softly, waving one paw in the air as if to say "come and see what I've found". Anu?'

'We raced over and there, in the middle of the bush, we found another piece of cloth, clinging to a dried branch – it's the same as the other three pieces. Whoever wore that shirt would have had to throw it away. Ricky.'

'The bush had broken branches and we found two "cigarette butts",' said Ricky, signing quotation marks. 'They're in the blue envelope on the table. The others joined us after that.'

'Whew! Lots of discoveries,' said Nimal. 'What next?'

'Let's clear up here and have dessert in the living room,' suggested Amy.

Within fifteen minutes everything was put away, and the dishwasher was running. The cubs were put in their basement playpen, with Codey beside them. Sam and Hunter lay down next to the children.

'Right,' said Rohan as the JEACs settled around the coffee table. He laid all the clues on the table and said, 'Discussion time, JEACs!'

'Give us a précis, Rohan,' suggested Amy.

The others nodded, so Rohan began. 'Very concisely, then, here's a summary. There's a gang of crooks targeting grizzlies. They've hacked out trails, deliberately camouflaged one of them, and have spent many hours around the firepit clearing, eating meals and drinking. They hid around BSC-1 for a few hours, killed two grizzlies there, and moved them to the firepit clearing via another hacked-out trail. We haven't found evidence that they're camping here, which indicates that they're possibly entering Manipau secretly – whenever they wish to do so. We haven't found a tunnel so far, and Group A didn't have time to explore the camouflaged trail going east from the firepit. The person wearing the printed shirt smoked something that could be drugs. Let's brainstorm.'

'May I examine the blue envelope, Rohan?' said Ricky hesitantly. 'While in rehab, we were taught about drugs, and I may be able to help.'

'Sure, yaar,' said Rohan, passing them over.

Ricky examined them, sniffed one briefly, passed them back to Rohan, and said, 'It's a weed of some kind – you smoke weed and inhale or inject other drugs. This is very mild and would relax you but, like most drugs, it's addictive. From what I recall, addicts have to take one every couple of hours.'

'Thanks, yaar,' said Rohan, 'that's really helpful. We now know that whoever smoked these was either in that bush for at least four hours, or was in there twice. Appreciate your knowledge.' Ricky turned red with pleasure.

'If crooks can enter Manipau freely, will they try to kill more grizzlies?' asked Mich.

'It's possible, hon,' said Amy. She rose and continued, 'But we're going to stop them. I'm going to make a quick call to Maddison and her brother, Kyle.'

'What about my friends Sorena and Corben who started a JEACs group a while ago?' said Mich. 'And Brinn, Corben's older sister, started a group, too. They were fundraising for World Wildlife Fund, Canada and the Calgary Zoo, and also creating awareness about polar bears in the North West Territories since a conservation lost fifteen bears to poachers.'

'I'll call them, hon,' said Amy. She went to the study.

'We must check the eastbound camouflaged trail Nimal found,' said Umedh. 'We may find the tunnel somewhere in that direction.'

'Sound idea, yaar,' said Rohan.

'Shouldn't we also search BSC-2, where the other three bears were killed?' said Corazon. 'We could look for a tunnel in that section, too.'

'Absolutely,' said Nimal. 'We'll do both searches tomorrow, but it'll take most of the day and we can't leave the cubs and Codey here all day – it's too far.'

'Is there some way we can take them with us?' asked Ricky.

'Carrying them could become a problem, yaar, since we need to keep our hands free as we trek through the forest, and we'll be carrying equipment,' said Rohan thoughtfully.

'There's also the risk of the cubs making a noise which could attract adult grizzlies to us – a bigger issue, I'd say,' said Nimal.

'BSC-2 is approximately 350 metres east of the Muskok, and we know we can't drive right up to it,' said Rohan, looking at a map of Manipau. 'How close to it can we get by car?'

'Approximately 25 metres west of the Muskok – a ten-minute drive from here,' said Corazon. 'There's a large clearing where we can park. Five minutes along a narrow trail to the river, across it, and then twenty minutes through shrubbery, to BSC-2.'

Umedh who was examining a map said, 'Is this the clearing, Corazon?' She nodded. 'And is this a little building near it?'

'It is,' said Corazon and Mich in unison.

'It's small, although fully equipped with kitchen, et cetera – we call it *Small Stop*. In your lingo it would be SS, right?' said Corazon.

'You catch on fast, kiddo,' chuckled Nimal. 'Can we use SS?'

'Yes. Every ranger has a key to it, and there are extra keys, too.'

'Great. We'll take the cubs and Codey, with lots of food for them, and install them in SS. We can then check on them every few hours,' said Umedh.

'Brill, yaar,' said Chris, who liked the word 'yaar' and had begun to use it frequently.

'Corazon, do you mind bringing us a key – perhaps two?' asked Rohan. The girl nodded and ran off.

Amy and Corazon both returned in a few minutes. Corazon handed over two keys to Rohan.

'Well, Amy?' asked Anu. 'You look big with news.'

Amy smiled and waved a piece of paper. 'First I spoke with Maddison and Kyle. Then I called Louise, Corben's mom, who said that she, Corben and Brinn were in the middle of a planning meeting with Sorena, her mom, Amaris, as well as the other members of their group. And she put everyone on speakerphone. By the way, all the others – Taite, Jette, Auslen, Kaplan, Ella, Bella, Aiden, Lucy and Tavin – said hi, and are eager to meet you. Do you want me to report now, Rohan?'

'Please,' smiled Rohan.

'Jump in with questions, JEACs,' said Amy. 'Maddison said Kanasu Reserve lost a total of nineteen grizzlies last year within a period of eight and a half months. The fencing surrounding the reserve was not secure, and they discovered large holes in the north and east sides of the fence.'

'Any construction going on there?' asked Rohan.

'Not on or next to the reserve,' said Amy, 'but a large mall was being built 50 kilometres south of the reserve, between two growing communities. There are good highways from the communities and mall to Kanasu, and a one-way trip would take less than half an hour – especially at night where there's hardly any traffic on the road. The mall was completed within a year, and the construction company dispersed.'

'Any more grizzlies killed after that?' said Nimal.

'No. And the reserve raised funds and put up high walls,' said Amy.

'What about the polar bears?' asked Gina.

'Corben, Sorena and Brinn said that Sheshawi Reserve in the NWT lost fifteen polar bears within three weeks in January of this year. This was only discovered because a man and woman were caught. They were moving three dead bears, via a chopper, in a sling. The chopper had problems and came down outside the northern wall of the reserve. A couple of rangers heard it and went out to help, but were shot at. They weren't hurt, but the shots made them suspicious, so they drove out of sight of the chopper, called the cops and then kept watch.'

'What did the crooks do?' said Nimal.

'One of them tried to fix the chopper, while the other kept guard. There was tons of snow, so the sling, which was also white, was not visible to the rangers. Two police choppers arrived just as the crooks' chopper rose into the air, and for the first time the rangers saw the sling. After a brief chase, the crooks were forced to land, and the rangers joined the cops. That's when they discovered the poor bears.'

'Construction companies in the area?' asked Umedh.

'One, 75 klicks away,' said Amy, 'building a road.'

'Did the crooks belong to that company, and if so, what was their role?' said Rohan.

'The boss identified them as supplies managers. They fetched weekly supplies from a community north of Sheshawi. A sled and rifles, with boxes of cartridges, were found in the chopper – but no notebooks or cell phones. The boss said they were hired because they were competent pilots, and she didn't have anyone else on her team who could fly a chopper.'

'This gang's shrewd,' said Anu. 'Did the crooks talk when they were caught?'

'Nope. Despite being promised a shorter sentence if they talked, both accepted a jail sentence of three years.'

'They were probably promised good money if they kept their mouths shut,' said Umedh.

'How could they manage without a phone?' said Mich. 'Wouldn't they have to contact others about the bears?'

'Good point, kiddo. But they probably had contacts in the community where they went for supplies,' said Rohan, 'and received their orders weekly. We *really* need to contact Remo.'

'I'll do that,' said Umedh, and the others updated Amy on plans for the next day.

Umedh returned in a couple of minutes. 'No luck – Remo left, unexpectedly, for meetings in Toronto. He is currently on the flight, so we can't reach him until tomorrow night.'

'Thanks, yaar,' said Rohan. 'Okay, we've lots to do tomorrow, JEACs. We'll prepare everything tonight, load up the Land Rovers, and leave around 5:30 in the morning – which means some of us need to be up by 4:30 at the latest.'

'It's nearly 9 p.m.,' said Nimal, looking at his watch. 'Give us instructions and we'll get started.'

A few minutes later, everyone was bustling around, and forty-five minutes later they were all fast asleep.

CHAPTER 11

Following up on Leads

The next morning, Amy, Anu, Rohan, Umedh and Nimal were up before four. Packages of food were prepared, and breakfast was nearly ready when the other JEACs, led by the dogs, trooped into the kitchen, dressed and ready to go. It was 4:45 a.m. The cubs had already been fed and were in their cage, supervised by Codey.

'Here's a final plan,' said Rohan, as everyone sat around the table.

'Amy and I'll drive. Once we've settled the cubs and Codey, we'll split into Groups A and B, with a slight change in the groups. Group A will be Umedh, Nimal, Corazon, Chris, Amy and Sam; they'll trek back, and follow the trail Nimal found yesterday. The rest of us will check BSC-2, look for a tunnel along the wall and anything else that might give us more clues. Each group needs TGs, darts and an air gun, and everyone should carry a WT. How deep is the Muskok and can we cross it easily?'

'No problemo,' said Amy. 'At this time of the year, from the wall to approximately 250 metres south where the river takes a sharp bend, it's not more than 0.3 metres deep. 150 metres south of the wall, along the river, there's a 6.5-metre gap in the forest, and the river's about 9.1 metres across – we usually cross there.'

'What about beyond the bend?' asked Umedh.

'There's a sudden dip where it becomes 3 to 4 metres deep, narrows to about 4.2 metres across, and is flanked on either side by heavy shrubbery. It's a fairly winding river,' said Amy.

'How far is it from SS to the clearing where Nimal found the hidden trail?' asked Chris.

'Just over a klick,' said Umedh, 'and with Amy and Corazon in the lead, we should get there in about half an hour, right, ladies?'

'Oh, yes, easily,' said Corazon. 'Unless we encounter animals and have to stop.'

The JEACs finished their meal, and ten minutes later they loaded up their knapsacks and everyone piled into the vehicles with the cubs and dogs. On reaching their destination, they parked the Land Rovers, and Amy opened the door to SS.

'The cubs are ready for a nap,' said Nimal as he, Mich and Gina quickly blocked a secure area for them in the kitchen. 'We'll put them down and leave Codey in charge.'

'Good. Everyone ready?' said Rohan.

'Yes, sir,' chorused the JEACs.

'It's nearly 6:15, and we'll rendezvous at 10:30, or earlier, depending on what we discover,' said Rohan. 'On each of your maps, Anu has highlighted the section where the bridge is being constructed on the other side of the wall, although we'll probably hear the workers and equipment quite easily. That's our RP this morning. Keep the WT earpieces plugged in, and we'll touch base hourly.'

'For any confused listeners, RP is Rendezvous Point,' grinned Anu. 'Gina and Mich are wired to SS, and we'll check on the cubs every hour, and feed them before coming to the RP. Any questions?'

'Everything's covered. Bye, Codey,' said Nimal, patting him.

They trooped out, Rohan locking the door carefully behind them.

'Keep a sharp lookout and stay safe, JEACs,' said Rohan, as the group split up and went in opposite directions.

*****

Group A followed several small but distinct trails. Sam went ahead with Nimal and Corazon.

'We'll try to circumvent the waterholes,' said Amy, 'so we don't disturb any animals, but we may see badgers, swift fox, deer, black bears and caribou. And, possibly, grizzlies. We need to stay upwind of any animals.'

'We're okay; the wind's . . .' began Umedh, when Sam growled.

Nimal placed a hand on the dog's head and the group halted, their tranquillizer equipment ready for action.

'I'll scout ahead with Sam – hide in the shrubbery,' whispered Nimal. The others nodded and slid silently into thick shrubbery, peering out ahead.

'Come on, Sam,' said Nimal, softly. Boy and dog moved off the trail, keeping among the trees for a few metres. Then they stopped quickly and hid under a bush, Sam growling softly. Nimal placed a hand on Sam's head and the dog became quiet.

A few metres ahead, ambling along sleepily out of the shrubbery, came a family of grizzly bears. The mother was leading two young cubs, and she stopped several times to sniff and call to them. It took more than five minutes for the bears to cross the trail and vanish into the forest. The JEACs didn't make a sound. After a further five minutes Nimal signalled the others to join him.

'That was awesome,' said Umedh, delightedly. 'That mother was humongous – at least 1.8 metres if she stood on her hind legs.'

'The cubs were adorable – I'd say they were three or four months old,' said Amy. 'We simply *must* stop the crooks from hurting the animals.'

The others nodded.

'Thank goodness we were upwind – she'd have objected strongly if she'd scented us,' said Nimal. It's nearly seven and they're probably on their way home for a nap since they're crepuscular creatures.'

'What's crepuscular?' asked Chris

'The periods around dawn and dusk,' said Umedh.

'If we did meet more grizzlies, Nimal would charm them,' said Chris. 'Look at the way Hurit responded to him.'

'Thanks for the vote of confidence, yaar,' grinned Nimal. 'But remember, Hurit was in an enclosure, didn't have her cubs with her and was injured. That's a world of difference – I'd be stupid if I imagined I could calm down a protective mother – animal *or* human!'

The others chuckled. Umedh touched base with Group B over the WT – all was well. A little later they reached the firepit clearing, ensured there was nobody around, and entered.

Umedh quickly checked the firepit, peering through the branches covering it. 'It's been used again – there are more ashes,' he said. 'Let's not hang around in the open.'

'Good idea, yaar,' said Nimal, quickly uncovering the entrance of the hidden trail and showing the others the sled tracks. 'Given that we don't know when the crooks move around our Centre, let's put the branches back so that they don't realize the trail's been discovered.'

'Sound idea,' said Umedh. 'You lead and I'll replace the branches behind me.'

'I'll help,' said Chris, and the two of them quickly covered the entrance behind them.

'It's quite dark,' said Amy, fishing out her torch.

The others pulled out their torches as well, and began examining the ground.

'If they had two sleds, each with a grizzly weighing around 220 kilos or more, there would definitely be tracks on the ground,' said Umedh. 'Question: could these branches in the pathway be camouflage?'

'Point, yaar,' said Nimal. 'Let's get off the middle of the trail and clear the branches; Sam – sit.'

The branches were cleared and sled tracks and footprints became visible.

'Brilliant, yaar,' said Nimal, high-fiving Umedh.

'Some of the tracks and footprints are smudged, but there are several clear ones,' said Corazon excitedly as Nimal, Umedh and Chris began sketching, while Amy took pictures. 'And the prints are different.'

'Look,' said Amy, pointing, 'there are actually two sets of sled tracks, with footprints between them. And see how deep the tracks are – the bears were heavy.'

'I found six different shoe prints,' said Chris.

'Actually, there are eight,' said Corazon, who was on the ground, examining the prints carefully. 'These two look similar, but they're slightly different. What do you think?'

Everyone knelt beside Corazon and examined the footprints. 'The pair next to Nimal has a smudged print at the heel, while the one in front of Chris has a defined heel – both have the same pattern, though – excellent tracking, kiddo,' said Amy.

'So there were eight people with the sleds,' said Umedh. 'Does that make sense?'

'Yes,' nodded the others.

'Let's cover up the path and simply follow the trail,' said Nimal.

The group moved on.

'It's a good thing we're moving faster now,' said Nimal, a little later. 'Although this trail's meandering all over the place, we're going steadily east.'

Twenty minutes later they stopped. There was no more trail, and heavy shrubbery lay ahead of them.

'I assume there's more camouflaging,' said Umedh, who was in the lead with Amy and Sam. 'Amy and I'll clear the path ahead and you three replace it behind you.'

'Here we are,' said Amy, entering a clearing – the wall was fifteen metres ahead of them. The noise of construction hit them immediately. 'We're right opposite the bridge site.'

'Those crooks obviously put a lot of effort into blocking the trail,' said Chris.

'And I'm convinced that they're out for more grizzlies – why else would they camouflage trails? Let's call the others,' said Nimal.

'I'll touch base with them,' said Amy, pulling out her WT.

'The others are okay; they'll be here soon,' said Amy a minute later.

'We'll wait for them before searching for a tunnel,' said Umedh.

'Okay – this is a large area and there's lots of shrubbery along the wall,' said Nimal.

'Let's sit in the shade inside the treeline,' said Amy, perching on a rock and looking at the wall. 'You know, I can't imagine where they could have tunnelled under the wall here – it's too rocky.'

'You're right. It would take heavy equipment to dig here,' said Umedh thoughtfully, examining the wall through his binoculars. 'There'd be signs of equipment if they'd used any, and I don't see a thing.'

'Good point, yaar,' said Nimal. 'What is it, Sam?'

The dog had pricked up his ears, and was looking at the eastern end of the clearing, growling under his breath. The JEACs tensed, ready for anything.

CHAPTER 12

Is There a Hidden Entrance to MWCC?

The shrubbery shook and out raced – Hunter! Sam leapt out to meet him and they greeted each other excitedly.

Anu, who was right behind Hunter, called out over her shoulder. 'It's group A.'

Group B emerged from the shrubbery, Rohan bringing up the rear.

'Good timing, JEACs,' said Rohan, looking at his watch. 'It's not yet 10:30. The cubs and Codey are okay. Let's pool info. Group A, you first.'

After Group A had finished their report and shown the others the sketches of the footprints and tracks, Group B gave their report.

'We found BSC-2 without a problem,' said Rohan, 'but it's like this clearing – mostly rocks, with patches of sand. We didn't find tracks of sleds or footprints, but found a few animal tracks. We went right up to the *eastern* wall, which is only about twenty metres east of BSC-2, and it's rock all around there, too. And yet, if the crooks came from BSC-2 towards this clearing, there should have been *some* tracks on either side of the river.'

'It was weird,' said Anu. 'It looked as if . . . hold it!' She thought hard for a few seconds and then said, 'Eureka! All traces of footprints or sleds were swept clean. Remember the hidden trail had plenty of camouflage? Bushes planted to hide the entrance and exit; branches and twigs on the trail covering all tracks. This is a clever group of crooks.'

'Right on, sis,' said Rohan. 'They must have wiped out all tracks on the river banks, confident that none would show on the rocks. The trails we took to this RP were regular ones, narrow but stony. Group A followed camouflaged tracks leading here. We really need to find the tunnel, but I doubt one could be dug here without heavy equipment.'

'That's exactly what Umedh thinks,' said Chris.

'We should still search the area,' said Umedh.

'Agreed,' said Rohan. 'We'll put the dogs on guard.'

The JEACs searched carefully along the wall. The sound of construction workers and heavy machinery was loud.

'No luck,' groaned Corazon, as they stopped for a quick drink. 'And it's boiling hot.' She splashed water on her face.

'There's definitely no tunnel here,' said Nimal.

'Hold it,' said Umedh, squinting away from the wall against which they were leaning. 'There's a slight indent in the ground ahead. Look to the right in that sandy patch.' He walked twenty metres away from the wall, and crouched down.

The others followed. 'Do you see that depression?' said Umedh. They nodded. 'It was caused by something heavy, and it couldn't be a rock which was rolled away, because the soil would have been dampish.'

'Heavy equipment?' asked Rohan.

'Not really, yaar,' said Umedh, walking around the depression and examining it closely. 'It would be challenging to bring something that heavy through this shrubbery, and make it disappear without a trace.'

'We'll keep it in mind and take a couple of pictures,' said Rohan, making a quick note.

Umedh examined the stones around the sandy patch and said, 'Some of these stones have brown patches, and I'm going to take a few back to GW.' He placed three stones in a plastic bag, and put it in his knapsack.

'What's next?' asked Chris.

'Based on what we've learned so far,' said Rohan, 'there *has* to be a tunnel – it's the only way in which crooks can enter and exit Manipau unseen. Let's return to SS, collect the cubs and Codey, and get back to

GW. We'll contact Jason, invite him over for a meal, and ask if we can meet the night supervisors tonight. We *must* meet Kylie.'

'I'm with you,' said Anu.'

'When we return from the construction site, we'll set up camp in SS, and check *along the river*, from the wall to the bend, looking for clues. Earlier we only searched around the gap in the forest where we waded across to get to BSC-2. You see where I'm going with this?'

'Got it,' said Amy. 'If the crooks were obliterating prints around the obvious place to cross the river, they'd have to walk *in the river* while removing all signs, and come out elsewhere along the banks – among the bushes.'

'Spot on, Amy!' said Rohan. 'Who's game for a night adventure?'

'Me!' chorused the JEACs.

'Let's hurry,' said Ricky, excitedly.

They set off for SS, and returned to GW just after 1:10 p.m.

'I'm going to analyze the discolouration on the stones,' said Umedh.

'I'll join you as soon as I contact Jason, yaar,' said Rohan.

The others prepared a meal and were ready to eat when Umedh and Rohan joined them.

'What did Jason say?' asked Gina.

'He'd love to join us at 6:30 p.m. and he likes *spicy* curries; he'll also organize a meeting with his supervisor, Santos, for tonight, and Kylie'll be there too,' said Rohan. 'Tonight's shift is from 4 p.m. till 2 a.m. – there's something urgent they *have* to complete. Usually the shift's from four to midnight.'

Nimal looked at Umedh. 'What were the results of the analysis, yaar?'

'It *is* grizzly blood,' said Umedh. 'Rohan and I wondered if the men stumbled over the stones and a bear fell off the sled – hence the depression and the blood. But I'm not satisfied that the depression was caused by the body of a grizzly.'

'I can't think of anything,' said Anu, after a few minutes. 'We need to get some rest, JEACs, especially if we're going to be up all night.'

'I wouldn't mind a nap, but what about getting ready for Jason?' said Mich.

'Chris and I'll make dinner, with Anu and Corazon helping, and since an Indian meal's quick and easy, we won't start till 5:15.'

'The rest of us will organize things for tonight while you're cooking,' said Rohan, as they finished the meal and cleared up.

The JEACs dispersed, agreeing to meet in the kitchen at 5 p.m., and within ten minutes there was not a sound in the house.

CHAPTER 13

Another Good Friend

By 6:15 the meal was ready, the table laid, and the vehicles loaded up, ready for their night adventure.

'Shall we ask Jason to join us tonight?' asked Chris.

'It could cause complications for him,' said Anu. 'If Kylie has it in for him, she might be suspicious if he hangs around with us, especially since everyone knows we're investigating the matter of missing grizzlies.'

'True, Anu,' said Rohan. 'We'll see what works out because it would be useful to have him join us.'

'I hear wheels,' said Umedh, looking out of the window. 'Man – that's some sports car!'

Everyone, excluding Anu and Amy, went out to examine the vehicle.

'It's good to see you folks again. Thanks for inviting me,' said Jason as they entered the house. 'Something smells absolutely delish. It's curry, right?'

'It is, it is,' chanted Mich and Gina, dancing around him.

'And Amy made it really hot and spicy,' added Mich.

'Come and meet Amy and Anu,' said Rohan, leading the way to the kitchen. 'There's a fire extinguisher handy in case the curry sets you aflame.'

'Are you saying nasty things about our cooking, Rohan?' said Amy.

'*Never*,' protested Rohan. 'This is Jason – you should see his car!'

The girls laughed, shook hands with their guest and took to him on the spot. He had brought flowers as well as two cartons of ice cream, and Mich and Gina seated him between them.

'Everyone's been singing your praises, and we're happy to meet you, Jason,' said Anu.

'We figured that if the terrible twins liked you, you must be okay,' smiled Amy. 'Now, I know Nimal's *starving* as usual, so we'll eat first. What would you like to drink?'

'Anything going: pop, juice or water works for me,' said Jason. 'I wasn't sure if I should bring a bottle of wine, as is the custom here, but realized that although Nimal, Umedh and Rohan are so tall, you're all still in school.'

'We'll get you a beer if you like,' offered Rohan. 'I believe there's some in the fridge downstairs.'

'No, thanks, mate. I actually *prefer* juice or water.'

'Join the club,' said Amy, pouring out juice for everyone. 'Please start serving yourself from the nearest dish, and we'll pass things around.'

'Here's a glass of water,' said Chris, 'just in case my cousin got carried away and put extra chilli peppers in the curry when I wasn't looking. She did that to me once, and *I* nearly had to be carried away.'

'Thanks, Chris. I'm used to very hot food, and this curry smells divine. Are those green chillies you have beside you, Anu?'

'They are. Would you like some?'

'Please.'

'Okay! We certainly don't need the fire extinguisher for him,' chuckled Nimal.

Everyone enjoyed the meal, and Jason was eager to hear about their various adventures. The JEACs liked Jason immensely; he was twenty years old, had a fifth level black belt in karate, and had visited over fifteen countries.

'I rarely get an excellent meal like this – curries this hot, I mean,' said Jason, as they cleared the table. 'My aunt's a super cook, but she can't eat spicy food; and our chefs have to cater for the group.'

'We'll give you some doggy bags and green chillies,' said Amy, as Umedh and Rohan put out a fruit salad and the ice cream Jason had brought.

'I'd love that,' said Jason, 'but only if you're sure you don't want it for another meal.'

'We'd be happier knowing that you were enjoying the meal,' said Anu, pulling out containers. 'Take the dessert into the living room, JEACs, and Amy, Nimal and I'll join you shortly.'

'Thanks for a splendid feast, folks,' said Jason, when everyone was served with dessert. 'By the way, who did the cooking?'

'Amy, Chris, Corazon and Anu,' said Nimal. 'I offered to help, but was thrown out.'

'Nimal's idea of helping is to eat as much as possible before the food's cooked,' chuckled Amy. 'Shall we brew a pot of coffee for you, Jason?'

'What are you folks going to have?'

'Hot chocolate,' said Gina.

'I'll have that, too. I should come and live with you – you eat and drink all the things I like.'

'You're welcome to stay with us – if your uncle and aunt don't mind,' said Umedh. 'You could go to work from here.'

Rohan glanced around at the eager group of JEACs and said, 'I know we'd all love to have you if you wouldn't find it boring. We've tons of room in the basement, where we boys sleep.'

'I'd like that, thanks,' beamed Jason. 'My folks will be glad I've made friends with you and won't mind at all. And if you like Korean food, I can make a few dishes.'

'Deal! So we won't give you doggy bags after all,' said Anu.

'And may I join in the adventure whenever possible?' asked Jason.

'We're hoping you will, yaar, starting tonight,' said Rohan. 'You'll be an honorary JEAC.'

'Hurray!' cheered everyone.

'Muchas gracias! A distinct honour,' laughed Jason. 'And will I see the cubs tonight? Are they friendly?'

'Almost too friendly,' grinned Nimal. 'They're fast asleep at the moment, but should wake up soon.'

The JEACs told Jason about the cubs, and he was keen to hear them humming and playing with a ball.

'Shall we update Jason on what we've discovered so far, JEACs?' asked Rohan.

'Sure,' said the others, and Jason nodded eagerly.

Rohan got the bag of clues and took out his notebook. Jason listened intently to their report, nodding his head now and then, and was eager to see the clues.

He was shown everything. When the pieces of cloth were placed before him, Jason picked one up, examined it carefully, and whistled. Everyone looked at him expectantly.

'These look like they're all from the same shirt, right?' said Jason. They nodded, and he continued. 'While I could be quite mistaken, I can't help thinking that these could easily be from one of Kylie's shirts.'

'Really?' gasped Corazon. 'How come?'

'She loves black and gold – I've seldom seen her in any other colours. She has several styles of shirts, but all of them have dragon prints.'

'I've never seen this print before,' said Amy.

'I have,' said Jason. 'I take my mom shopping now and then; there are several Chinese and Korean clothes shops she likes to visit and she says this print is currently in fashion – it's extremely expensive. The print's available in several colours, but I've never seen black before, and Kylie always wears black.'

'Amy and Anu, when we meet Kylie, try to get a feel of the texture of the fabric,' said Rohan.

'Will do,' said Amy. 'We'll ask her which store she purchased it from. Jason, how tall is Kylie?'

'About your height. Why?'

'I measured myself against the place where we found the first piece of cloth,' said Amy, 'and if the person was as tall as I am, it could have been ripped off the bottom of the shirt.'

'Excellent point,' said Nimal.

They told Jason about their plans for the night and he was thrilled to be included.

'We're focusing on the river,' said Umedh, 'and it would be useful to check the outside wall from the construction site towards where the Muskok branches off the Akie and goes under the wall. We might be able to locate the other side of a tunnel.'

'Good point, yaar,' said Rohan. 'Jason, is there lots of shrubbery along the outside wall?'

'Yes, going east; however, going west from the bridge they had to clear most of it, leaving about three metres of shrubbery along the wall.'

'What are the possibilities of us checking the outside wall with you tonight? Obviously we'd be undercover,' said Umedh.

'It could be tricky with Kylie. However, if we drive off and hide our vehicles under a grove of trees, we could trek back to the site through the shrubbery where there's a large tree just outside the fence. Some branches hang inside the site and we can get in and out via the tree – it's a dark corner and we won't be seen.'

'Excellent. What time's our meeting with Santos et al?' said Rohan.

'From 10 to 10:30.'

'Brill, yaar,' said Rohan. 'I'm glad you'll be with us.'

'Who's going to search the outside wall?' asked Amy. 'We should limit it to Jason and three others.'

'Agreed,' said Rohan. 'There are two crucial areas tonight, and we need more people on the inside. I suggest that Jason, Chris, Nimal and I check the outside wall, and the rest of you and the dogs look after the river and the inside wall.'

'Good plan,' said Anu. 'We'll synchronize our watches and plan to touch base at 1 a.m. via the WTs. RP will be on either side of the Muskok where it flows under the wall. Sorry, Jason, WTs are walkie-talkies, and RP is the Rendezvous Point.' Jason nodded.

'Good idea, Anu,' said Umedh. 'I'll get another WT for Jason; we'll each carry a unit in our knapsacks and wear the earpieces so that they don't beep out loud.'

'Great. It's exactly 8:45 p.m. by my watch.' said Rohan.

They had just adjusted their watches when Codey, who was with the cubs, barked. Hunter and Sam ran off to investigate.

'The cubs must be up,' said Nimal. 'Gina, Mich, please get the milk. Ricky, we'll get the cubs.'

A few minutes later an enthralled Jason was cuddling Ataneq, who investigated one of his pockets.

'They're used to us now, and love the dogs, too,' said Chris. 'Our main babysitter is Codey.'

'I wish I could see Nimal with Hurit,' said Jason, accepting a bottle of milk and feeding the hungry cub.

'You will once we've resolved this problem,' promised Amy.

Anu hummed as she fed Atka, and soon, to everyone's delight, both cubs started humming.

Once they were finished with their milk, the cubs wanted to play, and the JEACs had a fun time playing with them and the dogs.

'That was awesome,' said Jason, as they returned to the living room, once the cubs had been put back in their playpen with a couple of balls and teddy bears.

'Jason, is Kylie friendly with anyone in the team?' said Rohan.

'Funny you should ask, Rohan,' said Jason, 'because I was going to tell you about three workers who joined us recently – hired by Kylie since they worked together on a construction site in BC last year.'

The JEACs gasped, but Rohan asked Jason to continue.

'During breaks the four of them sit out of earshot of the rest of us, and appear to be in deep discussion. Rizvi says he's been in Canada for three years; Sheila's from BC; and Hing says he's been in Canada for ten years.'

'How did you discover this?' asked Umedh.

'Through Santos, who's my immediate supervisor and a good friend. He said he wouldn't have hired the three of them, but Kylie said she'd worked with them before and that they were good. None of them live on site, and Tina said they travel back and forth with Kylie and are the last people off the site. They keep to themselves.'

'Very interesting, indeed,' said Anu. 'We must try to chat with them tonight.'

'What's Santos like?' asked Nimal.

'Super nice guy! He's our overall supervisor – we generally work in two or three groups at night. Kylie oversees one group but reports to Santos. Of course, she has input as to what she and her group will handle for the night.'

Rohan's alarm beeped. 'Time to get moving, JEACs.'

'Tranquillizer equipment's already in the Land Rovers,' said Umedh. 'What about transportation? Do we leave your car here, Jason, since you're coming back?'

'Actually, perhaps you should drive your car, Jason,' said Rohan. 'We need people to assume you're going back to your place, and keep your connection with us on the QT for now.'

'And "on the QT" means?' grinned Ricky.

'Quiet,' chuckled Anu, and the others laughed.

'Excellent notion, buddy,' said Jason.

'Then you others can return in the Land Rovers, while we guys take Jason's car when we've finished our search, right?' said Chris.

'A bright blue, shiny Corvette's too distinctive to be driven on the highway late at night. If spotted, it would be recognized instantly, whereas a Land Rover wouldn't,' said Rohan. 'I suggest we keep one Land Rover and the other two vehicles are brought back.'

'I never thought of that,' said Jason, 'and it's a good point since we want to be inconspicuous – what an excellent detective you are, mate.'

'Good thinking, yaar,' agreed Chris.

Rohan smiled and continued, 'On the return trip, Amy can drive the Land Rover,' she nodded, 'and Umedh can handle a standard – if that's okay with you, Jason.'

'Absolutely!' said Jason immediately. 'As I discovered earlier this evening, Umedh knows more about cars than I do – and that's saying something. Are we ready to roll?'

They rolled!

CHAPTER 14

Cranes, Crooks and Captures

They stopped at the gate house, briefly, for Jason to grab a bag of necessities, change, and tell his family he would be staying at GW. Reaching the site at 9:35 p.m., they assisted Olivia, Jason's colleague, to prepare for the break.

Olivia left them for a few minutes, and Jason said, 'Santos is looking forward to speaking with you, Rohan. He's the guy beside the cement mixer. Kylie's the one in the black shirt. The three workers assembling machinery a few metres away from Santos are Rizvi, Sheila and Hing.'

'Listen up, JEACs,' said Rohan quickly. 'Amy and Nimal, focus on Kylie; Umedh and Jason, talk to Rizvi, Sheila and Hing. Chris and I'll speak with Santos. Anu and Ricky together; Corazon, Mich and Gina together – talk to the others. Any questions?'

They shook their heads. Five minutes later the break began, and the JEACs moved into action.

'Hey – fans!' grinned the first man in the queue. He and three colleagues served themselves and joined Anu and Ricky, who were seated at a picnic table.

'I'm Anu, one of the JEACs – and it's nice to meet you.'

'And I'm Ricky.'

'I'm Joe, this old man is Ralf, and the "kids" are Kelly and Alix,' said Joe, grinning around.

'Not PC at all, Joe,' said Kelly as everyone shook hands. 'Take two demerit points! Ignore him, folks; he's a nincompoop.'

'Kelly, he reminds me of my cousin, Nimal, said Anu. 'He's the chap approaching the cement mixer and striving, unsuccessfully, to look intelligent and serious.'

'I'm super intelligent and serious, too, and will definitely meet him,' said Joe. 'You JEACs are notorious – my daughter, Brooklyn, is eleven, crazy about animals and longing to meet you. She was very jealous of me this morning and asked if you would be holding meetings for interested kids.'

'Absolutely,' said Anu, giving him a notebook and pen. 'Write down her name and your email address; we'll be in touch.'

'My son, Vincent, is seven,' said Ralf. 'Is he too young to participate?'

'Kailah and Ashlee, my younger cousins, are seven and five, and adore all animals,' said Alix.

'So do my daughters, Abbey and Ally,' said Kelly.

'Put down their details,' said Ricky. 'Age is immaterial.'

'Ask us any questions. We're eager to assist you,' said Joe.

It was an informative discussion and the group parted reluctantly when the break was over.

'Do visit us again,' said Joe. 'We'd love to meet everyone.'

'Will do, sir,' said Ricky, 'and thanks very much.'

'Yes, thanks a ton – we've learned a lot,' smiled Anu.

'You're welcome. See you soon, JEACs,' said the group.

The other JEACs joined Rohan and Chris, who were walking towards the car park with Santos. The supervisor, delighted to meet everyone, told them they could visit any time, shook hands and returned to work.

'Let's move, folks,' said Amy. 'Jason, wave to us and drive off first – I'll explain later. There's a curve in the highway, a kilometre away, with a small clearing – we'll meet there.'

They did as she suggested, and a few minutes later the three vehicles parked under some trees. They were invisible from the highway, and the JEACs met briefly.

'Why didn't you want anyone to go with Jason, Amy?' asked Chris.

'Kylie was watching,' said Amy. 'She gives me the creeps.' She shuddered and looked at Nimal. 'What did you think?'

'That's one greedy megalomaniac,' said Nimal. 'But we'll talk later – we've a busy night.'

'When do we pool our information?' asked Gina eagerly.

'How about over breakfast, once we've had some sleep and are wide awake?' said Rohan.

'Okay,' agreed the others.

The group split up and the Corvette and one Land Rover drove off, while the four boys cautiously made their way back to the construction site.

*****

'Jolly good timing,' said Rohan as they reached the tree. 'Lead the way, Jason.'

A few minutes later the four boys were in the construction area. 'Our signals are one beep for safety, two for danger; if there's danger, take cover instantly,' said Rohan. 'Nimal, you're our best tracker; check ten metres ahead at a time – we'll await your signals before examining the wall.'

Nimal crept away, and his all clear came a few minutes later. Moving stealthily, they checked the wall but found no signs of a tunnel. It was tedious work, and when they had covered about 200 metres Nimal beeped twice and the others stopped ten metres behind him.

He joined them and said softly, 'There's a gap, about fifteen metres across, with only grass and a few low bushes along the wall. If someone's looking towards the wall and we walk across, they'll see us.'

'Okay, we'll take a break and think it through,' said Rohan.

They could see the bridge where work was progressing steadily. The boys drank some water and sat down for five minutes, watching the construction.

'That's a pretty large crane,' said Rohan, watching the machine move steel posts.

'Yes. We lost our only operator after the first bridge. He was seriously ill with food poisoning, and is off for a month. It's fortunate Hing's a crane operator,' said Jason.

'*That's* interesting,' said Rohan. 'When was the crane brought here?'

'Just over three weeks ago, when we'd finished using it at the first bridge.'

'How close to the wall does it need to be in order to reach over and either drop off or pick up something inside Manipau?' said Rohan.

The boys gasped.

'Gee whizz!' said Jason. He thought hard and said, 'This particular crane needs to be placed six metres away from the wall to reach over it and pick up something from the ground on the other side.'

'So, with one of Kylie's buddies being the *only* operator, there's another way in which dead grizzlies could be removed from Manipau.'

'Brill, yaar,' said Nimal. 'I concur.'

'Does it make sense to assume that the crane isn't always used at the river?' said Rohan.

'Absolutely. We use it mainly to set up the structure, which involves moving large, heavy materials.'

'Okay,' said Rohan thoughtfully, 'so would the crane be parked by the river when not in use?'

'Cranes take up a lot of space,' said Jason, 'and since there's other heavy equipment we need near the bridge, the crane's moved against the wall in the gap ahead.'

'Who decides where to park it? And for how long will it be on this side of the river?' said Rohan.

'Kylie, and . . .' Jason stopped with a gasp. 'Man, you're sharp! I see what you're getting at. The crane's probably going to be used for the next three weeks. Once half the bridge is completed, it'll be taken to the other side of the river.'

'Thanks, yaar,' said Rohan, 'that's valuable information. Now let's figure out how we get through the gap,' said Rohan.

'I'll crawl across on my tummy and check the wall,' said Nimal, 'while you keep a sharp eye on the workers – if they turn in my direction, beep twice and I'll freeze.'

'Will do,' said Rohan, and the boys put their binoculars to their eyes.

Nimal returned in ten minutes. 'No tunnel,' he said.

'Good work, yaar,' said Rohan. 'Chris and Jason, have you ever wriggled through grass and shrubbery on your tummy?'

'Never,' grinned the boys, 'but we're game.'

'Nimal, go first, beep when you're there and then keep an eye on the workers, and I'll do the same from here. Jason next, then Chris – watch Nimal – and use your binocs or you won't see him at all. I'll come last. Onward, JEACs.'

'That was fun,' said Chris, when they were safely across the gap.

'Sure was,' chuckled Jason, 'and I'm going to purchase camouflage clothing next time I'm in town – you boys merge so completely with the surroundings.'

'You chaps did well,' said Nimal.

By 12:30, they were in a small clearing, away from the wall, and took a short break. It had been a tough trek as the shrubbery was extremely dense.

'We're fifteen metres away from the Muskok,' said Rohan softly. 'That was some going, and it's even denser around the wall where the river . . . gosh! I realize where the tunnel could be!'

'Where?' breathed Chris.

'Gee – I need my brain examined!' whispered Jason. 'I remember Santos telling me about the wall and the culverts where the river flows into and out of Manipau – he was one of the construction supervisors.'

'Elucidate, yaar,' said Rohan.

'It was decided to build 3.05 metre-long culverts so that the river wouldn't become polluted; this would also reinforce the wall over the river. To facilitate regular maintenance of the culverts, they made cement platforms, 1.37 metres wide, on either side of the river, along the length of the culvert. The culvert is over 1.4 metres high. Perfect and safe access to Manipau! There's a grate at the Manipau end so animals can't escape through it. They also planted shrubbery around the culvert entrances and exits, so they weren't easily visible.'

'A perfect hideout for crooks,' murmured Nimal.

'Absolutely,' said Jason. 'Do you think they're camping there?'

'If they're not inside, killing more grizzlies, they could be there now,' said Nimal. 'What next, Rohan?'

'Nimal, get as close as possible and look for easy access; secondly, listen for any sounds or voices. I'll update and warn the others; they'll be approaching the RP shortly – it's 12:45 a.m.'

'Okay, although the others won't see the culvert until they're really close,' said Nimal.

'True,' said Rohan. 'Get back ASAP so we can update them on your findings.'

Nimal disappeared, and Rohan pulled out his WT, while the others listened on their headphones.

'Group A. Urgent. Come in. Over.'

'What's up, yaar?' said Umedh's voice immediately. 'Are you okay? Over.'

'Fine. Where are you? Over.' said Rohan.

'At SS checking on the cubs; starting for wall soon, over.'

Rohan updated them; as he finished, Nimal returned, looking excited. Rohan raised an eyebrow and Nimal winked back.

'Hang on,' said Rohan, 'Nimal's back with a report, over.'

'There's a hacked-out entrance through the bushes on this side. It's camouflaged; the stream's very shallow, so I stood in it and peered through the branches of a bush,' said Nimal.

'A lantern lit up the entire area, including the grate at the other end. It's a dry place, and there are three people in sleeping bags on this side. Loud snores woke up two of them, and a female voice asked someone, grumpily, to turn Nomaan over so that he'd stop disturbing them. A huge chap – would take two of us to hold him down – got up and pushed at the third sleeping bag. The man inside rolled over and stopped snoring, and the big guy returned to his sleeping bag, zipped himself in, and there was silence once more. There were guns beside each sleeping bag. Over.'

'Any phones? Over,' asked Umedh.

'Negative as far as I could tell. Over,' said Nimal.

'Good. We'll give them ten minutes to go into a deep sleep and then sneak in,' said Rohan. 'We're all good at karate, but the crooks will reach for their guns, so make sure to kick those away. Which of you are carrying TGs? Over.'

'Umedh, Amy, Corazon and I,' said Anu. 'Over.'

'Ricky, can you drive a Land Rover for a short distance? Over.'

'Yes, over.'

'Good,' said Rohan. 'Umedh, give the keys to Ricky. Ricky, Corazon, Mich, Gina, hide in thick shrubbery far from the culvert. You're our lookout: warn us by beeping twice if you see anything suspicious, like other crooks approaching the tunnel from inside Manipau. If we get into trouble, get back to GW ASAP and get help. Corazon, you know the best routes. Umedh, Amy and Anu, we need you and Hunter to assist us, over.'

'On our way. Keep talking and we'll signal when we're in place, over,' said Anu.

'Umedh, open the grate the second you hear one beep, and all of you join us fast. Try to get the crooks face down on their sleeping bags and gag them ASAP. Questions? Over.'

'None. Good luck,' said everyone.

'Keep tuned in, over,' said Rohan. 'Nimal, confirm the crooks are still asleep and signal us.'

Ten minutes later, everyone was in position. Nimal led his group into the culvert, and they spread out so that they could approach their targets fast. The opening grate did not make a sound – it was well maintained.

'Now!' signalled Rohan.

'What the . . .' grunted the big man, as Rohan and Umedh dropped on him. He reached for his gun.

'Oh, no, you don't,' growled Chris, stamping on the man's hand and kicking the gun out of his reach. The man groaned in pain and anger.

Jason and Amy tackled the woman; Nimal and Anu, along with Hunter, soon had the snorer begging that Hunter wouldn't bite him again. Stuck in their sleeping bags, half asleep and unable to reach their guns, the crooks still fought viciously. It took the combined efforts of the seven JEACs to subdue and gag them.

'Check them, their sleeping bags and knapsacks for phones,' said Rohan. 'We'll walk them to SS. Anu and Amy, ask the others to do the needful and, Anu, tell Gina . . .' he completed his sentence in Hindi.

'Right,' affirmed Anu.

'Lookout team, do you hear me? Over,' said Amy.

'We're tuned in, over,' said Corazon.

'Excellent. Take one vehicle and everything else, get to GW and call Shawn. Tell him to contact the police and get to SS ASAP. We have three bouquets of flowers. Over.'

'Will do, Amy. We assume you mean we should take the cubs and dogs, right? Over,' said Ricky.

'Correct,' said Anu. 'Gina, tell Shawn . . .' she spoke to her sister in Hindi. 'Over.'

'Right,' said Gina. 'Message received and understood. Lookout team over and out.'

The crooks were chivvied to their feet, and fifteen minutes later the group, with Hunter growling ominously if the crooks tried to stop, locked three angry, tied and gagged crooks in SS.

'What now?' asked Jason, as the JEACs moved out of hearing range.

'Hunter and Umedh will stay on guard here – Umedh, you've got a TG and darts, right?' said Rohan. Umedh nodded. 'The rest of us will return to the tunnel and clear up.'

'Are we taking everything out, Rohan?' asked Anu.

'No. We'll arrange the tunnel exactly as it was except for the crooks. Then Nimal and I will get back to the Land Rover and go to GW, while the rest of you return here. Once the crooks are collected, you folks come back to GW, too.'

'Super! Quick question, Rohan,' said Jason. 'Why did you make the crooks walk in the muddy section of the river with only Hunter growling behind them and giving them little nips so that they were forced to move – oh, never mind, I've got it!' He grinned and said, 'Footprints, right?'

Rohan nodded.

'What did you folks say in Hindi?' asked Chris.

'I asked if the police could use unmarked cars to collect the crooks so that nobody, neither the construction workers nor the crooks, would know that three people were caught.'

'We also suggested that Shawn request the police to keep the crooks separated, so they couldn't talk to each other,' added Anu.

'Are we going to try to get information from them?' asked Jason.

'Based on what we've heard, if it's the same gang as those caught in Sheshawi in the NWT, they won't say a word but will go to jail willingly,' said Umedh. 'They're a tough bunch and none of those caught, so far, had communication devices. They're probably extremely organized, follow tight schedules and are willing to risk being caught.'

'Now the other crooks will wonder what happened to their mates,' said Amy, 'and the obvious conclusions are that they've been killed by a grizzly, have given up and gone away, or that they've been caught.'

'That'll keep them guessing,' said Rohan. 'To work, JEACs.'

'Aye, aye, sir,' said everyone.

CHAPTER 15

Possible Assumptions Based on Pooled Information

The crooks were collected, the tunnel was in good order, and an exhausted but exultant group of JEACs returned to GW around 3:20 a.m. and fell into bed. The lookout team were fast asleep. Rohan stayed up making notes till 3:45 a.m., and then crashed.

'Thanks, you four,' said Amy the next morning, when she and Anu walked into the kitchen at 8:15 a.m. and found a hot breakfast nearly ready, while Gina and Mich fed the cubs. 'Where are you off to, Ricky?'

'To check on the guys,' said Ricky, haring out of the room.

'We knew you'd be bushed,' said Corazon, taking sausages off the grill and piling them into a large dish. 'How do you feel?'

'Bright-eyed and bushy-tailed,' grinned Anu, laying out plates. 'What about you lot?'

'We got lots of sleep,' said Gina, 'and we've already fed the dogs.'

'It was hard to stay awake after we'd called Shawn,' said Mich, 'so since you had a key, we went to bed.'

'We figured you'd be pretty late and agreed we'd go to sleep but wake up early to make breakfast,' added Corazon.

'The guys will be here in ten,' said Ricky.

Over breakfast, the lookout team were first updated on how the crooks were captured.

'Shawn was very impressed with all your suggestions,' said Ricky.

'The crooks had no idea of the plan,' said Jason. 'They were shocked when the police turned up in plain clothes and took them away in unmarked cars.'

'Sorry to rush you, JEACs, but we've got tons to do this morning,' said Rohan. The others looked up eagerly. 'Let's start with reports on our chats with the night shift group. Corazon, Mich and Gina, you begin.'

'We spoke to six very friendly people,' began Gina. 'We asked them whether they thought anyone from the construction company was involved with the killings. One of the group was Keith's cousin who was mad that he'd been badly injured, and suspicious because Kylie replaced Keith so quickly. They made cutting remarks about Kylie. Mich?'

'Others believe the three Kylie brought in are bad. One man, also Korean, said he'd overheard Kylie on the telephone, telling someone that her plan was going well; then Kylie saw him, started speaking about the bridge, and hung up seconds later. Corazon?'

'The other three, two men and a woman, share an apartment in Powela,' said Corazon, 'and mentioned that they've seen Kylie smoking something which they believe is weed. One guy was in a pub recently, and saw Kylie with Rizvi, Sheila and Hing chatting intently; they didn't see him.'

'Good job, girls,' said Anu. 'Shall Ricky and I go next, Rohan? Our info is similar.' Rohan nodded. 'Ricky, you start.'

'Joe and Ralf can't stand Kylie,' said Ricky. 'She's a lousy supervisor, frequently makes excuses to leave the site, and they believe she's taking drugs. Anu?'

'Kelly and Alix also suspect Kylie of taking drugs, though they haven't caught her in the act. Alix said that just over a week ago, before their night shift, she came out of the washroom to find Kylie waiting to go in. She had removed her jacket and Alix, who likes clothes, noticed that Kylie was wearing a black and gold print shirt. Kylie brushed past Alix rudely and as Alix turned to glare at her she noticed that the back of Kylie's shirt was in tatters. When Kylie came out she was wearing another black and gold print shirt, but *the style was different.*'

'Umedh and Jason?' said Rohan, making rapid notes.

'Jason introduced me to Rizvi, Sheila and Hing, saying that I was interested in mechanical things, and was eager to meet them since they operated such large equipment,' said Umedh. 'He also mentioned that I was one of the JEACs who were trying to solve the problem of the missing grizzlies. We were watching them closely and noticed Rizvi change colour and start perspiring profusely. However, they played nice and told me to ask away. So we asked them about their equipment.'

'Umedh's questions were highly technical,' grinned Jason, 'and they were shocked at the extent of his knowledge. Then Umedh asked where they'd worked previously, and that's when we heard the first lie – they didn't know that Santos had given me details of their background. Rizvi said he'd arrived in Canada a few months ago.'

'Sheila said she was from Ontario, and Hing said he was from Halifax,' said Umedh. 'All three said they'd only met each other when they joined *this* construction team. Since there wasn't any valid reason for their lies, we think they didn't want to admit their connection with one another.'

'We concluded by asking if they could guess what was happening with the missing grizzlies,' said Jason, 'but they just looked puzzled and angry and said that the sooner the crooks were caught, the better. We thanked them and moved away. When we turned to wave we saw two of them wiping sweat off their brows.'

'Chris, you next,' said Rohan.

'Santos was upset about the grizzlies. Rohan asked him about Rizvi, Sheila and Hing, and Santos said they were okay at their work, but he'd only hired them since Kylie sang their praises. Since she's a supervisor, he figured she might be right. Also, they needed Hing who operates large cranes. Rohan?'

'I asked Santos whether he felt Kylie was competent,' said Rohan. 'He was reluctant to say too much, but I assured him we wouldn't quote him and were merely trying to get a picture of the team, especially Kylie and crew, since they were the newest members. We also said that we'd spoken with his colleagues on the day shift, and that nobody appeared to like Kylie. He then relaxed and opened up, though he was still very professional.'

'He's a good guy,' said Jason.

'What did he say about Kylie?' asked Amy.

'He doesn't like her,' said Chris, 'and basically said that he thinks she's smoking weed, that she's not a very good supervisor, et cetera.'

'He can't jeopardize the timeline for completion of this bridge, but once it's done, he'll fire all four of them,' said Rohan. 'An interesting point was that Kylie's the last person off the site, responsible for locking up after all the others have left – *and her three mates leave with her*. Now, Amy and Nimal, tell us about Kylie.'

Amy looked at Nimal and he began, 'She's an utterly self-absorbed, self-centred megalomaniac. I'm pretty easy-going, as you know, but a minute in her company and I wanted to run away. When we approached, she was busy titivating in the side mirror of the cement mixer while talking on the phone. We overheard her say, "Oh, yes, naturally they'll obey me. I'll be chief one day. I've got to go now, darling; only three more weeks. Talk soon". She rang off and was admiring herself in the mirror, when Amy coughed. Amy?'

'She spun around, saw me and glared,' continued Amy. 'Then she spotted Nimal and became what I can only assume *she* thought was charm and sweetness. She giggled and held out her hand to Nimal as if she expected him to kiss it – Nimal shook it briefly. Then I shook hands, too. I prattled in an inane manner, admiring her and drawing Nimal's attention to her clothes. She fell into the trap and simpered in the most idiotic manner – I couldn't believe anyone would fall for that kind of stupidity.'

'Amy and I drew her out to the extent that she let Amy feel her shirt, and stand next to her, while we listened to the most boring details about the wonder that is Kylie,' said Nimal. 'One thing was confirmed – she's the only one *in a 300-kilometre radius* who wears that particular print. She loves black and gold, and apparently she has about 50 shirts in varying styles, all in that print. Also, she's only a quarter of an inch shorter than Amy.'

'The fabric feels and looks identical to the scraps we found,' said Amy. 'Then Nimal asked her if she had any idea as to who was killing the grizzlies – we struck gold! She froze, her eyes narrowed and she smiled coldly, looking like a cobra. She insinuated that the rangers were probably morons who couldn't do their job properly. Oooh! She makes me mad!'

'I felt Amy boiling and stepped on her foot,' said Nimal. 'Changing topics, I asked if she'd travelled a lot, and she unbent a bit saying she'd travelled all over Europe; but when I asked about travel in

Canada she just said, abruptly, that she'd lived in every province. Then she said she had work to do, and beetled off.'

'At least we know that she was wandering around Manipau,' said Anu.

'Shall we have some coffee or hot chocolate before reporting on our discoveries last evening, prior to the excitement of catching crooks?' asked Amy.

'Good idea, Amy,' said Umedh. 'I'll help you and we'll take it to the living room.'

'Now, tell us about your discoveries last evening,' said Nimal, when everyone had a mug of something hot.

'Anu, you start,' suggested Amy.

'We got back to GW, picked up the cubs and dogs and settled them in SS,' said Anu. 'We split up and searched south of the gap along both banks of the river, for footprints and sled tracks. About five metres before the bend in the river where it becomes deeper, Umedh, who was searching on the eastern side of the Muskok, called us.'

'I found both sled tracks and footprints emerging from the river,' said Umedh. 'We traced these prints away from the river, and although they disappeared after two metres because the ground became stony, we put Hunter on to them. He led us directly along a trail we figured would take us to BSC-2. Amy.'

'We returned to the river, and Umedh found a large print of something under a bush. It was three metres long, two metres wide, and had a pattern of lines,' said Amy.

'We decided to search in the vicinity of the bush,' said Corazon. 'Gina and Mich, who had been crawling around under the bushes, scrambled out, each with a handful of grizzly hair.'

'It was caught on the branches,' said Gina excitedly. 'Mich and I were shining our torches into the bushes when we noticed many clumps of hair.'

'We couldn't figure out why grizzlies would have crawled under the shrubbery,' said Mich, 'but Umedh asked us to bring out all the hair we could find.'

'Umedh placed it on a cloth, and examined it,' said Ricky. 'He found one clump of hair which was stuck together and kind of icky. He thought it was blood and that it should be analyzed for confirmation.'

'We obliterated our footprints near the river,' said Anu. 'Then Umedh's watch beeped and we realized we needed to check on the animals and then chat with you.'

'You need to see that large print, Rohan,' said Umedh.

'Sure. We'll . . .' began Rohan, when the telephone rang and he answered. 'It's Shawn, Tulok and Hassan,' he said, and put it on speakerphone. 'Okay, go ahead. Anything new?'

'No, we're just checking you're okay,' said Shawn.

'We're fine,' the JEACs assured him.

'Any report from the police?' asked Rohan.

'I spoke with Inspector Geraldine a few minutes ago. Not a word out of the big guy or the woman,' said Hassan. 'They're tough. However, the third man spoke in his sleep, but didn't make sense. He mumbled a lot, and one time he said, "That stupid raft cut my leg".'

'Look, JEACs, we have to run to a meeting,' said Shawn, 'but I'll be in the vicinity of GW at eleven and can drop in for five minutes. Do you need anything?'

'Yes,' said Rohan, to everyone's surprise. 'Could you take Codey and the cubs back with you, Shawn – perhaps leave them with Rani or Lisa for the next couple of days?'

'Sure, mate – anything wrong?' said Shawn.

'Nope, but we're going to be all over the place the next couple of days and don't want to endanger the cubs or leave them alone too often,' said Rohan.

'Sure. What are you folks up to?' said Tulok.

'We want to split up in smaller groups,' said Rohan, 'and keep an eye on the north culvert and other areas. We'll be careful, I promise.'

'We trust you, JEACs,' said Hassan. 'Do you need any more guns for protection?'

'No, thanks,' said Nimal. 'We'll use the TGs, air guns and our martial arts to defend ourselves; if necessary, we'll turn their guns on them. We also have Hunter and Sam.'

'I wish we could help you,' said Shawn, 'but you know our situ.'

'No worries, mate,' said Umedh.

'And please don't tell Mom too much as she'll only worry,' said Amy.

'Everybody's really busy,' said Shawn reassuringly, 'so we won't have to give details. I'll be over at eleven; have to run, JEACs.'

The men rang off, and the JEACs looked at Rohan, wondering what he had in mind, but Rohan was squinting into space, as was Umedh.

'Raft?' muttered both boys and looked at each other.

'The large print you found under the shrubbery beside the river,' murmured Rohan, raising an eyebrow.

Umedh, his eyes gleaming, nodded, and said, 'The large print under the bush was made by a raft. Presumably, grizzlies are killed, brought to that location and the bodies are hidden under bushes until other members of the gang arrive, via boat, to collect the animals. The bodies are placed on the raft, towed down river, through the lake, and taken outside through a culvert similar to the one we found. It would be easy to load the bears into vehicles which transport them to their destination.'

'Brill, yaar,' said Nimal. 'It's a perfectly logical plan.'

'Makes sense! What now?' asked Anu.

'Tell us how you anticipate events unfolding, Rohan,' said Jason, and everyone looked at Rohan eagerly.

'Based on all we've heard and discovered, we need to do a number of things,' said Rohan slowly. 'Jump in with questions, since they'll clarify our thinking. I believe the crooks have only three weeks left in which to kill as many grizzlies as possible, so let's discuss entrances and exits.' He looked at Umedh and said, 'Last night Jason said that when the crane's not in use, it's parked beside the wall, opposite the clearing we checked yesterday. What do you think, yaar?'

Umedh thought hard for a few seconds and then said, 'After the night shift, someone operates the crane and can drop people into Manipau, as well as take things or people out. The depression we saw in the ground is where the crane basket rested inside Manipau; while the blood patches on the stones near the depression could mean that the bodies of grizzlies were loaded into the basket and taken over the wall.'

'Agreed,' said Rohan. 'And as Kylie and her gang are the last to leave, it makes perfect sense. They have two methods for removing grizzlies from Manipau.'

'Why do you think they have only three weeks left?' asked Ricky.

'We overheard Kylie say she had to put up with something for another three weeks,' gasped Amy.

'Correct,' said Rohan. 'I realize that while most of it is pure conjecture, we have a number of clues pointing to Kylie and her gang being the crooks. I also believe that they're part of a larger group of crooks – possibly an international gang.'

'And they'll kill as many grizzlies as possible in the next three weeks?' said Amy.

'Yes, so we need to catch them ASAP,' said Umedh. 'Tell us your plans, Rohan.'

'Right: we need to watch the north-east culvert. We should check the south-east culvert, come up river to the curve where the raft prints are, and time the trip. Check outside the south culvert for tracks of any kind, and keep an eye around the firepit, the crane basket imprint clearing, and BSC-1. These crooks will try to kill bears at any time of the day or night. Since they're probably aware of Manipau's shortage of staff, they'll likely go all out this week in particular. We *must* prevent them from killing any more grizzlies. Have I missed anything?'

'You've covered everything, mate,' said Jason. 'There are eleven of us and two dogs; how do you suggest we divvy up?'

'I can drive through Manipau and check the location outside the south culvert,' said Umedh. 'On my return I can scout around BSC-1. If I leave here at noon, what's the fastest route?'

'Out through the north gates, east past the CC and south on Highway 22Z,' said Jason. 'Ten minutes on that road and you'll meet the highway to Manipau. The highway's faster than driving through Manipau.'

'But I'm not permitted to drive on my own outside Manipau,' groaned Umedh.

'Give me a few minutes to make a couple of calls,' said Jason. 'May I use the phone in the office next door?'

'Sure,' said Rohan.

Jason went off, returning with a wide grin on his face.

'What's up, yaar?' said Umedh.

'*I'll* drive you, Umedh,' said Jason, 'and we'll take my car. I called my friend, Olivia, whom you met last night, and asked if she'd cover me for a week – she agreed. Then I checked with Santos, explained the situ to him, and *he* agreed. So I took a week's vacation.'

'You're using your *vacation* to help catch the crooks?' said Chris.

'Can you think of a better reason?' smiled Jason. 'Come on, JEACs. I love animals as much as you do, and I'm dying to be part of this adventure – pretty please?'

'Well, since you said "pretty please" you're in, Jason,' smiled Anu.

'And we and the bears *love you* for it,' shouted Gina and Mich, hugging him exuberantly, while the others expressed their delight, too.

'That makes a world of difference to our plans, yaar,' said Rohan slapping him on the back. 'This is a tricky, vicious group of crooks, and we're thrilled to have you. Okay, so Jason and Umedh will check the south culvert outside Manipau, and then get back and keep watch around BSC-1. What next?'

'Gina and I can watch the north-east culvert,' said Mich.

'Easy-peasy!' chimed in Gina.

'Good idea, kiddos,' said Rohan gently, hating to disappoint the girls. 'The problem is that you'll need a couple of TGs, and you've never used them before, right?' The girls nodded glumly.

'Ricky, Chris and I can keep watch with them,' said Corazon. 'We'll take Sam, too.' The boys nodded eagerly while Mich and Gina beamed. 'Also, I'm used to the forest.'

'That would be perfect,' said Rohan. 'You're Team A, and while you're on duty, Corazon can give you lessons in using a TG.' The youngsters cheered.

'I'll go with them but will hang around the CBI clearing – crane basket imprint,' said Nimal. 'If I see anything suspicious, like the crane dropping crooks inside, I'll contact Team A. They'll be within WT range.'

'Okay, yaar. Take Hunter and you'll be Team N. I'll drop you and Team A at SS,' said Rohan. 'Everyone should have their WTs with the earpieces plugged in at all times, and each team should have TGs and darts.'

'Anu and I will be Team B,' said Amy. 'We'll drive to the lake, pick up a boat, check the south culvert, and then time our trip up the Muskok.'

'Excellent,' said Anu. 'We'll figure out how many trips can be done in a night. Then we'll get back ASAP, and wander around SS and BSC-2, keeping an eye on the river where the raft print was. We'll keep in touch with Teams A and N.'

'There are several waterholes south of SS, frequented by grizzlies, which we'll monitor as well,' added Amy. 'What will you do, Rohan?'

'A few things,' said Rohan. 'I'll first hang around BSC-1 and the firepit clearing and see who comes there for a meal. When Umedh and

Jason return, we'll make further plans as required. None of this is cut in stone and some of us need to be flexible in case another group needs help. Who knows how things will pan out.'

'What will the other teams be named?' asked Ricky.

'Jason and Rohan had better go by their initials, too, and Umedh's known as Q,' said Amy.

'Here's a suggestion about communication, so please pull out your WTs,' said Umedh. 'So far we've been using frequency 56.8, but these are high tech units and we can choose which frequency to use, so we're all on the same band. Since we're splitting up, let's change frequencies on a regular basis.'

'Excellent notion, yaar,' said Rohan. 'That'll prevent the crooks using one of our WTs to tune into our plans if one of us gets caught.'

'Precisely! There are thirteen of us, including the two dogs. We'll begin at frequency 13 and every hour, on the hour, we'll go up by thirteen. Example, at noon, we'll move to 26, at 1 p.m. we'll change to 39, and so on – does it make sense?' The others nodded. 'Let's synchronize our watches and set them for hourly reminders.'

'Brill, yaar,' said Chris, as they made the adjustments.

'Another point,' said Umedh, giving Rohan a quick look, 'if possible, avoid contacting anyone five minutes prior to the hour or on the hour.'

Rohan studied his friend for a second and said, 'Good point, Umedh. We'll check in at half past the hour. Teams A and N check in with each other hourly – you're all within the WT range; Nimal update the rest of us once you've checked with the others. Teams B, J and Q, on your return, contact one of us the minute you're within range.

'And,' Rohan hesitated, before continuing, 'unlikely though it is, if any of us get caught pretend the earpiece is for an iPod and at first opportunity turn it off. If we can't reach anyone we'll know something's happened and will take action.'

'Will do,' agreed the JEACs, although none of them were concerned about the possibility of being caught.

'Right, folks. It's nearly eleven, and Shawn will be here shortly,' said Anu. 'Let's get organized so we can leave once he's gone.'

'SS has a good stock of food,' said Amy. 'Gina and Mich, please get the cubs and Codey ready for Shawn. We'll make packets of sandwiches for lunch.'

'We'll help,' said Chris and Ricky.

'The rest of us will deal with necessary equipment,' said Rohan. 'Also, Shawn's in a hurry, so Gina and Mich, look out for him, hand over the cubs and Codey, and tell him we'll be in touch when possible.'

'Okay,' chorused everyone, and left the room.

At 11:30 a.m. the JEACs met in the living room, fully equipped, and formed a circle. The cubs and Codey were gone.

'JEACs – attention!' said Anu, putting her hand into the circle. The others put out their hands, too – one on top of the other. 'On the count of three,' said Anu. 'One, two, three! JEACs to the rescue!' The group raised their hands in a cheer, with Hunter and Sam barking loudly, and a few minutes later GW was empty.

CHAPTER 16

Teams at Work

'Do you have a hiding place in mind, Team A?' asked Rohan, as they drove to SS.

'There's heavy shrubbery on the east side of the Muskok,' said Corazon. 'We can hide in it and get a good view of the bushes around the culvert as well as SS. If required, I can trail anyone who comes out of the tunnel – without being seen.'

'Be careful, kiddo, okay?' said Rohan. 'If you do follow anyone, take Sam along.'

'Sure, Rohan,' grinned Corazon, petting Sam. 'I promise I won't be reckless. I'll also give the others a briefing on which darts to use, and make sure that we have loaded TGs.'

'Great,' said Nimal. 'What's the shrubbery like, Corazon?'

'It has multicoloured leaves: green on the top and red underneath.'

'I know where it is,' said Mich. 'I crawled underneath and there was lots of room.'

'And we'll need to keep watch in all directions,' added Gina.

'Excellent point, kiddo,' said Rohan, pulling up near SS. 'Who's got a key?'

'Me,' said Chris.

'Hunter and I'll check the shrubbery and surroundings before we take off,' said Nimal, in response to a quick glance from Rohan.

'Good luck, everyone; stay safe,' said Rohan, and drove off.

The others waved and then set off, creeping through shrubbery until they were a few metres from the river.

'Hunter and I'll go ahead and make sure it's clear,' said Nimal.

The others nodded. Nimal and Hunter quickly checked everything, including the grate at the culvert and the tunnel.

'Nobody around,' he reported. Corazon led them across the river. While Nimal and Hunter kept watch, the others crept under the heavy bushes.

Watch alarms sounded softly, and everyone changed their WT frequency.

'Nimal, will you check from the outside and make sure none of us can be seen or heard? We'll talk softly,' said Gina.

'Also, say something in a normal voice, without the WT,' said Mich, 'and walk towards us from the culvert.'

'Of course, kiddos,' said Nimal, pleased that they were becoming aware of security. He crept away with Hunter. 'Nobody can see or hear you,' said Nimal quietly, into his WT, after he had walked all around the hiding place talking to Hunter. 'Did you hear me?'

'We heard you and can see both of you clearly,' said Mich. 'And we've a great view of the tunnel entrance, despite the shrubbery surrounding it.'

'Brill. I'll touch base with you once I'm settled in my zone,' said Nimal softly. 'Stay safe, Team A. Come on, Hunter.'

Team A wished him luck, and settled down. Corazon began to explain darts and dosages to the others. It was 12:45 p.m.

*****

In another section of Manipau, Anu said, as she and Amy reached the boathouse, 'That was a quick drive.'

Amy pulled out keys from her pocket, unlocked the door of the boathouse and went inside. 'Here's the perfect little motor boat for us,' she said, and they climbed into a boat and set off. 'We'll go south first and check the culvert.'

'Good!' said Anu, pulling out her binoculars, as Amy zoomed eastwards on the lake.

A few minutes later the lake narrowed considerably and joined the river, and the girls turned south. Amy turned off the motor, and using paddles, allowed the river to carry the boat along. Five metres from the wall, she manoeuvred the boat into the east bank where there was a small clearing, and they climbed out and made their way to the culvert.

As they reached the culvert Amy whispered, 'I hear something.' The girls froze.

'Sounds like someone's in the tunnel,' murmured Anu. 'Should we scram? Our TGs are in the boat.'

'No, let's hide,' said Amy, pulling her under a bush. 'Shh.'

They heard machinery working and realized the grate was being opened.

'Nothing here,' said a low voice.

The girls gasped, crawled out of the bush hurriedly and peered into the tunnel.

'Umedh?' said Anu, softly.

There was a moment's silence and then, 'Anu? Amy?' said Umedh's voice.

'Yes,' responded the girls.

Umedh and Jason parted the bushes covering the entrance and looked out at the girls. 'You nearly gave us a heart attack!' said Jason.

'And we nearly had one,' said Amy. 'Thank goodness it's you guys! I thought it was the crooks. Did you find anything?'

'Plenty of signs that bears are sent down river and pulled out about a kilometre from here,' said Jason. 'We found a matching print of the raft, vehicle tracks, sled marks, and blood spots.'

'It's also evident that this tunnel's being used,' said Umedh, 'so let's get moving. The crooks could arrive any moment.'

'Yes – good luck, boys,' said Amy.

'You, too,' said Umedh.

'We'll fill up gas and then head back,' said Jason.

The boys closed the grate and disappeared, while the girls quickly launched their boat and set off up river.

'There's a canopy of trees just beyond the first curve,' said Amy as they went through the lake again.

'Like that green tunnel,' said Anu, looking ahead, and Amy nodded. 'Let's slow down when we're in the tunnel, and check the banks for raft prints, or anything else.'

'Okay, but why?' said Amy.

'Since the days are longer, the crooks would have to be cautious that people on the lake don't see them. So they might hang around until dark or wait till people are at dinner, before heading for the culvert.'

'Brill!' said Amy, rounding a curve in the river. 'Here we go – binocs ready?'

'Set,' replied Anu, as they entered the arboreal tunnel and everything turned a soft green. The river was 4.6 metres wide.

Amy navigated the boat towards the east bank and slowed down. 'It's dead quiet here,' she said.

'Sure is,' murmured Anu, her binoculars glued to her eyes, examining the bank.

Three minutes later Anu said, 'Stop! Get closer to the bank where there's no shrubbery and those branches come down low.' She pointed to the spot.

Amy turned off the motor, used the oars and steered the boat right up to the bank. 'What did you see, Anu?'

'A shirt on a branch and a coil of rope,' said Anu, stepping onto the stony bank and taking several pictures.'

'Do you think they stop here until it's dark?' said Amy.

'Probably; I'll check the rest of the area,' said Anu, moving away from the shirt which had obviously been put out to dry. Amy saw her bend, brush aside leaves, and take more pictures. 'Lots of empty food cans and beer bottles,' she said, waving one at Amy. She returned to the edge of the river and got into the boat. 'It's too stony to see raft prints, but the rope could be used to tie it up under the branches. I'll hold the boat steady and you look down river through my binocs.

'Gee whizz,' said Amy. 'There's a clear view of the lake and river through that gap in the trees; the crooks could ensure nobody was in sight before they went to the south culvert. Good spot! Do you want to check anything else?'

'No. We'll continue to check the banks, but I think we've found what we're looking for,' said Anu.

'Let's hope we don't meet any crooks – although I see you're ready to deal with them,' she added with a chuckle, as Anu waved her TG.

The rest of the trip was uneventful, and by 2:50 they were moored. 'Team A, come in,' said Anu, softly. 'We're in the vicinity. Over.'

'Location please, over,' said Ricky.

'West bank, two metres north of where the river deepens, under an overhanging tree – can you see us? Over,' said Anu.

'No, you're well hidden, over,' said Ricky.

Team B quickly updated Team A on what they, as well as Umedh and Jason, had discovered. 'Anything at your end? Over,' said Anu.

'Nothing,' said Corazon. 'Nimal and Hunter are okay. I scouted around twice, going right up to SS, and all's well. Gina, Mich and Chris are napping, and we told them to turn off their WTs. At three, Ricky and I'll have a nap, over.'

'Good thinking,' said Amy. 'We're going back now and . . . oops, time to change frequencies. I assume you'll change the rest of the teams' WTs? Over'

'Yes,' said Ricky. 'What time will you get back here? Over.'

'It's three now, so I'd say around five,' said Amy. 'Umedh and Jason should get back to GW around 4 p.m. and will go to BSC-1. Stay safe, over.'

'And you, over and out,' said Ricky and Corazon.

Team B set off, reached the boathouse in good time, and then headed for SS.

CHAPTER 17

Divide and Conquer

Umedh and Jason reached GW at 4:15, locked the car in the garage, contacted Rohan and met him at a waterhole south of BSC-1.

After updating Rohan on their discoveries, Umedh said, 'Anything at this end?'

'No. Half an hour ago Nimal had nothing to report for himself or Team A, but gave me Team B's news,' said Rohan, and told them what Amy and Anu had found.

'What are the next . . .' began Jason, when their WTs beeped.

'Come in, R! Come in! Over,' said Nimal's voice urgently.

'What's up, yaar?' said Rohan quickly.

'I can't reach Team A. I've tried them for ten minutes with no luck. Hunter and I are off to investigate, but I wanted to update you first. Over.'

'Two of us will meet you in the shrubbery near SS – we'll beep when we're there,' said Rohan. 'Umedh will remain here. We should be there in twenty minutes. Comments, anyone? Over.'

'Sound plan,' said Umedh. 'Change frequencies *immediately*. We'll start at 104, and then change again on the hour. It's 4:35; Team B will be in my WT range soon, so I won't change until I contact them. Over.'

'Right,' said Nimal. 'On my way, over and out.'

'Umedh, meet Amy and Anu at GW and the three of you get to the firepit ASAP,' said Rohan. 'I'm positive the crooks have Team A, and they may bring the kids to the firepit. We'll check around SS and give you an update. Take my air gun.'

'Okay, yaar – good luck,' said Umedh, and watched the boys disappear into the forest, before making his way to GW. He was seven minutes away from GW when his WT beeped.

'Team R, Q or J, come in, we're three minutes from GW, and on the way to SS, over,' said Anu.

'Stop at GW, park in the garage, and enter GW *through the garage entrance*. Let me in at the basement door in five. Over.'

'Problems?' asked Anu. 'Over.'

'Probably. Over and out,' said Umedh, and raced along the trail.

'What's happened?' asked the girls anxiously, as they let Umedh into GW.

'Team A can't be contacted,' said Umedh, and quickly explained the situation. 'We need to get to the firepit. We'll split up around the clearing, but ensure that we're not too far from each other. Agreed?'

'Okay,' said Amy. 'We can't afford to get captured, if that's what's happened to the others.'

They made their way out of the door, locking it behind them, and reached the outskirts of the firepit clearing by 5:20.

'We're six metres away,' said Anu softly. 'I'll scout ahead.' The others nodded. Anu was an excellent tracker.

'Beep once if there's nobody around, and twice if there is,' said Umedh. 'If we don't hear from you in five, we'll come looking for you – stay tuned.'

Anu nodded, and crept forward. She was soon in hiding under a thick shrub and was barely in position, when she heard a grunt of pain. Beeping twice on her WT, she scanned the area, trying to locate the direction from which the sound had come. The bushes on her right, covering the false trail Nimal had discovered, shook violently and some of the fake branches were thrown aside.

'Two women entering clearing from false trail and approaching firepit,' murmured Anu into the WT. 'One's limping, other's supporting her. Talking loudly in foreign lingo; limper's in pain, assisted to sit on a rock. Over.'

'Stats on size of females, communication equipment, et cetera, over,' said Umedh.

'No sign of phones. Limper five foot, slim, fit; other about five foot seven, sturdy, broad. Broad one replacing false trail; has bound up limper's ankle, moving her to rocks near firepit and is preparing food. Over.'

'Can we take them? Over,' said Amy.

'Affirmative! Strategy?'

Fifteen minutes later, the JEACs stood over the two women, both of whom were tied and gagged.

'Good work, team,' said Amy. 'Let's get rid of all signs that anyone's been here, before we decide what to do with these beauties.'

They organized the clearing and Anu said, 'We can't leave the women in the forest; they'll be mauled by bears.'

'We'll take them back to GW, put them in one of the empty sheds next to the garage, contact Min-jae, and get him to organize the police to pick them up. I'll help the limper,' said Umedh.

'Perhaps we'll get news of Team A shortly,' said Amy.

'Hope so. What next?' said Anu, as they made their way to GW.

'We'll make further plans after dealing with these two,' said Umedh.

'Okay,' agreed the girls.

*****

Meanwhile, Rohan and Jason reached SS in under twenty minutes. 'Nimal, we're in the shrubbery beside the parking lot, over,' said Rohan softly.

'Great. Two chaps have crawled into our team's hideout. I'll ensure they're going to stay put – stay tuned.' Five minutes later Nimal said, 'I'll be there in three. Over and out.'

'Man, you're so quiet,' gasped Jason, as Nimal and Hunter joined them. 'What's the situ?'

'Clearly, our group's been captured and moved. Those chaps are waiting for something, and they have rifles.'

'Could we grab them?' said Rohan. 'Would diversionary tactics work?'

'Yes, to everything, yaar,' grinned Nimal. 'They're in their early twenties, and nervous. I watched them come through the culvert, and they jumped at small noises.'

'You know the layout. Suggestions?' said Rohan.

'Entice them out of the shrubbery first,' said Nimal.

After a quick discussion, the boys and Hunter moved into position. Jason stepped out of the shrubbery as if he had just come along a trail, crossed the river, went up the bank past the shrubbery and approached the bush from behind.

'Come on out, kids,' he said, cheerfully. 'Anything . . .' He stopped and jumped back, taking up a karate position, as a rifle emerged from under the bush, followed by one of the crooks.

'Hands up – my mate's got you covered,' said the man, picking up his rifle. 'I have him now, Bali.'

'Where are my friends,' growled Jason, raising his hands and inching backwards slowly.

'You'll soon find out,' said Bali, joining them. 'Don't try anything or we'll shoot.' Jason remained still and Bali grabbed his arms, saying, 'I've got him, Taga. Help me tie him up.'

Taga put down his rifle, and went to help his partner. They were gleefully tying up Jason, when Rohan, Nimal and Hunter leapt out from behind trees. The boys and the dog were too strong for the men.

'Hunter, on guard!' said Nimal, pointing to Taga who was flat on the ground. Hunter immediately stood over the man, growling fiercely, and Taga didn't move.

Freeing Jason, the boys gagged and tied the men. Nimal and Hunter checked the surrounding area, gave the all-clear, and within minutes the crooks were pushed inside SS and the window curtains drawn. The entire operation took only ten minutes from the time Jason had walked out into the open.

'Remove their gags,' said Rohan, pointing one of their own guns at the men – although, unseen by them, he had put on the safety catch. Hunter stood by, and Jason and Nimal whipped off the gags.

'Start talking,' growled Rohan, 'and fast, or we'll encourage our dog to bite. Don't try shouting for help – this room's soundproof. Where are our friends?'

The petrified men looked at the three angry boys and the dog, and began speaking fast. 'They were taken to a cave outside the centre,' said Taga.

'We didn't want them to be hurt . . .' began Bali, but stopped when the boys laughed derisively.

'How considerate,' said Jason. 'Who took them there and where's this cave?'

'A few of us,' muttered Bali. 'The cave's east of the river.'

'You need to be more communicative,' snapped Rohan. 'Details, NOW!'

'The cave's where the north and east walls meet,' said Taga. 'It's only five minutes east of the tunnel, but . . .' He trailed off, looking nervously at Bali.

'But what?' growled Nimal.

'We can't tell you anything else,' muttered Bali sulkily.

'Who are your leaders?' asked Jason.

'We don't know, and anyway, what's in it for us?' said Bali, trying to play tough.

Nimal and Jason looked at Rohan who shrugged his shoulders and said casually, 'No worries, chaps. Gag them. We'll leave them near the den we saw earlier; the grizzlies will start moving soon.'

'You mean the den with the mother and three cubs?' said Nimal, pretending to look horrified. 'But, yaar, she'll be as mad as fire if she finds anyone near her cubs. You sure?'

'Absolutely, yaar,' said Rohan, and Nimal and Jason approached the men, gags in hand. 'They're no use to us and . . .'

He stopped as the men began talking very fast.

'We don't know much,' whimpered Taga. 'A guy named Rizvi hired us two months ago, and offered us lots of money if we worked for them.'

'He told us that even if we were caught and went to jail, we weren't to say a word, and the money would be waiting for us when we got out,' muttered Bali. 'But I don't want to be eaten by bears – please don't leave us in the forest.'

'What sort of work have you done?' asked Jason.

'We drove a truck with goods to BC and followed instructions,' said Bali. 'We went to a particular truck stop on a specific date and time, parked the vehicle and left the keys on the seat. Inside the restaurant was an envelope addressed to us, with a note giving the make, model and licence plate, along with keys to a car which we drove back to our lodgings in Powela. By the time we returned to the parking lot, the truck was gone.'

'Didn't you see who took your truck?' asked Rohan.

'No. The parking lot's behind the restaurant, and can't be seen from inside. Also, we were told that both of us must go in or we wouldn't get paid,' said Taga.

'What were the goods?' growled Nimal.

'We don't know,' said Bali. 'The containers were always sealed.'

'How many trips have you done?' asked Jason.

'Five. We were supposed to do ten more over the next few weeks, but nothing happened this week,' said Bali.

'You must have some idea of what your goods are,' said Rohan sternly. 'Are they killing grizzly bears?'

The men glanced at each other nervously – Hunter and the boys looked fierce and determined. 'Yes – but it's only a guess,' whispered Bali, 'based on the other work we've done. One night Rizvi took us by boat to the south tunnel, pulling a loaded, covered raft behind us. At the tunnel, three people opened the grate and moored the raft inside the tunnel. We were sent outside the Centre, to wait in a truck parked out of sight of the tunnel, and given some food. After a couple of hours, the raft was floated along the river and we helped load a sealed container into the truck.'

'As I was pushing the container, I saw blood and fur on a corner of the raft,' said Taga. He shuddered. 'It was horrible!'

'We needed money badly,' said Bali.

'So you decided to become crooks and kill innocent animals? Smart!' said Jason angrily.

'Now, give us the exact location of the cave where our friends are, and what your orders are for the rest of the day,' said Rohan. 'Speak fast! It's nearly . . .' He broke off as their WTs beeped, handed over his gun to Jason, and said, 'Get more info.'

He left the room quickly, and went out of earshot. 'I'm inside SS, folks. Where are you? Over.'

'The girls and I are in the shrubbery beside the parking lot near SS. Instructions? Over,' said Umedh.

'Join us fast – and be careful. There are too many unsavoury characters around. Over and out.'

Minutes later, the group was together, along with Hunter. The crooks looked astonished to see three more JEACs. Rohan raised an eyebrow at Jason and Nimal, and the boys nodded.

'Gag them again,' said Rohan. 'We'll confab in the other room. Hunter, on guard and bite them if they make a sound or move!'

Hunter wagged his tail and sat down in front of the petrified men, as Jason and Nimal gagged them. The JEACs then assembled in the kitchen.

'The kids are gagged, tied hand and foot, and poor Sam was tied by Corazon since the crooks threatened to shoot him if she didn't,' said Nimal angrily.

'One man's on guard outside the cave,' said Jason. 'Apparently he's 6 foot 5 inches tall, and weighs around 115 kilos. He has a gun, a cell phone, and specializes in combat. He'll be there until 9 p.m., and then someone will relieve him. These two don't know what'll happen to the kids after that. They were asked to stay in hiding and wait for some other crooks – but they don't know timings or numbers of crooks involved tonight.'

'The cave's surrounded by huge trees and dense shrubbery and is directly outside the north-east corner of Manipau,' said Nimal. 'Easy to get to, but we'd have to use surprise tactics on the guard.'

'Is there a way to get over the wall from inside – perhaps a tree with branches drooping outside Manipau, like at the construction site?' said Anu.

'Excellent idea, sis,' said Rohan. 'We don't need to leave anyone to guard these chaps for a bit. Anu and Jason, go outside Manipau, through the culvert and hide in the east side shrubbery from where you can see the entrance to the tunnel. Take Hunter with you. We'll reconvene there at 7 p.m. at the latest. Anything else?'

'Quick update,' said Umedh, and told the boys about capturing the two women. 'We also asked Min-jae to get to GW, along with a few police officers, so that they can keep an eye on the crooks – you know, food, bathroom breaks, et cetera. They'll be within range of the WTs; we gave him the frequencies.'

'And the police can gather any other crooks we capture from time to time?' grinned Rohan, and Umedh nodded back. 'Excellent thinking, yaar!'

'Min-jae should be at GW by now – I'll call him and ask him to have someone collect the two here,' said Amy, going to the telephone.

'Okay, JEACs – let's go,' said Rohan, once Amy had finished updating Min-jae. 'Remember to stay tuned in.'

*****

By 6:40 p.m. the group reconvened and after a rapid update, further plans were made. Ten minutes later, Umedh and Rohan, who were the biggest and heaviest of the group, went back inside Manipau, taking strong ropes with them. The others, with Hunter, waited for their signal.

'We're set,' came Rohan's voice, twenty minutes later. 'Zero hour is 7:20 p.m. sharp. Questions? Over.'

'None. Over,' said Amy, after a quick glance around the group.

'Excellent. Over and out,' said Rohan.

The JEACs outside Manipau were hiding in heavy shrubbery surrounding a clearing in front of an outcrop of rocks. The rocks obviously had caves, both large and small, but the entrances were concealed by more shrubbery. Behind the rocks were several large trees, some of which were inside Manipau with branches hanging over the wall. They were heavily foliaged.

It was quiet except for the sounds of birds and crickets. The large crook looked fierce and alert, his gun at the ready, as he paced a wide trail leading to the river, pausing occasionally to use his night-vision binoculars.

'Not an easy capture,' muttered Nimal to Hunter. 'But let's see what our Tarzans can do.' Hunter licked him enthusiastically.

The crook strode to the end of the clearing, west of the rocks, turned and returned to midpoint, looking towards the river through his binoculars.

'WHOOSH!' The sound took him by surprise, and a split second later he was sent flying, falling face down on the trail.

'Get him, JEACs,' yelled Rohan, who had swung down on a rope tied to a tree, and hit him in the back.

'Amy and Anu, keep those guns trained on him,' shouted Jason, as everyone raced to help Rohan.

'He's incredibly strong,' panted Nimal, as the boys jumped on the man. 'Hunter, bite him!'

'Oww!' yelled the man, as Hunter nipped him first on one arm, and then danced around, nipping him on each leg. The crook swore as he tossed and turned, struggling to free himself and flailing out with his limbs as he attempted to find his gun which had flown a couple of metres away from him. But Umedh, who had swung down from another tree, had kicked it out of reach. Amy put down her TG, grabbed the man's gun, put on the safety catch, and aimed it at him. Anu had her TG trained on the crook, too.

The combined weight and strength of the four boys along with some hard punches, karate chops, and Hunter growling ferociously near his face, finally subdued the crook.

'Jason, keep his arm twisted while I gag him – he's not very polite,' said Umedh, who had a knee in the man's back and had bent one of his arms backwards at a painful angle.

'You ruffians,' growled the man furiously. 'Wait till I'm free.'

'Sure,' said Nimal cheerfully. 'We'll wait; and much as we enjoy hearing your dulcet tones, do put a sock in it, old bean.'

A gag was forced into the crook's mouth, and he was trussed up so that he could not move or get free.

'He's incredibly strong,' said Jason, as everyone stood back, panting, and looked at their prisoner. 'What shall we do with him?'

'Umedh, Jason and I'll deprive him of any communication devices,' said Rohan. 'Amy, give me his gun; the rest of you find the kids and bring them here.' He turned to the man and added, 'You'd better hope they're unharmed.' The crook glared at him.

Five minutes later the JEACs were reunited, with a joyful Sam being fussed over by everyone, including Hunter. The younger JEACs were all right, although they were still rubbing their arms and legs, after being tied up.

'Are you all right? Not hurt?' asked Amy anxiously.

'We're fine,' said Chris. 'Sorry we messed up – they took us by surprise. They threatened to shoot Corazon and Sam, so we surrendered. By the way, there was a cell phone in a bush outside the cave, which they used to call this guy – we've got it.'

'You did the right thing, yaar,' said Rohan. 'It would've been too risky not to obey. Glad you got their phone. Before we update each other and make further plans, Amy, Mich, Corazon – where can we put this crook? We can't risk taking him to SS or GW, and we obviously can't leave him in the caves, since the others know about them.'

'There's a grotto 150 metres east of us,' said Amy. 'Although it floods during spring it'll be okay now. Nobody would dream of looking for him there and even if his gag gets loose, nobody would hear him.'

'Excellent,' said Rohan.

'Are we going to release his legs – he's too heavy to carry?' said Ricky, eyeing the huge thug.

'Too risky,' said Umedh. 'He's trained in combat and probably has all kinds of tricks up his sleeve.'

'We'll drag him,' said Jason.

'It's a stony trail for about 100 metres, and then it's muddy . . .' began Amy, but stopped and shrugged. 'Given what he's been doing to our poor grizzlies, a bit of roughing up won't hurt him.'

'Amy, lead Umedh, Jason, Nimal and me to the grotto,' said Rohan. 'The rest of you ensure that there's nothing to show any of us have been around this area or the cave.'

'We'll be back soon,' said Amy, and she and the others set off, the boys dragging the crook easily.

By 8:15 p.m. the JEACs were together again.

'Can he get free?' asked Corazon anxiously.

'Not a chance,' said Nimal grimly. 'We tied him to a sturdy rock in the grotto; he can't move an inch – we had to be harsh.'

'We also checked to make sure there weren't sharp objects or anything else with which he could cut his ropes,' said Umedh.

'Then we rolled a huge rock in front of the opening so that even if he does get loose, he can't get out,' added Rohan. 'How many crooks were there and did you five hear anything?'

'We saw seven of them, plus Hogni – that's the big guy,' said Chris. 'They said two would hide in our spot, awaiting further orders. Some of the group were going to the firepit, others on various errands, and the leader and more crooks are scheduled to arrive at one in the morning – nothing will happen before then. Nobody gave specifics of numbers.'

'Okay. We've dealt with the two from your hideout and two at the firepit. Let's return to GW, get detailed updates, and make further plans,' said Rohan. He contacted Min-jae and told him they were returning to GW.

Hunter, Nimal and Corazon scouted ahead, and by 9:05 p.m. the group reached GW and were greeted cheerfully by Min-jae and five police officers. Chris peered into the shed and verified that the two females were the ones who had captured them.

Everyone assembled in the kitchen, drew the heavy curtains, and sat down to a hot meal of leftover food, during which they briefly updated Min-jae and the police officers on what had happened, without going into too many details.

'Great work, JEACs,' said police officer Juanita, who was in charge of the team. 'Since you know how to move around in wildlife centres better than we do, and we're short of officers until 2 a.m., Inspector Geraldine instructed us to take direction from you. What would you like us to do now?'

'Could you make arrangements for Hogni to be collected from the grotto, and the four captures to be taken away?' said Rohan. 'Also, if some of you remain here, we'll communicate with you via WT; Min-jae knows his way around Manipau.'

'Sound ideas,' said Juanita. 'We'll get on it and I'll stay here with Min-jae until our team returns.'

The police officers left the kitchen. Rohan turned to Team A and said, 'What happened?'

'It was my fault,' said Corazon miserably, but the others negated this instantly. 'Everything was quiet, and we got hungry so I said I'd take Sam and a TG and get food from SS. When I was returning . . .' She broke off with an angry sob. Anu gave her a hug, and Ricky continued.

'The rest of us were watching the culvert as well as down river. The crooks had obviously come up river, and since the bend in the river hides the place where the raft was hidden, we didn't see or hear a thing. We saw Corazon emerge from the shrubbery on the west bank and wade across the river.'

'Then a female voice shouted: "We have you and your dog covered, don't move or we'll shoot!" Corazon had no choice,' said Mich. 'She commanded Sam to stop. Two women went up to Corazon; one kept her gun trained on Sam, while the other grabbed Corazon and twisted her arm behind her back; but Corazon didn't cry out.'

'The woman asked what Corazon was doing with a gun,' continued Gina, 'and Corazon replied that she was tracking bears and wandering around Manipau as she always does. The women spoke together in a foreign language, and then checked the bag which had two dozen sandwiches; they guessed there were more of us.'

'When five men arrived through the culvert and joined the women,' said Chris, 'the women threatened to break Corazon's arm if she didn't talk. But one of the guys threatened to kill Sam, so the rest of us came out of hiding.'

'We couldn't risk Sam or Corazon being hurt,' said Ricky. 'The crooks forced Corazon to tie Sam up; we were also tied up, gagged and taken to the caves. There they contacted someone via the hidden cell phone, and half an hour later, Hogni arrived. The two younger men were sent back to keep watch from our hiding place.'

'Did you hear anything else?' asked Umedh.

'Before Hogni's arrival, they discussed matters, speaking in English since the men didn't know the other language,' said Corazon. 'They were in awe of their leader, and although they didn't mention a name, they were obviously speaking about a female.'

'They spoke about more people coming tonight, but didn't give numbers or locations,' added Chris.

'Did they mention Hogni's role?' asked Anu.

'I think he was called in specially to guard us,' said Mich.

'The guy who called him apologized and said an unexpected situation had arisen and they needed him for a few hours,' added Gina.

'Okay, thanks. Here's an update of what we've been doing,' said Rohan, and brought them up to speed. 'Now, before we go any further, are you sure none of you need to sleep?'

'We slept while in the cave; we couldn't do anything else,' said Gina.

'I just want to catch these horrible crooks before they kill any more of our grizzlies,' said Mich.

'Agreed,' chorused the JEACs.

'You JEACs are amazing!' said Min-jae, who had been listening attentively. The youngsters smiled.

'Okay, as far as we can guess, there'll be a large number of crooks in and around Manipau tonight,' said Rohan. 'We know they'll start from the firepit around 1 a.m. There are eleven of us and I think we should continue our successful strategy of *divide and conquer*. My guess is that Kylie's the leader. The others could be Hing, Rizvi and Sheila – unless Hing's needed outside Manipau to operate the crane. There must also be more crooks to take the raft to the south culvert, et cetera, and who knows where their location is at the moment.'

'Makes sense,' said Anu.

'I see three key venues where action will take place,' continued Rohan. 'For ease of reference, I'll use acronyms: CBI – which stands for crane basket imprint – is the section *inside* Manipau, opposite the construction site; CO – crane outside – is the crane parking spot *outside* Manipau; F is the *firepit*.

'The crooks have between half past midnight and 5 a.m. to use the crane since the morning shift begins at six. From 10 p.m. to 5 a.m. they can use the culverts and river without being seen, and can roam around Manipau safely. By now those at the firepit may be aware that something's going on, but they don't know exactly what's happened. Obviously, none of these crooks, except for Hogni, carry phones or WTs, but use phones hidden in strategic places. Comments? Ideas?'

'I concur,' said Amy.

Everyone contributed to a fast-paced discussion and Rohan made rapid notes.

'That's solid input,' said Anu, finally. 'May I imagine a scenario?' The others nodded. 'After the night shift, when everyone but Kylie and her team have left the construction site, three of them will be dropped over the wall at CBI, via the crane; Hing may join them at one of the sites. Just a second. Jason, how would we know if the crane is being used tonight?'

'It'll be parked facing the wall,' said Jason. 'Usually it's parked facing the river. Actually, Anu, you've reminded me of something. Over the past two weeks, the crane was usually parked facing the river, but on four days I noticed it was parked facing the wall. It's a weird thing to notice, but I like efficiency, and while it takes time to back a crane into place, it saves time in the morning. I may be wrong, but those four days were when Santos had meetings from 11 p.m., and left Kylie to wrap up the shift.'

'Does Santos have a meeting tonight?' asked Nimal.

'I'll check,' said Jason, going to a telephone. He spoke to Santos, and hung up. 'He does and will be off site from 10:30.'

'Can you operate a crane, Jason?' asked Umedh.

'Not for work,' grinned Jason, 'but I can move it if required.'

'Excellent,' said Rohan and Umedh. Everyone looked at Anu and she continued.

'If they're moving grizzlies over the wall tonight, Hing may stay at CO, to operate the crane. Kylie et al will join the others at the firepit, then split up and look for grizzlies from 1 a.m. onwards. Since CBI and south of it is also grizzly territory, and the crooks may use the crane, they'll likely operate around that section of Manipau. I wouldn't be surprised if they have a backup plan to move grizzlies down river, too.'

'Good thinking, Anu,' said Umedh. 'Jason, it's nearly 10:30 p.m. How late is the crane usually operated?'

'For this week, it should be parked by 10:45,' said Jason. 'I see where you're going; we can check to see which way it's facing, and if Hing's there, we'll capture him.'

'But how would Hing *know* when the crane's required to pick up grizzlies if they don't use cell phones?' asked Chris.

'Point, Chris,' said Rohan. 'These crooks appear to plan things down to the minute. They hid one mobile phone near the caves; they could hide a cell phone around the CBI location, and when ready, contact Hing or have some other signal.'

'Do you think Hing will remain near the crane?' asked Gina.

'Possibly,' said Jason.

'Rohan, do you have a plan?' asked Amy.

'Yes, and it's based on our discussions,' said Rohan, looking round at the eager JEACs. 'Here are my suggestions: Jason, Umedh and Amy, get to the construction site just before the shift's over, climb in via the tree, and check on the crane. If it's facing the wall do whatever's necessary to ensure that it cannot be used by the crooks; capture Hing if he's there and get his phone.'

'And if we don't think the crane will be used tonight, we contact you?' said Jason.

'Correct,' said Rohan. 'Your group will be team CO. If it looks like the crane will be used, alert AGM – Anu, Gina and Mich, and CNH – Corazon, Nimal and Hunter, so they're prepared for action. If you capture Hing, deliver him to Min-jae.

'AGM stay around CBI, climb trees for safety. Keep close contact with CNH – who will be on the ground in the same location. CNH, follow any crooks moving towards the firepit – they'll probably use the camouflaged trail. Update AGM and GW on a regular basis. AGM remain in hiding and be prepared for anything.'

'If we see a phone being hidden, we'll take it and turn it off,' added Anu.

'Good. Ricky, Chris and I will be team F. We'll communicate via WTs. By 1 a.m. teams CNH and F should be hidden around the firepit. If in danger, signal two quick beeps on the WTs or fire an air gun into the ground; any team in your vicinity will come to your aid. If attacked, use your martial arts and the butt end of your TG to protect yourself. The usual on synchronization, code names, et cetera. Everyone should have at least four lengths of rope in their knapsacks or around their waists – plenty of rope in the storage room – a penknife and scarves for gags. Any questions so far?'

'Carry on, yaar,' said Umedh.

'We know that after 1 a.m. the crooks will separate and hunt for grizzlies. Be alert for instructions on your WT.'

'Are we going to try to capture everyone, Rohan?' asked Mich, looking at him wide-eyed.

'We'll do our best, kiddo,' said Rohan, putting an arm around her and Gina, who were on either side of him. 'Remember, stay safe, protect each other, and *please, don't play with the grizzlies!*' The tension broke as everyone burst out laughing.

'Is there anything else we need to think of?' said Jason. 'What about the river?'

'At the moment, for safety reasons, we won't split up the group further,' said Rohan.

'We've covered all known contingencies and the rest depends on how things pan out,' said Anu. 'Time to move – it's a quarter to eleven.'

'JEACs to the rescue, once more,' cheered Gina. 'Let's save our grizzlies!'

CHAPTER 18

So Many Crooks

It was 10:55 p.m. when the teams left GW. Sam, still sore from being tied up, was left behind with Min-jae.

'Good luck, everyone!' said Min-jae and Juanita, and seconds later everyone was out of GW and on their way.

*****

Team CO arrived at the construction site and were inside it before 11:30 p.m.

Jason led the way through the shrubbery, to the crane. 'Nearly there – see that leafy tree near the wall? If we climb it we'll see the crane.'

'Okay,' said Amy. 'Just twenty minutes left for the shift. At ten to midnight I'll contact AGM and CNH.' The boys nodded.

A few minutes later they were up in the tree, looking at the crane and giving each other the thumbs up. Amy began taking pictures.

At ten to twelve Amy spoke softly into her WT. 'AGM, CNH, come in, over.'

'AGM here, CNH on another mission. We're fine, you? Over,' replied Anu.

'Crane parked *facing wall*; Hing's pottering around it. Kylie's speaking to him but we can't hear them; they're looking at wall and their watches; Kylie's moving away. Keep alert and stay safe. If crooks come over wall, we'll signal two beeps through WTs. Meet you at CBI. Over.'

'Change of plans; get to F and make contact. Over and out,' whispered Anu.

'Stay up here?' signalled Amy to the boys.

'Yes,' nodded Umedh.

The three of them watched silently. A few minutes later the shift was over and ten minutes later everyone, except for Kylie, Hing, Sheila and Rizvi, had left the site. Rizvi and Sheila drove two trucks from the parking lot and parked them close to the crane; Kylie and Hing attached an open basket to the crane, and Kylie climbed into it, followed by Rizvi and Sheila. Amy immediately signalled AGM.

The crane lifted the basket over the wall and returned empty. His task done, Hing went towards the cabin where there were washrooms. At Jason's signal, the JEACs shinned down the tree.

'Grab him as he comes out of the cabin?' asked Umedh.

'Yes,' breathed Jason and Amy.

'I'll get the Land Rover inside as soon as you've got him,' said Amy.

They raced through shrubbery; the boys hid in the shadows beside the cabin door, while Amy waited beside the gate with Jason's key. The cabin door was slightly open, and a sliver of light streamed out.

Then the light from the cabin was turned off, the door closed and locked; as Hing reached the last step, Umedh rugby-tackled him, bringing him down with a thud that shook the breath out of the man.

'Good work, yaar,' said Jason jubilantly, gagging Hing, while Umedh tied him up.

'Way to go, team,' said Amy, halting the Land Rover near them, and Hing was lifted into the vehicle.

'Shall I move the crane?' asked Jason.

'Yes – hop in; I'll deal with the trucks,' said Umedh, as both boys climbed into the vehicle. Amy drove towards the crane and trucks.

'What are you going to do to the trucks?' asked Jason.

'Perform surgery,' grinned Umedh.

'He's a brilliant surgeon,' laughed Amy. She stopped and the boys leapt out.

Jason moved the crane away from the wall, and was climbing into the Land Rover when Umedh joined them, throwing distributor caps and spark plug cables into the back seat.

'Are your patients dead, doc?' laughed Jason.

'Fortunately, yes!' chuckled Umedh. 'Let's go. Good timing, folks – it's only 12:25.'

Amy raced along the road, heading back to GW. They handed over Hing and hastened to the firepit.

*****

Meanwhile, Gina, Mich and Anu were all in the same tree, their binoculars glued to their eyes, while Nimal and Corazon scouted around on the ground with Hunter – it was 11:20 p.m.

'All clear,' muttered Nimal into his WT. 'We're . . .' Hunter sniffed hard, growled fiercely, then stopped as Corazon touched him. 'Hold it,' the boy murmured into the WT.

A thick forsythia bush, ten metres away from CNH, shook violently and they heard an anxious male voice groan, 'I heard a growl. Was it a bear?'

'Don't be stupid, and get out of the bush,' said a female voice, impatiently. 'There aren't any bears at the moment. We have to wait here for the other two before going to the firepit.'

'But they don't know we're here – and we're not allowed any phones and things,' whined the man. 'They might shoot us thinking we're bears, and if we meet a bear . . .'

'I hope it eats you!' interrupted the woman angrily. 'I don't know why I was saddled with you. Now get out of the bush, and watch for bears. At least the other two guys are good fighters. I'm going to make a lookout for us in these bushes.'

'I wish I'd gone to Vancouver yesterday,' grumbled the man emerging from the bush suddenly. He looked around the clearing nervously, and moaned, 'Where did all the people scheduled for today disappear to? I wasn't scheduled until next week. Aren't there any more of the gang coming?'

'Nobody knows where the others are, moron,' snapped the woman, 'which is why the four of us were called in urgently. Don't you want to earn big bucks?'

'Not this way,' groaned the man.

There was a brief silence except for the sound of branches being broken. Everyone saw the crooks clearly before they crawled into the bush – the woman was under five feet in height, while the man looked timid and weak.

'Let's get them,' said Nimal.

'Okay,' said Anu, 'I'll join you; Mich and Gina – you're on lookout.'

'Beep when you're close,' murmured Nimal. 'Mich, Gina, signal if you see bears approaching.'

In the silence that followed, Nimal whispered something to Corazon, who disappeared through the shrubbery with Hunter, and hid opposite Nimal – they were now on either side of the forsythia bush.

Nimal's WT beeped; he gave Anu directions to his location, and a couple of minutes later the four of them were ready for action.

'Two bears entering the clearing; crooks preparing to shoot,' said Mich urgently over the WT.

Nimal fired the air gun into the ground and the bears disappeared before the crooks could get a shot at them.

The female crook leapt out of the bush, yelling to her companion to follow her, but the JEACs converged on them.

'Got you!' said Nimal, rugby-tackling the woman from behind. She fell like a log, but wriggled furiously out of his grasp, and kicked out.

'She knows karate,' gasped Corazon, racing up while Hunter helped Anu who had brought the male down with a karate kick. 'Get her, Nimal.'

Nimal hesitated for an instant, reluctant to hit someone so much smaller than himself. But when the woman leapt into the air and kicked out at him, Nimal avoided the kick and went for her, using his own karate skills, while Corazon, who was a purple belt, joined him. Two minutes later, the woman was gagged and bound.

'Phew! What a spitfire,' muttered Nimal, as he and Corazon dragged her into the bush, and tied her securely to the sturdy trunk.

'And here's our brave lad,' said Anu. She and Nimal tied the cringing man to the trunk of another bush, out of reach of the woman, and gagged him. 'Girls, come in, over.'

'You folks were awesome, over' said Mich and Gina gleefully.

'Anyone else, or any more bears, in sight? Over,' said Anu.

'Not a dicky bird, over,' said Gina.

'Good. I'll join you shortly. Keep your eyes peeled and stay tuned. Over and out,' said Anu.

'Thanks, Corazon. You were wonderful; I couldn't have managed without you,' said Nimal.

'My pleasure, Nimal,' grinned Corazon, 'although, honestly, if you were less "gentlemanlike" you wouldn't have needed assistance.'

'Mea culpa,' said Nimal meekly, making sure the knots were secure. He winked at the girls, and continued loudly, 'Do you think it's safe to leave them here? What if the bears get them?'

The male crook shook with fear and began to whimper; the entire bush shook, too.

'Good point, bro,' said Anu. 'What do you think, C?'

'They'll be okay if they stay still,' said Corazon. 'If the bears see the bushes shaking they'll investigate.'

The crook promptly stopped shaking, and Nimal said kindly, 'Good man. We're taking your guns, so if you're found by bears, you'll only have yourselves to blame. Goodbye!'

A few minutes later, the JEACs and Hunter left the bush. They had gone through the crooks' pockets and removed everything.

'We'll go to the secret trail entrance and wait for the other two,' said Nimal, as they reached the foot of Anu's tree. 'Agreed that we just follow them instead of trying to capture them?'

'Definitely,' said Anu. 'We need more muscle to tackle two strong guys. I'll update Min-jae and Juanita about the new captures, once we're all in place.'

When Anu had disappeared from sight, CNH made their way to a good hiding place, a short distance from the secret trail entrance.

'AGM, we're set,' said Nimal softly. 'It's 11:40. Any . . .'

'Hold it,' interrupted Gina. 'Bushes moving on east side of clearing. Can see two huge chaps, both wearing jungle green, about five foot eleven and over 100 kilos; one's bald, and the other has a moustache.'

'They have bottles in their hands and are sitting down on rocks at the edge of the clearing,' added Mich.

After five minutes Anu said briefly, 'They're up – moving – *staggering*, towards secret entrance. I think they're drunk. Follow them, over and out.'

'I hope the crooks don't catch them,' said Gina anxiously.

'What if Hunter barks?' added Mich.

'Catch those two and Hunter?' grinned Anu. 'No way! Relax, kiddos, they'll be fine; also, drunk men have deadened senses and slower reflexes. I'll contact GW to collect the two we captured here.'

*****

Team F – Rohan, Chris and Ricky – were in place by 11:15 p.m., under heavy shrubbery with a good view of the firepit.

'Only two and they don't look very tough,' said Chris quietly.

'They could be martial artists,' murmured Rohan. 'Shh. Listen.'

'How long will it take the others to get back?' grumbled the woman, talking as she ate. 'I wish they'd give us details.'

'They've got to bring three boats up river, and Gar has to take another truck to Hing,' said the man. 'They should be here by 1 a.m. to meet the boss.'

'How are we transporting the goods tonight?'

'Crane and trucks; the boats are for us since the trucks will be full. Cover the pot of food for the others. I'll set my alarm for 12:30 and we'll get some sleep; the sleeping bags are near the waterhole.' They disappeared from sight.

'Those snores will frighten away anything,' grinned Ricky, five minutes later. 'What's our plan?'

'Disable two more,' said Rohan, making his way to the waterhole along the edge of the forest, the boys on his heels. 'I'll tackle the guy; you two get the woman – don't let her scream.'

'Piece of cake, that,' said Chris, as they gagged and tied up the crooks. 'I love it when they're taken by surprise – are we going to clear the food, et cetera?'

'No – too risky,' said Rohan, as they tied each crook securely to bushes away from the waterhole, ensuring they could not move an inch. 'Let's get back to our hideout.'

The boys chuckled softly, and were soon hidden once more. At 11:45 Rohan scouted around the clearing, and returned within ten minutes.

'Nothing to be seen or . . .' began Rohan, and broke off when the WT beeped twice, a low owl hoot was heard, followed by two more beeps.

'What's up?' whispered Ricky.

'It's a warning signal we use which means "stay alert, danger",' said Rohan. 'Probably someone coming down the trail.'

Ten minutes later, the camouflage from the secret trail was thrown aside, and two big men staggered into the clearing, not bothering to move quietly.

'Where are the others?' growled the bald man. 'We were told there'd be someone here. I'm hungry.'

'Probably taking a kip,' said the moustached man. He crossed the clearing, checked the shrubbery around the waterhole, and said as he carried two sleeping bags over to his companion, 'Nobody around.'

'They must be close by,' grumbled baldy, pulling a lid off the pot of food.

'Let's eat,' said mustachio. 'And I know where there's beer.'

'Bring it on, mate,' said baldy enthusiastically.

A few minutes later they were eating and drinking; their speech became more slurred. After the meal they threw the plates on the ground, fortified themselves with more beer, and lay on the sleeping bags, boasting about how they would spend the money they would earn from this job. Their rifles were out of reach, near the firepit. Clearly they were more than halfway under the table, and not expecting trouble.

'F, this is CNH,' came Nimal's voice quietly. 'Where are you? Over.'

'Opposite the firepit in a thick bush, five metres east of a forsythia bush. Over.'

'There in two. Over and out,' said Nimal.

Chris and Ricky jumped when Corazon, Hunter and Nimal joined them.

'Man, you're quiet,' gasped Ricky.

'Who are these chaps, yaar?' asked Rohan quietly, patting Hunter as the dog licked him thoroughly.

'Replenishments for the disappearing troops,' grinned Nimal. 'Their boss won't be pleased – they're high as kites.'

'Any others?' said Rohan.

'We got two more,' said Corazon.

'We knew these two were coming here, since they were shouting it out to the world, so we used a quicker trail. Anu's going to update Min-jae and ask CO to join you after capturing Hing. AGM are safe in a tree,' said Nimal.

'Where are the other crooks?' asked Corazon. 'I thought there'd be more.'

Rohan updated them. 'It should be easy to put these two away before the rest arrive.' He outlined his plan and the group split up, and moved into action.

'Good evening. Who are you?' said Corazon, entering the clearing from the shrubbery near the waterhole.

Both men sat up and turned towards her; seeing who it was, however, they laughed and lay down again.

'What are you twins doing in the forest at this time of the night?' slurred baldy. 'Aren't you scared of the bears?'

'I think there's only one girl,' mumbled mustachio. 'Did you see any beers – I mean, bears?'

'I came after my dog who ran away. I'm hungry, and I think I'm lost.'

'Silly girls,' said baldy. 'Grab plates and help yourselves. The food's on the rock.'

'Thanks,' said Corazon, and went towards the firepit and the rifles.

The men began arguing about whether there was one girl or two. When the four boys and Hunter charged them, the crooks attempted to rise, but staggered and fell down.

'Pure walkover!' chortled Ricky, as they dragged away the now unconscious men, securely tied and gagged, and tethered them under two separate bushes deeper in the forest. Corazon and Chris tidied the place.

'They'll sleep it off. Good work, everyone, and well played, Corazon and twin,' grinned Rohan, when they were in their hideout once more. 'Nobody would guess anyone had ever been around here.'

'I threw away the pot of food, too,' chuckled Corazon. 'The boss and the others will be mad.'

Rohan asked Min-jae to make arrangements to collect four more – after 1:30 a.m. 'The GW group are tickled pink,' reported back Rohan. 'They like our *divide and conquer* strategy.'

'How many to go, Rohan?' asked Nimal.

'As far as we've heard, two with Kylie and three returning from various tasks,' said Rohan. 'It's 12:25; Kylie et al should arrive in ten minutes or so, and Gar may come here via the culvert. CO should join us soon.'

'Did you see any bears?' asked Chris.

'Yes – and we got Hunter to make a noise and scare them south of GW,' said Nimal. 'I hate frightening animals, but it was a necessity.'

'How do we make sure no grizzlies . . .' began Ricky, when Hunter growled, and everyone froze.

'Something's moving near the secret entrance,' whispered Nimal.

A head peered into the opening cautiously – it was Kylie. She looked all around, muttered something over her shoulder, and emerged warily, followed by Sheila and Rizvi. They carried rifles and didn't bother to camouflage the secret trail.

Ricky began to take pictures. The crooks circled the clearing and returned to the rocks.

'Where's everyone?' said Kylie angrily.

'Perhaps they're sleeping behind the waterhole,' said Rizvi, going over. He returned, looking puzzled. 'It doesn't look as if anyone's been there.'

'The firepit's not been used either,' said Sheila. 'It's covered with sand.'

'Something's up,' said Kylie. 'Everyone, other than Gar, Len and Tig should be here. Get some cans of food, and let's eat while we wait for the others.'

'It's 12:40 and those three should be here by 1 a.m., right?' said Rizvi, opening cans with a penknife.

Kylie took a plate of food from Sheila without a word of thanks. 'Yeah, and I asked for four more. This is the worst operation I've ever been in – and those kids are a menace.'

'At least some of the kids were caught,' said Rizvi viciously. 'That guy, Jason, seems to be very friendly with them.'

'Yeah – I don't trust him. I tried to get him fired,' said Kylie, 'but Santos and Remo think he's a good worker because he can operate any piece of machinery, and learns fast. However, I made sure he wasn't given too many night shifts.'

'If we can get two or three bears tonight, and another four over the next two weeks, we'll meet our quota,' said Sheila. 'I can't wait to finish this job – grizzlies are scary.'

'I'm not scared of anything,' boasted Kylie, finishing her meal. 'I just want a break before the next . . .' She broke off and all three grabbed their rifles.

'Thank goodness,' said Kylie, lowering her gun as a man and woman joined them. 'How many boats did you get?'

'Three,' said Tig. 'We stole two speedboats from their boathouse.'

'Excellent,' said Kylie, smiling approvingly. 'What about Gar?'

'He was dropping off the truck and should be with us soon. Where's everyone else?' said Len.

'Who knows! For all I know they've gone on vacation. We arrived a few minutes ago, and the clearing looked like nobody'd ever been here,' said Kylie, sitting on a rock.

'Ho Chi and Cita should have been here,' said Len, eating hungrily.

'Hopefully they've gone after bears,' grunted Kylie, 'but they should have waited for my orders.'

'What's the plan, boss?' asked Tig.

'Once Gar arrives, we pair up and go to the three waterholes south-east of the clearing opposite the crane. We'll drive the bears to that clearing and kill them there. Gar would have parked his cell phone in the usual spot near the entrance to our secret trail, and as soon as we get even one bear, we'll alert Hing – the crane basket can take two at a time.'

'What about fire this time?' asked Len.

'You're a pyromaniac,' said Kylie with a grim laugh. She seemed to like him and Tig. 'No. Heard about all the forest fires? It's too risky and we can't get . . .' She stopped abruptly. Everyone picked up their rifles, staring towards the east trail.

'Only me,' said a male voice, and Gar emerged, rifle in hand.

'Good – grab some food and eat fast,' said Kylie. 'All set?'

'Yeah. I didn't see Hing and couldn't waste time trying to find or call him,' said Gar. 'The truck's parked next to the other two, and the cell phone's in place.'

'He's probably in the cabin having a nap, knowing nothing will happen before 1:30 a.m.' said Sheila.

'Right,' said Kylie. She updated Gar and continued, 'If those kids are around, get them – but for goodness' sake don't kill anyone; we can't risk a major felony.'

'But we got five,' said Tig. 'How many brats *are* there?'

'Too many,' said Kylie. 'You got the younger kids; there are five more – three strong-looking boys who are nearly six feet or over, and two girls.'

'You think they'll be wandering around tonight?' said Len.

'Doubtful – they're teens!' said Sheila snippily. 'My son's seventeen, and only wants to sleep. It's the younger kids who have more energy and probably thought they'd have fun while their elders slept.' The others laughed and agreed.

'What about that guy Jason, and Centre staff?' said Gar.

'I think Jason's on vacation since he wanted some days off,' said Kylie, 'and the Centre's short-staffed. Now listen up.

'At 4 a.m. sharp, quit everything. Len, Gar, get to the construction site via the north tunnel and meet Hing – cover up the goods properly and get out of there fast. The rest of us will meet at the boats and get to the south tunnel. Our ride won't arrive until 7:30. If everyone's not at the boats by 4:30, whoever's there, take a boat and go immediately – we need to get through the lake before daylight. Clear?'

'Sure,' said Tig.

'It's 12:55,' said Kylie. 'We'll give the others twenty minutes more. The pairs are: me and Tig, Gar and Len, Rizvi and Sheila. Sheila, call Hing – don't forget to put the cell back in place.'

'Right,' said everyone, and fell silent.

'Wonder if Anu et al got the mobile,' muttered Nimal. 'I . . .' he broke off as their WTs beeped.

'Teams CNH and F here; update, over,' said Rohan, softly.

'We're at GW. Hing captured, disabled two trucks, moved crane, cops also covering construction site and north culvert. You? Over,' said Amy briefly.

'Good job,' said Rohan. 'Six crooks at F waiting for cops. Crooks stole two Manipau boats which we must recover, over.'

'Okay. Do we join you? Over.'

'Negative,' said Rohan. 'Ask cops to cover south culvert, inside and outside Manipau, and be ready at the eastern lakeside. Q, join us; Amy, Jason, go to CBI, contact AGM and CNH; CNH will get to CBI. Strategy – chase bears from three waterholes south of CBI. The rest of us will join you ASAP. CNH will update you further at CBI. Over.'

'On it; our ETA at CBI approximately 1:10 a.m. – we'll take shortcuts and run. Anything else? Over,' said Amy.

'Chris, Ricky – can either of you handle a boat?' said Nimal.

'I can,' said Chris, 'and what's ETA?'

'Estimated Time of Arrival,' explained Nimal. 'Rohan, can these chaps, Mich, Gina and Hunter, take one boat and hide in the shrubbery on the south shore, or is it too dangerous with the kids?'

'We'll look after them,' said Ricky eagerly.

'Okay,' said Rohan. 'CNH, get going; update AGM; Ricky and Chris will come with Q, and I'll join you ASAP.'

Nimal, Corazon and Hunter crept away, and there was silence for fifteen minutes.

'How long before Umedh . . .' began Chris, and broke off as the WTs beeped again.

'F, come in, Q in vicinity, over,' said Umedh.

Rohan gave Umedh their location. 'Six in clearing, over and out.'

'Man, you guys are so quiet,' murmured Ricky, when Umedh joined them two minutes later.

'Experience, yaar, and I didn't want to get eaten by a grizzly,' grinned Umedh. 'Everything arranged. Su-bin will contact Aunty Janet and the others.'

'Brill, yaar,' said Rohan.

Umedh listened as Rohan gave him a concise update of the situation, and then said, 'You'll stay until the crooks start moving?' Rohan nodded. 'You'll need this for later – press down and push,' and Umedh handed him a package.

'Good man, Q,' grinned Rohan.

'Let's go, boys,' said Umedh, and Ricky and Chris, who were dying to know what the package contained, left reluctantly with him.

Rohan kept watch, listening intently to last-minute instructions from Kylie. At 1:15 a.m. Kylie rose, and they left via the secret trail, this time camouflaging it behind them. Rohan sped off to join the others.

CHAPTER 19

The Victorious Chase

At CBI, the JEACs quickly updated each other.

'We have their mobile – it's turned off,' said Anu. 'I used a hanky in case there were fingerprints.'

'We have six to deal with,' said Umedh. He looked at Amy and Jason who had large packages on their backs. 'What have you got there?'

They unstrapped the packages and gave them to Nimal and Chris. 'Water skis, Q – two pairs,' grinned Amy. 'If Corazon and Nimal go with the boat crew, Nimal and Mich know what to do, right?'

'Yes,' chuckled Mich. 'You want us to fix these so you can chase the crooks.'

'Absolutely, hon,' smiled Amy. 'Although it's a bit cloudy, there's a full moon tonight and Rohan and I are good waterskiers. Once the water skis are fixed, take our speed boats down river, beyond the first curve; hide the one with the water skis so it's not visible from the river, and you kids and Hunter take the other to the south shore. Nimal and Corazon, return to us. The rest we'll play by ear.'

'Brill,' gasped the JEACs.

'The crooks will have to manage in one boat – theirs,' said Jason.

'Let's get moving,' said Umedh. 'Nimal and Corazon, be careful, okay?'

'Sure, and we'll join you in half an hour,' said Corazon. 'I know lots of shortcuts.'

The six of them, with Hunter, sped away.

'I guess . . .' began Umedh, when the WTs beeped. 'Q here, over.'

'Where are you? They'll be at CBI soon, over,' said Rohan.

'Do we need anyone to stay here? Over,' said Anu.

'Negative,' said Rohan. 'They're going to the three waterholes, but aren't familiar with area. Update, over.'

'Four here, and we'll cover the three waterholes: Anu, Jason middle, Amy and you west; I'll do east and CNH will join me, over,' said Umedh.

'Okay. Four minutes from west waterhole, over,' said Rohan.

'If you see any bears, frighten them away – preferably *south* of us. Over and out,' said Amy.

The JEACs sped off, ensuring that they were upwind of any animals. There were more than ten grizzlies, and some cubs, around the three waterholes, but the JEACs made sufficient noise and chased them southwards.

'AR in position,' said Amy.

Seconds later Umedh reported. 'CN with me; kids should be at south shore in twenty minutes. Over.'

'Good. Stay tuned – I hear noises,' said Rohan. He listened hard, and said, 'Crooks arriving, splitting up to come to other locations. Over and out.'

The JEACs tensed. The crooks didn't lower their voices as they went into hiding, and were clearly disappointed there were no bears at the waterholes.

'It's 2 a.m.,' said Kylie, a little later, not bothering to speak softly. 'I suppose they're still eating.' She and Tig were in a tree opposite Rohan and Amy.

'Probably – they're huge,' said Tig. Clearly neither of them knew much about bears. 'How will we load them into the basket?'

'As soon as we hear shots, we'll know someone's got a bear. Everyone gets to the clearing to help push them into the crane basket,' said Kylie. 'Six of us should be able to do that. Hopefully the others are chasing bears towards the clearing even now, and we'll hear shots soon,' said Kylie.

'Wonder what happened to the cell. You think Gar forgot where he put it but doesn't want to admit it?' said Tig.

'Probably,' said Kylie. 'He's rather dim. Anyway, no biggie; Hing knows that if cell phone reception is out, we'll chuck stones over the wall when we have a bear.'

The JEACs went into a low-voiced conference over the WTs, and then crept out of their hiding places. Ten minutes later, shots rang out north of the waterholes – one, two, three, four!

'Let's go,' said Kylie, quickly scrambling down the tree. 'Maybe we've got at least two.'

Within minutes the six crooks were hiding around the clearing.

'Who's there? If you shot a bear, where is it?' shouted Kylie, peering cautiously out of the shrubbery.

'We heard four shots and came running,' called Len. 'We haven't seen any bears.'

'Neither have we,' said Sheila.

'Must be one of the other groups,' said Kylie. She and Tig cautiously entered the clearing, guns at the ready. 'Come out, everyone, and stay alert.'

'Only six of us,' said Len, as they gathered in a tight circle, looking around nervously as the moon came out from behind a cloud and lit up the clearing. 'Didn't any of you fire a gun?'

'No,' said the others, looking puzzled.

'Cita! Ho Chi! Are you here?' called Kylie.

More gunshots were fired, and the crooks crouched instinctively. 'GET THEM!' shouted several stentorian voices. The shrubbery in six or seven places around the clearing rustled and glaring lights hit the group of crooks.

'I can't see,' yelled Rizvi and Tig, covering their eyes.

'Run! To the boats,' screamed Kylie, shielding her eyes, and shooting indiscriminately into the rustling shrubbery.

She grabbed Tig, while Gar caught Rizvi's arm, and the six of them raced eastwards into the forest, still shooting.

'Excellent work, JEACs; now to *our* boat,' chuckled Rohan. 'Everyone got their ropes back?'

'Yes,' they smiled, wrapping lengths of rope around their waists, and following Corazon south-east.

'That was a super trick – tying our ropes to bushes five metres away so the crooks shot into them and not at us,' chuckled Jason.

'Done it before, yaar,' said Nimal, 'and it works like a charm.'

'What were those lights you flashed?' asked Corazon.

'Q's invention, completed earlier today,' said Rohan, showing them the implement. 'Like spotlights or car high beams which blind anyone for a few seconds. Q put them into a casing which looks and acts like a torch. Do you have a name for it, yaar?'

'Waiting for one of you to name it; I've done my part,' grinned Umedh.

'Brill, Umedh,' said Anu. 'How about *sporch* – combination of spotlight and torch?'

'Perfect!' agreed everyone.

'It's nearly 2:40,' said Rohan.

'And here we are,' said Corazon, as they reached the river and the hidden boat.

Nimal took the wheel and they set off. By 3:02 a.m. they were moored in a good hiding spot, close to where the river flowed through the lake. Rohan and Amy put on their waterskis.

'Will all six crooks fit in their boat?' asked Anu.

'At a squash, which will slow them down,' said Nimal.

'Tie yourselves to the boat, so you can't fall out – we're going to do some trick skiing,' said Rohan. 'Nimal, begin the routine as soon as they enter the lake – we'll have lots of moonlight. Corazon and Anu, stay down and flash the sporches so the crooks can't see properly to shoot. Umedh and Jason, use your air guns to put holes in the boat; Amy and I'll ski behind.'

'But you'll be targets,' protested Corazon.

'No way,' chuckled Nimal. 'They've been training to do various stunts. Wait and see!'

'This'll be some chase!' said Jason. 'Will they be here soon?'

'Judging by the direction they took off in, they'll have to go north-east to reach their boat,' said Amy.

It was nearly 3:25 a.m. when a boat came in sight.

'All six of them with Kylie at the wheel – excellent, she can't shoot,' muttered Anu. 'Hope the kids won't try to join us too soon.'

'I told them to wear lifejackets, and stay clear,' said Umedh.

'Good thinking, mate,' said Jason. He and Umedh were secured by ropes, crouching low in the boat, guns at the ready; Anu and Corazon were also secure and had a sporch each.

'Ready everyone?' asked Nimal.

'Yes!' chorused the others, and the chase began. Nimal increased speed, and the motor roared into life. The crooks looked back fearfully.

'JEACS TO THE RESCUE!' yelled Nimal.

'Faster, Kylie,' roared Gar.

'Shoot them!' yelled Kylie, speeding up and turning into the lake as the JEACs had guessed she would.

Anu and Corazon shone their sporches at the crooks. Gar and Tig, trying to aim at the JEACs, were blinded and their shots went wide, but Jason and Umedh scored.

'Something hit the boat near me,' screamed Sheila, 'and we're taking in water.'

'Stick something in it,' shrieked Kylie, trying, unsuccessfully, to increase speed and beginning to weave in the middle of the lake.

There was utter confusion in her boat. The crooks' bullets were useless: they were unused to shooting from a speeding, weaving boat and were blinded by the sporches, and Nimal was also weaving at an unbelievable speed. Jason and Umedh kept up a steady fire, and more bullets hit Kylie's boat. Amy and Rohan were also jumping and weaving all over the place.

'Watch out!' roared Len, as a motorboat sped out from the north shore, and a megaphone was heard over the sounds of the chase.

'This is the police! Pull over and surrender!' came a stentorian voice, as the police motorboat prevented the crooks from approaching the northern shore of the lake and a floodlight was shone on their boat.

Kylie turned her boat in a tight circle and raced east again. The JEACs turned, too, and sped past the crooks, forcing them northwards again. Nimal accelerated.

Amy and Rohan jumped! They flew right over the crooks, who ducked in fright. Kylie lost her focus, swerved sharply, and with a loud CRASH, rammed into the north bank. Releasing their waterskis, Amy and Rohan dived safely into the lake.

The crooks, thrown out of the boat, were stunned by the impact and lay groaning on the ground. Police and Manipau staff captured them easily.

'HURRAY! WE GOT THEM!' shouted several voices, as Chris and the others sped up, Hunter barking excitedly.

The JEACs and police moored their boats near the crash scene, and everyone jumped out. 'That was awesome!' chorused the JEACs, as Rohan and Amy swam up.

'And scary!' exclaimed Janet.

'Excellent work, JEACs!' applauded Chief Inspector Geraldine.

'Did you collect everyone we captured tonight?' asked Rohan.

'We did, JEACs – your strategy of "divide and conquer" has worked well with so many crooks.'

'It certainly did, and we have an excellent team,' grinned Rohan.

'We had a superb time,' said Jason, 'and I'm sure there'll be a tightening of procedures in the hiring process from now on.'

'Definitely,' said Inspector Geraldine.

'Let's meet at Tranquillity when you're done,' said Janet. 'We all want details.'

'Gee whizz, it's nearly 4:30, Mom,' said Amy. 'Could we have a big breakfast? I'm sure . . .'

'Nimal's simply STARVING!' shouted the JEACs.

'*Rem acu tetigisti!* It's a growing boy I am, mes amis,' grinned Nimal.

'*Rem* whatter?' chuckled Chris.

'It's Latin and means "You hit the nail on the head",' chorused Mich and Gina, and everyone burst out laughing.

CHAPTER 20

We Saved Our Grizzly Bears!

By 5:30 a.m., everyone gathered to enjoy a hearty breakfast in the large dining room at Tranquillity, including Inspector Geraldine and two of her team. They ate quickly and adjourned to a large meeting room.

'Please give us details,' said Inspector Geraldine, setting up a recording device on the table.

'Anu, why don't you do the usual?' suggested Rohan.

'Jason, Corazon, Ricky and Chris,' said Anu, 'I'll be the narrator and will ask each of you to participate, okay?' They nodded, and Anu began.

Everyone listened intently as Anu competently pieced together the tale, and each JEAC participated.

'Very skilfully related, JEACs,' praised Inspector Geraldine, when they had finished. 'And thanks to your pictures and sketches, we have good evidence. Needless to say, you've done an excellent job!'

'It was our pleasure, Inspector!' chorused the JEACs.

'Please let us know if you need more from us,' added Rohan. 'Also, do you think Kylie was the "big boss" of the gang or is she reporting to someone higher up?'

'Good point, Rohan,' said Inspector Geraldine. 'Unfortunately, it sounds like she was in charge of this particular assignment, but isn't the ring leader.'

'An international gang?' suggested Rohan.

'Possibly,' said the inspector. 'We'll keep in touch, if you like.'

'Yes, please,' said Rohan.

'Won't you find the rest of your stay boring after this adventure?' said Inspector Geraldine, smiling around the group.

'I'm for a quiet life, Inspector,' said Nimal. 'Bed and food – that's all I . . .'

'. . . and a few million animals, including bears, reindeer, foxes, badgers, dogs, et cetera,' chuckled Janet. 'THANK YOU for saving our grizzlies, JEACs – which obviously includes you, Jason . . . it means a lot to . . .' she choked and held out her arms to embrace them all.

Joyfully everyone hugged one another.

'We'll make sure you don't find life too slow . . .' began Kafil.

'We'll put them to work,' said Sheri promptly. 'Education sessions for the animals, especially grizzlies, on how to use WTs, duck bullets and . . .' She disappeared amidst the group of JEACs who hugged her till she cried for mercy.

'We have a fundraiser coming up, more animals to meet at the animal nursery and observe in the wild, plus exploring all around Manipau,' said Umedh.

'And *we're* going to learn how to waterski,' said Mich.

'Yes, we want to do stunts like Rohan and Amy,' added Gina.

'Sounds great,' chuckled Inspector Geraldine. She rose and shook hands with everyone. 'Thanks, again, JEACs. Have a good rest and I'll see you at the fundraiser.'

'Bed, everyone,' said Janet. 'You'd better sleep here – it's 9 a.m. and everyone looks sleepy and dopey.'

'I . . . think I'm t-too tall for a-a d-dwarf,' stuttered Nimal, trying, unsuccessfully, to stifle his yawns.

'BED!' said Sheri, pushing him out of the room.

A few minutes later, the JEACs were fast asleep.

*****

'I love meeting C-ites,' said Nimal, two days later. It was 5 a.m. and the group, including Jason and Sheri, were at GW, preparing for a work session with a group of 33 youngsters, most belonging to Manipau staff. The families had returned from their various vacations, and the kids were eager to meet the JEACs.

'I'll ask,' sighed Chris, winking at Jason and Ricky. 'C-ites, yaar?'

'People who live on conservation centres, yaar,' said Nimal, looking astonished. 'Get with it, kids! It's high time . . .' He collapsed under the combined weight of the three boys.

'Kids, my left foot, as Anu would say,' chuckled Corazon.

'Hey, JEACs – order!' said Anu sternly. 'We have 33 JEACs, ranging in age from four to twenty-four, arriving at 8:30 a.m., including Sorena, Corben, and their group of JEACs, as well as Sorena's younger brothers, Gabriel and Joel, and Corben's sister, Brinn. Maddison, who recently started a JEACs group with some friends, is joining us as well. So, unless you want to spend the morning cooking, while we make decisions without you, *behave yourselves*, or my left foot will . . .'

'Aunty! Are you *threatening* us?' interrupted Nimal, pretending to be horrified.

'Naturally!' said Anu attempting, unsuccessfully, to look grim. 'Now, shake a leg, folks, and . . .' She stopped and burst out laughing as every one of them shook a leg vigorously. 'You're incorrigible.'

'Agreed,' chuckled Amy. 'Blame Sheri – she told us to shake our legs next time you used that phrase.'

'*Sheri!* You little wretch!' gasped Anu, wiping away tears of laughter. 'And now I have a stitch in my side.'

'I'm as good as gold,' grinned Sheri. 'But you do use the weirdest expressions.'

They chuckled as they got back to work; they were in high spirits, and the joking and teasing was endless. There would be over 45 people attending the meeting and having lunch, before splitting up into smaller groups.

The JEACs, C-ite kids, and a few other special guests were responsible for the entertainment at the fundraiser. To add to the fun, Remo was back; Chris Larkin, his brother, Jack, parents from India and friends from Australia had all arrived; Chris-J and Ricky's parents would join them in a few days.

The dogs and cubs were hilarious: Sam kept trying to herd the cubs; Codey was an anxious babysitter since the cubs could now climb out of their playpen – they wandered around freely, and were thoroughly spoilt. Hunter was never hungry because everyone knew about his unusual method with watermelon and grapes, and fed him constantly, watching gleefully as he carefully spat out the seeds.

'Brekker's ready, kids,' yelled Sheri, at 6:30 a.m., playing a loud solo on a dinner gong, and everyone rushed into the kitchen.

'We're simply STARVING!' shrieked Mich, Gina and Corazon, trying to yell over the sound of the gong.

'And now I'm simply DEAF!' said Sheri, ceasing her efforts.

The group ate, cleared up, and then went upstairs to prepare for the meeting.

'Gina and Mich, would you teach the others to sing both our theme song as well as *The Humming Bear Cubs* song?' said Amy. 'Mom said she'd do three training sessions prior to the fundraiser.'

'Sure,' said Gina. 'Chris and Ricky, would you help us with the singing and music? Corazon's playing the piano.'

'No problemo,' said Chris. He and Ricky were good guitarists.

'I hear wheels,' said Mich running to a window. 'The JEACs are arriving!'

A few minutes later, groups of youngsters began arriving in batches and were greeted warmly by the JEACs. Once everyone was seated, Sheri, who was chairing the meeting, suggested a round of introductions.

Everyone was delighted to meet the GW JEACs, and gave them a round of applause for saving the grizzly bears. After the meeting, and a session where the singers learned the songs, they stopped for lunch and got to know each other better.

The small group sessions began after lunch, and each group planned their segment of the programme. At 5 p.m. the entire group gathered together, once more, to report on their plans. An hour later everyone, except for three C-ites, reluctantly left GW.

'We heard about the killings, through Dad,' said Suzanne, Shawn's oldest daughter, who was a vivacious nineteen-year-old, 'and it nearly ruined my trip to Ireland.'

'That's too bad,' said Jason. 'Was it the first time you'd been there?'

'The second,' smiled Suzanne. 'I called Dad daily, and danced for joy when I heard how all of you caught the crooks. Thank you so much. I'm going to be working with grizzlies when I've finished my degree in anthropology.'

'That's awesome,' said Jason. 'My recent adventures made me eager to learn more. I could use some help.'

'I'd love to help you, Jason,' said Suzanne.

Nimal looked from one to the other, winked at Anu, and began to hum 'Bachelor Boy' loudly. Jason grinned, but ignored him. Amy threw a cushion at Nimal.

'Suzanne, Fadi and Marco, do stay for supper,' said Rohan hospitably.

'We'd love to,' said Fadi eagerly, 'but my dad's picking us up at seven.'

'I'd like to stay,' said Suzanne.

'We could drive all of you home afterwards,' offered Jason, eagerly. 'Don't you live fairly close to each other?'

'We do,' said Suzanne, 'but I'd hate to inconvenience you.'

'No problemo,' said Rohan, when Jason looked at him. 'What do you suggest, yaar?'

'You and I could take a Land Rover; we'll drop the boys first and then Suzanne,' said Jason, gratefully.

'Sounds good,' said Umedh. 'I'll call the parents.'

They had a merry supper and the three C-ites fit right in with the JEACs.

'What was it like in Dubai, Fadi?' asked Anu. 'It looks very exotic in some pictures, and so Disney-like in others.'

'It's a combination,' said Fadi. 'The UAE has tons of money, and does everything in style. It was fun!'

'The sheikh invited us to his palace for a meal,' said Marco, 'and it was sumptuous! He was a very nice man. When he heard about the JEACs, and how all of us were involved in conservation work, lived on centres, and endeavoured to create awareness and educate people about the importance of saving our planet, he seemed very interested. He asked for Dad's phone number.'

'Why?' said Mich.

'Don't know,' said Fadi. 'Marco and I were thrilled when we met with some relatives; they're going to start three JEACs groups in their schools.'

'Yeah, that was cool,' said Marco. 'Have any of you been to Dubai?'

'No, but I'd love to visit,' said Amy.

'Time to move, folks,' said Rohan, looking at his watch. 'We told your parents we'd bring you back by 9:30.'

'Wow, time flies when you're having fun,' said Fadi, as they thanked everyone.

'See you tomorrow, folks,' called the JEACs, as Jason drove off, Suzanne beside him, the other three in the back.

'So much for our *bachelor boy*,' grinned Nimal.

'You're not to rag or embarrass him, Nimal,' warned Anu.

'He won't be embarrassed, Anu,' said Nimal. 'In fact, if we *don't* tease him, he'll wonder what's wrong with us. He's cool, and Suzanne's got a wicked sense of humour – did you hear her teasing some of the others? It's a perfect match.'

'Agreed,' admitted Anu, while Amy and Umedh nodded. 'And thank goodness he's not the soppy kind. I wish we weren't all growing up so fast,' she added with a sigh.

Amy gave her a hug, winked at Umedh and Nimal, and said, 'Cheer up, hon! Remember we're going to stay "forever young" in your books, and you can remove every hint of romance from them, if you wish.'

Anu hugged her back as the others laughed. She said, with a chuckle, 'Darling Amy, my brother would murder me if he was forced to stay a kid forever! Now Nimal's a completely different matter.'

'Little wretch,' said Nimal, grinning at her. 'You just wait until I doctor your bed . . .' He broke off as they heard wheels. 'I'll be good, Aunty, for now.'

Jason and Rohan walked into the kitchen.

'Anyone for a last cup of chocolate before we hit the sack?' offered Nimal. 'The kettle's on the boil, and I know the kids will have some.'

'Yes, please,' said the group, and a few minutes later everyone was in the living room, sipping companionably.

'You know, reflecting on this holiday, there was a very interesting feature which stood out,' said Anu thoughtfully.

'What was it, Anu?' said Corazon, who liked trying to figure out Anu's ideas. 'Is it the way the crooks behaved and their psychology?'

'Or perhaps the way Jason . . .' began Nimal, breaking off when Amy, Ricky and Chris threatened to choke him.

'It just happened again!' chuckled Anu. 'It's been a holiday of unfinished or interrupted sentences. I'm . . .' she broke off, and ran out of the room, leaving the others in splits of laughter.

*****

The day of the fundraiser dawned – it was a gorgeous day!

'Rise and shine, JEACs, all,' sang out Amy, waking the girls in the two rooms they shared.

Anu ran down to the basement to wake the boys.

'It's 4 a.m., Anu,' groaned Nimal.

'And you have a million things to do, amigo,' said Anu, throwing a pillow at him. 'Spit spot, kiddo! Brekker in half an hour.'

She raced upstairs to join Amy and Sheri in the kitchen, and they started preparing breakfast. The others joined them quickly.

The fundraiser would be held on the south shore of the lake. Since a huge crowd was expected, flat screens and loudspeakers had been set up so that everyone could see and hear what was happening on the big stage.

'I can't wait to meet our chief guest, Dr. Doug Wrightman,' said Nimal. 'When's he coming?'

'Around 1 p.m. for the opening at 2,' said Amy. 'He's such a wonderful man and highly qualified. He's a passionate conservationist and renowned vet in Canada, and travels to other countries to perform life-saving surgery on animals, speak at numerous conferences, lecture at universities, et cetera. Listing all his accomplishments would take hours. His wife, Kestra, and kids – Braedon and Kasen – are lovely, too.'

'Yes, and we're lucky that they'll be spending a week at Manipau,' said Rohan. 'We won't have time to chat today.'

'It was very kind of him to agree to lunch with us tomorrow,' said Anu. 'I'm longing to hear about his experiences with wildlife.'

They finished breakfast, and then it was time to leave – 5:30 a.m. did not seem too early, given all the work to be completed prior to the opening.

Needless to say, Dr. Doug opened the fundraiser with an inspiring talk on the importance of conservation, and Manipau rang with cheers at the end of his speech.

Once the cheers had died down, Chris Larkin said, 'Before Dr. Doug declares the fundraiser open, I have an announcement. Some of you know what occurred at Manipau recently, and we wouldn't have had the heart to hold this fundraiser if not for a very special group of youngsters. Could the founding group of JEACs, as well as those who joined them and worked to save our grizzly bears, please come on stage – that includes Hunter, Sam and Codey.'

'Lead the way, kiddo,' said Sheri, pushing a reluctant Rohan forward. 'Follow him, kids; you too, Jason.'

The group climbed onto the stage, along with the dogs. Obeying Sheri, they stood in a row.

'First, let me inform everyone that Hurit, the mother grizzly that was badly injured some weeks ago, is recovering well, as is the male bear that was injured a few days ago. Secondly, these JEACs have resolved a problem which would otherwise have resulted in the tragic loss of many more grizzlies,' said Chris. He introduced the JEACs individually. 'These youngsters have varying talents, but in one cause they are identical – in their love for all animals and nature, and their eagerness to educate the world about the importance of saving our planet. Let's give them a cheer!'

Manipau rang with cheers again: for the JEACs, for their dedication, for the safety of their animals, and just in general joy and enthusiasm.

'JEACs, we had lengthy discussions on how to express our thanks,' said Chris, 'although I know you don't expect anything. But I'd like the following to join me: Dr. Doug, Jack, Janet, Lisa, Rani, Remo, Sheri, Hassan, Kafil, Shawn and Tulok! Also, JEACs: Corben, Sorena and Brinn.'

Once they were gathered on the stage, Dr. Doug drew back a curtain, revealing another section of the stage. Each of the adults wheeled a trolley to the front of the stage, while the three JEACs brought out smaller trolleys. At a signal from Chris, the trolleys were uncovered.

'CHOCOLATE CAKE! Hurray!' shouted the JEACs, and a collective whoop of delight went up from everyone. The icing on the cakes read: WELL DONE, JEACS – AND THANK YOU!

The dogs set up an excited barking – on each of the smaller trolleys were doggie dishes with wonderful treats in them. Brinn, Corben and Sorena placed the dishes on the stage and the dogs tucked in.

'And there'll be a piece of cake for everyone,' announced Chris.

'I always *knew* Canada had a good recipe for chocolate cake,' said Nimal, cheekily, as everyone on stage hugged the JEACs. 'When do we taste it?'

'Soon,' said Chris. 'But first, we have a special song, composed and produced by Gina and Mich.'

A stand with a keyboard, guitars and a drum set was rolled forward. A team of 50 JEACs took the stage, with Janet as conductor, and began to sing.

At Manipau in Canada, we're happy to be here;
We're having so much fun you see, we simply have to cheer –
Hurray!
There's Codey, Sam and Hunter – and a cuddly cub or two
Who, when you're feeding them their milk, will hum along with you!

With Ataneq and Atka we are having quite a blast;
Their mother Hurit was quite hurt but she's recov'ring fast.
And when it looked like grizzlies were being killed at Manipau,
We had to stop those horrid folks, and give them to the law.

Our group of JEACs have resolved a mystery or two,
And Jason soon became a friend, he joined our human zoo.
With crooks emerging left and right, we changed accordingly:
'Divide and Conquer' was the name of our new strategy.

We checked out culverts, rivers, cranes, and found some hidden trails,
Then we all searched for evidence – clue hunting never fails.
And when they captured some of us, and tied us hands and knees,
The older JEACs rescued us, some swinging down from trees.

The boss of all the crooks was in the final group of six;
They tried to kill more grizzlies, but we JEACs played some tricks.
With water skiing stunts and sporches, plus a speedboat chase,
We raced after the nasty crooks, and won the final race!

So let's rejoice and sing, dear friends, we've saved our grizzly bears!
Some sentences are incomplete, and really no one cares.
The most important thing we know is animals are GREAT;
We'll have a grand old time today. *Come on – let's celebrate!*

Cheers filled Manipau. Then everyone joined in singing the song with the JEACs – several times.

The fundraiser was a HUGE success! People from all around Canada, the United States and a few other countries had flocked to Manipau, and over two million dollars was raised for wildlife conservation.

The programmes and events were a success. Sorena, Corben and Brinn, along with the rest of their JEACs group, were thrilled to participate with the founders, and delighted to spend the next three days with them.

Rohan, Umedh, Amy, Nimal, Anu, Gina and Mich, together with Hunter, were taking a well-earned rest, when Fadi and Marco raced up.

'Come quick,' shouted Marco.

'Where, kiddo?' said Amy, as he tugged her hand and Fadi pulled Rohan and Umedh.

'To the lake,' yelled Fadi. 'Somebody wants to meet you.'

'Ah, they want our autographs,' said Nimal. 'Will they pay well?'

'Nutcase,' laughed Marco, who was nearly as crazy as Nimal. 'Hurry!'

They followed the boys, and saw Hassan, Jim Patel, Jack Larkin, Chris and Janet speaking with a man who was wearing a dishdash and keffiyeh. He looked very elegant.

'Who's that?' whispered Mich to Gina as they neared the group.

'Don't know,' said Gina. 'He looks Arabian.'

'Shh,' said Anu, as Fadi and Marco raced ahead, calling out to Hassan.

The group of adults turned to greet them.

'JEACs, this is Abdul Al Sami, one of the sheikhs in Dubai,' said Janet. 'Marco's father works for him.'

'I am delighted to meet you, JEACs,' said Sheikh Abdul Al Sami, shaking hands with each of them, including Hunter who very politely offered a paw. 'I've heard about you, and your parents, and also about Jack's work in setting up conservations all over the world.'

'It's an honour to meet *you*, sir,' said Rohan. 'Is this your first visit to Manipau?'

'Yes. It is also my first visit to the province of Alberta, although I have been to Toronto and Vancouver several times. This is a beautiful centre.' He paused, looked at Jack, who nodded, and continued, 'I know that you're very busy today, so thank you for allowing me to take up a little of your time.'

'Not at all, sir,' said Umedh. 'It's our pleasure.'

'Thank you,' said the sheikh. 'I have asked Jack to set up a conservation centre in the UAE, and he will be coming over in December. I wondered if all of you, including Hunter, would like to visit us? Marco and Fadi will be there, too. Naturally, I will pay all costs involved. I think you will enjoy seeing a bit of my country.'

'Wow!' gasped the JEACs. 'Thank you *so much*, sir!' Hunter gave a polite bark as well and stood up on his hind legs.

'You are most welcome,' smiled the sheikh, 'and feel free to shout, if you wish! I have nephews and nieces, now young men and women, and I wasted a lot of time telling them to be quiet!'

The JEACs laughed and gave him a rousing cheer.

'Would we also go dune bashing, sir?' asked Mich and Gina.

'Definitely,' said the sheikh. 'And you will see belly dancers, have your hands painted with henna and go sandboarding. I will also send you to visit all the sights in the UAE. I've invited your parents, and they will arrive on the twenty-first of December, so you can spend Christmas together.'

'Awesome!' said Nimal. 'Thank you so much! I've heard that Arabic food is delish, sir.'

'I am sorry to disappoint you, Nimal,' said the sheikh with a straight face, 'but we only eat western food nowadays.'

'Oh, er,' began Nimal, at a loss for once, and then he saw the twinkle in the sheikh's eyes, and grinned. 'Well, sir, I will then have to teach your cooks how to make some good Arabian dishes!'

Everyone burst out laughing, and Nimal had the last word, when he said, 'I'll also teach them how to make a good chocolate cake!'

Sheikh Abdul Al Sami chuckled over Nimal's cheekiness and cuffed him playfully. The JEACs left the adults to their talk, after thanking the sheikh once more.

'*Dubai* – Arabian Nights come true! Another country, adventure, animals, and a new conservation to be set up,' said Anu dreamily, as they walked along the shore for a few minutes with Fadi and Marco.

'Earth calling Anu!' said Rohan, grabbing his sister as she was about to walk into the water. 'Sounds fun, doesn't it?'

'ABSOLUTELY!' chorused the others.

Let's leave the JEACs in their happy dream. A visit to Dubai, that exotic land! Who could ask for more?

* * *

GLOSSARY

Word	Meaning
°C	Celsius or Centigrade – a unit of measurement for temperature
Acronym	A word formed from the initial letters of other words
Altruism	Unselfish concern for the welfare of others; selflessness
Amigo mio	My friend – Spanish
APs	Aged Parents – acronym
ASAP	As soon as possible – acronym
ATV	An all-terrain vehicle
Aunty	When used by a kid to another kid – fun usage
Binocs	Binoculars – short form
Biscuits	Cookies
Boot of his car	The trunk of his car
Brekker	Breakfast – short form
Cell phone	Mobile phone
Chopper	Helicopter – short form, casual
C-ite(s)	People who live on conservation centres – fun word, pronounced see-ite
Comfy	Comfortable – short form
Creep	A feeding enclosure for young animals, containing a long, narrow entrance so the mother can't get through, often installed in zoos or conservation centres which have breeding programmes
Cuz	Cousin – short form
Delish	Delicious – short form
Dishdash	An ankle-length garment, usually with long sleeves, similar to a robe. Generally worn by middle eastern men.
ETA	Estimated time of arrival – acronym
Et al	And others – Latin
Exactimo	Exactly – fun usage
Gas/gas station	Petrol/petrol station
Grazie	Thank you – Italian
Grotto	A grotto (Italian) is any type of natural or artificial cave
Hindi	One of the languages of India
Hols	Holidays – short form (vacation)
Hon	Honey – short form
In the offing	Idiom, meaning 'In the near or immediate future; soon to come'
Info	Information – short form
JEACs – CBCK	Canada British Columbia, Kamloops
Je ne comprends pas	I do not understand – French
Jiffy	Unspecified short period of time
Keffiyeh	A traditional Middle Eastern headdress fashioned from a square scarf, usually made of cotton

Word	Meaning
Kilos	Kilograms – short form
Klicks	Kilometres – informal (military) usage
Lab	Laboratory – short form
Lingo	Language – slang
Loony bin	Mental asylum – fun usage, not meant offensively here
Machang	Mate/buddy – used most often in Sri Lanka by males
Mea culpa	My fault – Latin; the direct translation is 'Through (or by) my fault'
Megalomania	A condition or mental illness that causes people to think that they have great or unlimited power or importance
Merci	Thank you – French
Mes amis	My friends – French
Mobile phone	Cell phone
Moi	Me – French
Mon ami	My friend – French
Nineteen to the dozen	Talks a lot – idiom
No problemo	No problem – fun usage of word 'problem'
Non compos	Non compos mentis – Not of sound mind – Latin
Omnivores	Animals that derive their energy and nutrients from a diet consisting of a variety of sources that may include plants, animals, algae and fungi. These animals are called omnivorous.
Oui	Yes – French
Précis (also precis)	A summary or abstract of a text or speech
Pusillanimous	Showing a lack of courage or determination; timid; fainthearted
Put a sock in it	A request to be quiet
QT	Acronym – on the quiet
Queue	Line up
Rem acu tetigisti	Translates as 'You have touched the matter with a needle' – Latin expression meaning 'You have hit the nail on the head'
Sec	Second – short form
Situ	Situation – short form
Spit spot!	Hurry up! – phrase used by Mary Poppins
Sotto voce	In a quiet voice, or as an aside – Italian
Torch	Flashlight
Truck	Lorry
UAE	United Arab Emirates – acronym
Yaar	Mate/buddy – most often used in India by males
You take the entire bakery	To 'win the cake' for being special; to be an extreme case – used here in fun

Poem inspired by the book *Peacock Feathers* by Amelia Lionheart

School is out, but we are not in a pout, at home, but we're getting about
Poachers are low, but we're not going to slow,
      we were careful and we got real low
As we hid in a cave, we really felt brave
Hunter was guard, he was smart, and sometimes they got split apart
Anu and Gina, they loved the arts, we all played our parts
The helicopter flew up but they sent it down,
      then they went to the jail in town.
From: Alexa – Age 10, Canada

Dear Ms. Lionheart, Your book was very good and really interesting. I liked the adventure in it, and how the children planned and caught the poachers. I was sorry for the peacocks when they were caught and left to die, so I was really glad when they got saved. I would like to read another book about the same children solving another animal mystery. *From: Alina – Age 9, France*

Dear Amelia, I enjoy reading your books and going on the adventures with your characters. I can't wait for the next book to come out. *From: Alix – Age 18, Canada*

Dear Ms. Lionheart, I loved your book, *Peacock Feathers*, because it includes my two favourite subjects: animals and mystery. I found the story so exciting I did not want to put it down. My favourite character was the dog Hunter, because he played a key part in stopping the poachers. I am looking forward to reading your next book. *From: Alya – Age 12, France*

Dear Ms. Lionheart, My name is Amanda. I am nine years old. I liked your book because it was about saving animals. I especially liked Gina because she wrote good poems. She helped solve the mystery. It was an exciting mystery book. I hope you write another animal book soon. *From: Amanda – Age 9, Canada*

As an adult, I have thoroughly enjoyed reading Amelia's books. From the beginning to the end of each book the suspense and adventures of the JEACs is incredibly eventful. I had a hard time putting each book down until I was finished reading. I'm looking forward to her next book. I would highly recommend reading these stories. *From: Annley W., Canada*

Dear Ms. Lionheart, I think your book is amazing because it was awesome that those kids could solve and figure out the mystery of the *Peacock Feathers*. Every time we stopped reading I was always on the edge about what comes next! I can't wait to read the next book! It won't surprise me if the next book is as OUTSTANDING as this one! *From: Brayden – Age 14, Canada*

I really like the JEACs books because they are filled with adventure and conservation approaches. I care about animals and our environment and the books focus on those important topics. The characters in the books are very committed to saving animals and I especially like Nimal because he is smart but he has character. *From: Corben – Co-Leader, JEACs–CAC–No.3 – Age 10, Canada*

I like how Hunter became part of the JEACs and helped them rescue animals. *From: Elsa – Age 5, Canada*

Dear Amelia, I love your first book! I surely am going to buy your next book. I love it too much to choose a part because I love every part, but if I had to I would choose the end when the thieves are captured because then the peacocks were safe. *From: Eve – Age 7, Canada*

Dear Ms. Lionheart, I like this book because it is fun and exciting. You always want to know what happens next. I'm excited to know what the next book is going to be about. *From: Joshua – Age 11, Canada*

My children really enjoyed the series. They learned more about various endangered animals and different cultures. On a recent trip abroad to Sri Lanka, my children happily used the new Sinhala word, 'Ayubowan', that they learned while reading *An Elephant Never Forgets*. *From: Joyce V. – Mother of Elsa and Vareed, Canada*

Dear Amelia, We like your books. We really like Hunter because he is funny. *From: Kailah and Ashlee – Ages 7 and 5, Canada*

I like the books because they teach me about the importance of protecting animals. In *Peacock Feathers*, I found the part with the wimpy crook funny. I am glad the JEACs capture the bad guys. *From: Kathleen – Age 10, Canada*

I *love* Ms. Lionheart's book series. It is about all my favorite things: adventure, beautiful animals, faraway places and kids making a difference in the world! After the first book I was inspired to create a real life JEACs group at my school. *From: Maddison – Age 10, Canada*

I love animals. I love the books because of the different age groups and how they grow, and the various countries and the differences in life. *From: Mikala – Age 11, Canada*

Dear Amelia, I have truly enjoyed reading your books. They are very well thought out and are very easy to follow. You have such wonderful characters with some very amusing quirks and traits. It is lovely that each book is based in a different country as it gives children a chance to discover the world without leaving home. *From: Sheri G. – Mother of Alix, and aunt to Kailah and Ashlee, Canada*

I like the JEACs books because they are mysteries and they use a lot of descriptive language. They take place in different countries, which is interesting. I love animals, conservation, plants and nature. My favourite character is Anu because she loves books just like me! *From: Sorena – Co-Leader, JEACs–CAC–No.3 – Age 9, Canada*

I like how the JEACs used their karate skills to rescue the animals. The JEACs have really exciting adventures! *From: Vareed – Age 7, Canada*

AN AUTHOR AND FOUNDER'S DELIGHT IN PRESENTING
JEACs – CAC – No. 3

You are UNIQUE! This means **YOU** have special gifts to help change the world.
(Amelia Lionheart)

This is inimitably true of *JEACs – CAC – No. 3*. Congratulations: Aiden, Auslen, Bella, Brinn, Corben, Ella, Jette, Kaplan, Lucy, Sorena, Taite and Tavyn, who formed the official group in May 2013.

I met eight-year-old Sorena in November 2012 (she had already read the first three books in the series and was eager to form a group), and nine-year-old Corben in April 2013, at book signings. After reading the books, Corben sent me an email at the beginning of May 2013, informing me that he and Sorena were forming a group with some of their classmates. I met Corben, Sorena and their respective mothers, Louise and Amaris, towards the end of May, in order to formalize the group.

The dedication of these two young leaders never fails to thrill me. Corben and Sorena are *true conservationists*. From the ages of six and seven, these two youngsters have supported World Wildlife Fund by adopting animals. Read about this on the WWF blog article which appeared on July 17, 2013 – http://blog.wwf.ca/blog/2013/07/17/these-junior-environmentalists-and-conservationists-jeacs-raised-660-for-wwf/.

At our meeting, I was informed that they wished to raise $5,000 for WWF over the year. They had various plans as to what type of fundraising events they would hold and the crafts they could make; they also asked pertinent questions about the percentage of funds they could use to cover costs of posters, et cetera. We agreed that since fundraising dollars were precious, up to 10 percent could be used for administrative costs. We spoke about recognition and appreciation being key characteristics of JEACs groups, and they chuckled when I asked their moms to 'tune out of our conversation' while Corben, Sorena and I discussed the importance of thanking our families for supporting us – including our moms.

At their bake sale at the end of May 2013, they raised $660 for WWF. Then the Alberta floods occurred and the children were upset about the damage done to the Calgary Zoo. So they changed their earlier goal and began to raise funds for the zoo. Another point which impressed me was the methodical way in which they organized their group. Sorena and Corben would meet to discuss plans on one day of the week, and then meet with the rest of the group on another day of the week, to share information and gather input. They take attendance, hold all members accountable and expect everyone to participate.

This group have raised nearly $4,000 for WWF, the Calgary Zoo, the Fish Hatchery and the Bird Sanctuary, and they have carried out this hard work during the period commencing end of May 2013, up to June 6, 2014. Other group members, and their parents, have also participated in events whenever possible; they are a dedicated, enterprising and awesome group of JEACs.

Despite the fact that Sorena has moved to a new school, the group continues to work well together. The group's comprehension of what the JEACs are all about is quite clear, thanks to parental guidance.

Please read the articles Corben, Sorena, Brinn and their moms, Louise and Amaris, have written. I am humbled, beyond words, that they took time out of their busy schedules to honour me in this way – thank you all.

As for Amaris and Louise, it is a pure delight to work with you, learn from you, and enjoy the talents of your children and their incredible group. I have a glorious time whenever we meet, despite the serious work we are undertaking. Thank you both for your support, care, encouragement, teaching and generosity – not only of your time and talents, but for sharing your children with me.

My heartfelt thanks also go out to all the other JEACs in this group, as well as their parents, teachers and school administrators. The success of this group is due to your hard work.

Please contact me if you wish to know more about the JEACs and would like to set up a group, so that you can receive your unique identity name and number and become part of this global network.

The name JEACs is trademarked: JEACs™. It is owned by me, and you need permission from the JEACs Advisory Board *prior* to carrying out fundraising under the JEACs name.

Thank you for caring about our planet.

Amelia Lionheart
Author and Founder of **the JEACs**
Website: www.jeacs.com

HOW **JEACS – CAC – NO. 3** CAME TO BE

by

SORENA
Co-Leader of the Group

I have always loved animals and wanted to help them. When I was in grade 2, my mom had bought me one of Amelia Lionheart's books, *Peacock Feathers*. I read it and I really liked it so I read the rest of the books Amelia had written. Then one day I went to Chapters with my dad and we got to meet Amelia. I found out that she was launching her next book, *Can Snow Leopards Roar?* I went to the book launch and Amelia signed my books and I had a chance to meet and hear about the first JEACs group. I really wanted to start my own JEACs group but I couldn't find anyone who had read the books or was interested at that time. A while later, when I was in Grade 3, I was talking to my friend Corben at school and he told me that he had also met Amelia Lionheart and was reading her first book. We decided to start our own JEACs group. We met Amelia with our moms and officially started *JEACs – CAC – No. 3* on May 25, 2013.

We have had lots of meetings and other kids in our school wanted to join as well. Our first fundraising event was a craft and bake sale at our school; we raised $660 for WWF. WWF then did a blog about JEACs – CAC – No. 3 and our efforts. Then the flood came and flooded the Calgary Zoo. We decided to help the zoo and we had a lot of events for them. At the last big event Dr. Doug Whiteside, the Senior Staff Veteranarian of the Calgary Zoo, came to support us. He offered us a tour of the Calgary Zoo's Animal Health Centre. There, we presented Dr. Doug with a cheque for $2,310. Now we will be raising money for the Inglewood Bird Sanctuary, which was also affected by the flooding. I can't believe what we have accomplished! I have always wanted to do something like this and am so grateful to Amelia, our teachers and school and especially our parents for supporting us. I am so proud of JEACs – CAC – No. 3!

Sorena – Age 9

MY DAUGHTER – SORENA

Co-Leader of **JEACs – CAC – No.3**

by

AMARIS

It all started when I was searching for a new book for my daughter Sorena to read. I noticed a book with a peacock on the cover; Sorena loves animals so naturally, I picked it up to have a look. I read the synopsis on the back cover; it was about a group of children who saved animals; perfect. Sorena has had ideas of this type of thing since she was very young. She had been asking to start an animal club with her friends at school to educate people on endangered species. So I bought the first book, *Peacock Feathers*. I read some of it to ensure it would be appropriate for Sorena, but before I had finished the book, she found it and read the whole thing. We proceeded to get the rest of the books from the library; she read all of them and enjoyed them very much. She and her little brothers, Gabriel (5) and Joel (2), would pretend they were the characters in the books and go on rescue missions. Sorena talked about starting a JEACs group, all of the time.

One day Sorena and her dad, Steve, had returned home from a trip to the bookstore and she was very excited to tell me that she had met Amelia Lionheart. Bookmarks in hand and smiling from ear to ear, she told me all about it and that the first JEACs group had been started. Now she was even more enthused about the idea. Steve had given Amelia his email address because Amelia had told them that she had a book launch coming up for her newest book. Sorena persistently asked him every day if he had gotten an email from Amelia Lionheart; she couldn't wait. Steve was very happy to be a part of her excitement. When the email came and we knew the date of the book launch, her excitement grew. I took Sorena to the book launch with her little brothers. We listened to the inspirational story of Amelia and the first JEACs group. Sorena stood in line with her books to be signed and I felt so appreciative that she had the opportunity to meet the author who had inspired her so much. After that day we looked at the website for the JEACs and talked a lot about starting a group but the only obstacle was she didn't know anyone who had read the books and who shared her passion to start a group with.

Time passed and one day Sorena came home from school and eagerly told me about her friend, Corben, who had met Amelia Lionheart and picked up her first book. Corben was as encouraged as Sorena was by Amelia and her books. And so it began: JEACs – CAC – No.3. We all met – Amelia, Sorena and I, and Corben and his mom, Louise – to make it official and discuss the children's plans with her. I think the proudest moment for me was hearing all of the thought Corben and Sorena had put into the JEACs group from fundraising ideas to their goal to raise $5,000. The kids had chosen to support WWF, a cause that was familiar to Sorena. She had adopted a tiger from WWF with her birthday money when she was six and was saving for more animals.

The two talked a lot about their plans for the group at school, and other kids who had heard about it wanted to join too. They now have eight other members and meet once a week at school. Their teachers and school administrators are very supportive of the JEACs and we were able to hold our first fundraiser, a bake and craft sale, at their school. Sorena and Corben made an announcement to the school, and other kids in the group made posters and handmade crafts. The sale was a great success and we raised $660 for WWF, which motivated WWF to post a blog about the initiatives of these amazing young people.

Amelia had crocheted hats for our first fundraiser; they were immensely popular, so Sorena decided to start learning to crochet for future fundraisers. Sorena and Corben know that they can't do all of this on their own and have learned, with Amelia's support, how important gratitude is. They give handmade cards to everyone who contributes to their fundraisers. They have been busy making cards to sell at our future fundraisers, too.

Their cause this time was the Calgary Zoo, in light of the extensive damage the zoo suffered due to flooding in Calgary. We held many events for the zoo and at our final event in November 2013, Sorena and Corben introduced Amelia and Dr. Doug Whiteside, who came to support their fundraising efforts. At that event Dr. Doug invited the JEACs on a tour of the Calgary Zoo's Animal Health Centre. We went on the tour as a whole group in December and presented Dr. Doug with a cheque for $2,310! It was a very proud and exciting time for all of us.

I have thoroughly enjoyed being involved in the JEACs group and look forward to the future. It has been such a pleasure to meet and get to know Amelia, Corben and Louise, all motivating, talented and fabulous people. Our meetings together are so much fun, we lose track of time. I also know that none of this would be possible without such a phenomenal group of people around us. It has been enlightening for Steve and me to see our child so engrossed in saving the planet and the co-inhabitants of our earth – something that has always been my dream; we have such a responsibility as human beings to respect and care for all of the life around us. Sorena has gone from donating her birthday money to thinking of bigger ways she can achieve her goals and follow her passion; and she is actually carrying it all out. We are so happy to be right there with her. We are also thankful to Louise and Corben and their family and all of the JEACs. We are especially grateful to Amelia for the guidance and support she provides and for the fantastic opportunity she has given us all.

by

CORBEN
Co-Leader of the Group

I became a JEACs member after meeting Amelia Lionheart at a bookstore. She inspired me to form a group the next day at school, with my friend Sorena who is also interested in animals and conservation. The group decided to raise funds for the World Wildlife Fund (WWF), which made me happy because every year for my birthday I would ask for money instead of presents to give to WWF. The bake sale at our school raised $660 for WWF. In relation to this donation, WWF wrote a blog about our donation and our JEACs group. "Despite their young ages, Sorena and Corben have been WWF supporters for a number of years already. Sorena adopted a tiger when she was six and Corben regularly donates his birthday money to WWF instead of buying presents" (quote from WWF blog). This was very exciting to our group!

Our group was planning our next goal when a tragic flood happened in Calgary. Due to the flood, the zoo was very damaged. So we decided to fundraise for the zoo. The plan was to hold three events: two at Chapters/Indigo stores and one at our school during our annual Art Harvest Celebration. Over the summer, we worked hard to make cloth bags and greeting cards; and Amelia crocheted many hats. From all this hard work, we raised $2,310 for the zoo. We were lucky enough to meet Dr. Doug Whiteside, the zoo's Senior Staff Veterinarian, and present him with the cheque. Dr. Doug then invited us to have a behind-the-scenes tour of the zoo hospital. It was cool!

Sadly, Sorena moved schools, which made it more challenging to hold JEACs meetings and plan the next fundraising events. We got creative and Skyped quite a few times and made some plans. I hold regular meetings at school with another co-leader, Jette. Our new goal is to raise money for Calgary's Bird Sanctuary and the Fish Hatchery. They were both affected by the flood and need help. We plan to hold another bake sale and craft sale at our school. We hope to raise $1,000 in total and give half to each conservation place.

I love being a member of the JEACs and hope that many more people can form groups because we need more help to save animals and their environments.

Corben – Age 10

by

BRINN
Active Member and Senior Supporter of the Group

I joined the JEACs group because I think it a great conservation group and I love to help animals. I have helped the JEACs in many different ways. All of the JEACs members made homemade cards and I helped my brother make the cards with beautiful pictures of animals and plants. Either my brother or I took some of the pictures. I attended all of the JEACs fundraisers where I helped sell the goods. The stands required at least one person at the table at all times, so if the parents wanted a break or had to help someone else, I would always take over for them.

I also contributed ideas regarding what we were going to sell. I attended the meeting and helped in the decision-making process. I also attended all the fundraisers for the zoo, of which there were three, and I really enjoyed helping out. I found it was fun to sell goods. I enjoyed it because I knew it would be going to a great cause: the flooded zoo. I also helped to watch the younger siblings if the parents were busy, making sure they were safe and entertained.

Speaking of younger siblings, I am so proud of my little brother, Corben. He has put so much effort into the JEACs group. He is one of the leaders and is a very hard worker. He has done so much for the zoo and has made a great impression on others.

Brinn – Age 12

CORBEN – MY CONSERVATIONIST SON

Co-Leader of **Jeacs – CAC – NO. 3**

by

LOUISE

Growing up, I was always interested in animals and felt very protective and loving towards them. When I had children, those feelings and interests appeared to have been passed on to them, particularly to my son, Corben. From a very young age, he showed a strong interest in learning about animals and he became more concerned about animals' well-being as he began to understand the negative environmental impacts they face. As a result of this increased awareness, Corben began to ask his friends to give money to him at his birthday parties, rather than gifts, so he could use that money to adopt endangered animals through the World Wildlife Fund. He began that tradition on his seventh birthday and continued on through to his tenth; this will likely become a lifelong tradition.

The day that my children and I were at Indigo and we met Amelia Lionheart, I knew immediately that my son had found someone who was going to be able to inspire him to greater levels. She told him about her books and about the JEACs and he was immediately hooked. The next day at school, he formed a JEACs group, along with a friend of his, who coincidentally also knew Amelia Lionheart, her books and the JEACs. He and Sorena began to gather ideas to help raise funds in support of animals and their habitats. I was thrilled to see him take such initiative and wanted to help him in any way that I could. All of the JEACs members and their parents worked hard to put together a bake sale that helped raise $660 which was given to the WWF. As a result of their donation, WWF recognized Corben and Sorena by writing a blog about the fundraiser:

*"The 8- and 9-year-old leaders of the newest group, Sorena and Corben, with the help of their families, fellow JEACs, and Amelia, raised $660 for WWF-Canada through a bake and craft sale at their school recently. They registered their fundraiser through WWF's **Community Panda program**. Community Panda events are a lot of fun, and the money they raise supports WWF's efforts to protect wildlife and wild places. When asked what their favourite part of the fundraiser was, both kids answered with an enthusiastic, 'everything!' Thanks so much to these JEACs, their families, and Amelia for helping us to protect species at risk!"*

The next plan set out the by the JEACs was to raise money for the zoo, particularly as it was ravaged by the June 2013 floods. With much enthusiasm, the children and parents set out to create cards and cloth bags to sell at the three events: two at Chapters/Indigo stores and one at the Annual Art Harvest at the kids' school. We all worked diligently over the summer in making signs for the table, posters for advertising and the all-important cards and bags. In addition, Amelia Lionheart generously crocheted literally hundreds of hats, which were a huge hit! We raised $2,310 and were particularly delighted when given the opportunity to meet Dr. Doug Whiteside from the zoo. He is the Calgary Zoo's Senior Staff Veterinarian and he attended the last fundraiser at Chapters, providing an informative talk to the children and patrons who were present. The JEACs members presented him with a cheque, and the smiles on their faces strongly indicated their delight and pride in such an accomplishment.

The JEACs group continued to meet regularly at school, despite changes in the group's membership. One notable and sad change was Sorena's departure from the school. Corben and Sorena decided to continue to keep the group running, with Corben holding meetings at the school, which the two then discussed during Skype sessions. From their small meetings and group meetings, the JEACs have decided to raise money for the Bird Sanctuary and the Fish Hatchery, two conservation areas that were also affected badly by the floods. In June, the children once again will sell the remaining hats, cards and bags, along with baked goods provided by the parents of the families involved. Some of the JEACs members are going to create more crafts, such as rainbow loom creations and stuffies to sell at the fundraiser. They have an ambitious goal of $1,000, which will be split between the two organizations.

I have felt honoured and privileged to be part of this group, working with these wonderful children as well as Amelia Lionheart and Amaris, Sorena's mom. We have forged a strong bond throughout the hours of preparation and discussion, for which I am extremely grateful. I look forward to more adventures in conservation!

ABOUT THE AUTHOR

Amelia Lionheart has been writing for many years and is the published author of five books for children. She has a diploma in writing from the Institute of Children's Literature, Connecticut, USA.

Amelia, who has lived and worked in several countries, believes very strongly in the conservation of wildlife and, in particular, the protection of endangered species. She is convinced that awareness of this issue, when imbued in children at an early age, is a vital step towards saving our planet.

As a member of several nature/wildlife preservation organizations, including the Durrell Wildlife Conservation Trust, she invites children and their families to become involved with local zoos and conservation centres and to support their important work, both by creating awareness and fundraising. To encourage this, she created a group called the 'Junior Environmentalists and Conservationists' (the JEACs) in the first book of her JEACs series, *Peacock Feathers*. In the other books, the JEACs travel to various countries, having adventures while enlarging their group and encouraging local children to start groups of JEACs in their own countries.

As of June 2014, Amelia has five groups of JEACs in Canada. The JEACs continue to evolve and are currently involved in fundraising for established organizations such as the Calgary Zoo, WWF Canada, the Whooping Crane Foundation, Calgary Rehabilitation Wildlife Centre, Humane Society, the Bird Sanctuary, the Fish Hatchery, and other local and international groups.

Amelia's other interests include environmental issues, volunteer work and fundraising. She believes that if people from different countries explore the diversity of cultures and learn from one another, they will discover that they have more similarities than dissimilarities. Many of these ideas are included in her books.

Please check out http://www.jeacs.com, Amelia's website for children.